THE GOLD

Death
at Castle
Wolf

ANNA PENROSE

First published 2024 by Mudlark's Press

First paperback edition 2024
Cover design by Deranged Doctor Design

ISBN 9781913628178

Also by Anna Penrose

The Golden Murders Series

1.The Body in the Wall
2. Dead Winter Bones
3. Death at Castle Wolf

Writing as Liz Hurley

The Hiverton Sisters Series

Dear Diary (novella)
A New Life for Arianna Byrne
High Heels in the Highlands
Cornish Dreams at Cockleshell Cottage
From Ireland with Love
Aster's Story

Prologue

Mal tried blinking, but the darkness was total. One of her eyes remained closed as she gingerly explored her face with her fingertips. A thick sticky substance had coated one eye, and she followed the liquid up to the brow of her hairline. Her head was throbbing as she discovered a gash on her temple. She didn't think she was still bleeding, and she stopped touching her head. Instead, she rubbed at her eyelashes until she felt that eye open, but the darkness remained.

Groaning, she tried to come to her senses. She had been following... Who had she been following? It was hard to gather her thoughts. She decided to ignore that for a second and try to understand where she was. Her trousers were wet, and she appeared to be sitting on a stone floor. Using her fingers, she began to explore her surroundings. Clambering to her feet, she held her hands out in front of her, feeling the cold, rough walls under her palms; now and then, they brushed over something slimy and organic hanging from the stone. Leaning forward, she sniffed the plant and realised it was seaweed. As she slid her hands across the wall, she felt the familiar undulating surface of mussel shells.

Fear gripped her as she raised her hands above her head and felt the wall above. Everywhere she touched, the walls were wet and covered in seaweed. Shells and seaweed could only thrive when submerged in seawater.

1

Wherever she was, she knew that in a few hours the tide would return and this room would fill up with water. And if she couldn't find a way out, she would drown. Trying not to panic, she began to look for a way out.

Time and tide waits for no man. But sometimes a canny woman can beat the odds.

DAY ONE Chapter One

Dear Oppy,

It is not a dirty weekend! Sorry to start my letter so abruptly, but honestly, I nearly had to pick up the phone to tell you off!

I tell you that I'm simply going for a bridge weekend with Jacques and you jump to all the wrong conclusions.

You know how much I love playing cards. Jacques just thought I might enjoy the opportunity to have a whole weekend of bridge, and I have to say I am very much looking forward to it.

Putting her pen down, Mal drummed her fingers and wondered if she was protesting too much. Malachite Peck, disgraced City trader, ex-convict, and now bookseller, sat in the little flat above her bookshop and twitched her lips. Maybe she was being overly defensive. The truth of the matter was that she was looking forward to Jacques Pellofey's company as much as the cards, and as usual, her sister had gone straight to the heart of the matter.

Over the past few months, they had become regular companions, visiting the Truro market together, and the odd Sunday walk and lunch. She turned down as many invitations from him as she accepted for fear that her enthusiasm for his company be misinterpreted as anything more than a desire for like-minded company. She would rather be lonely than give him the wrong impression. But when he invited her to join him on his annual bridge weekend, she had completely caved.

Beyond the opportunity to play bridge all weekend and spend time with Jacques, the location was utterly appealing: an island hotel, a boat ride off the Cornish coast. Her very own Alcatraz. The thought made her laugh; she had spent five years in prison, now she was dashing off to an island set adrift from the Cornish mainland. She imagined the accommodation would be very different indeed, and she was looking forward to some stimulating company.

Finishing the letter and adding it to the pile, she set off to finish her last-minute chores. Jacques was picking her up at ten, so all she had to do was post her letters and wait. She had already put a sign up in the shop saying, 'Closed for a few days'; told Sophie she was away; filled Mack's bowl with food; and asked the postie to leave any parcels at the pub next door. Sophie was the local police officer and, despite Mal's recent brush with the law, she had found her to be a lovely young woman and a credit to her uniform. Sophie had no inclination to become a detective and was Mal's first port of call when situations became tricky.

Grabbing her suitcase, she began making her way down the steep and narrow staircase. Jacques would have been happy, no doubt, to bring her suitcase down for her, but she'd be blowed if she let him think she was the sort of woman who couldn't carry her own luggage.

That said, these stairs were an absolute nightmare to navigate. Just her luck, if she were to break her neck before her holiday even started. She had spent the past week refining her suitcase until she had whittled it down to a single carry-on piece of luggage. She would have to rotate a few items for a range of outfits and had picked out clothes that went with a few pairs of shoes rather than shoes for each outfit. Even so, Mal felt dreadfully under-prepared and wished she had a further suitcase, but was determined to show Jacques that she wasn't a total clothes horse.

Despite her mutterings, she was looking forward to the opportunity to dress up once more. As a City trader, life had been a never-ending round of dinners and social events, and Mal loved to dress up. One time she had arrived in high heels and ripped denim and caused a sensation. When her host had gently remonstrated her attire, Mal pointed out that she had made three million for her hosts that year and they had responded by cutting benefits to their workers. Mal wondered if her hosts had wanted that on the press release?

Mal knew how to use clothes to create impact as much as a well-constructed portfolio of stocks and shares. Nowadays, she had to work out if James Patterson was a crime writer or a thriller writer. Her life had changed immeasurably.

Leaving her alarmingly small suitcase by the front door of the shop, she headed out into the village.

'Is that all you've packed?'

Jacques raised his eyebrows at Mal's small blue suitcase. He placed it in the back of his Land Rover, trying to obscure the fact that both of his cases were considerably larger.

'You said pack light,' Mal shrugged. 'Besides, it's just a weekend. Not all women are clothes obsessed.'

Jacques gave her an old-fashioned look, which she ignored and climbed up onto the Land Rover seat, sweeping the seat before she sat down. Given she had a very limited amount of clothes, she didn't want to start the trip with dirty clothes, even if it was a long raincoat. As Jacques made his way to the front of the car, she settled in quickly, making sure he hadn't spotted her actions. There was no point declaring she didn't care for her appearance whilst trying to make sure his car didn't mess up her outfit.

'I put the potatoes and fishing pots in the back, you know,' said Jacques meaningfully. 'The seat is perfectly clean.'

Mal was about to protest, then laughed.

'Guilty as charged. I may have under-packed.'

'We've got time if you want to grab some more clothes?'

Mal looked over her shoulder into the back of the car and saw the size of Jacques' case.

'It is just three nights, isn't it?'

'It is. What can I say? I'm a bit of a clothes horse from time to time.'

Given that she and Jacques had so far only met in the village for beach walks and home cooked-lunches, she had little to go on. They had started playing bridge with some of his friends and he was always very smart. Maybe this was a side to him she hadn't spotted.

Today he had on a knitted navy jumper with a red-coloured collar peeking out over the top. Navy chinos matched dark leather ankle boots, and he was wearing a smart wax jacket as opposed to his fish-stained sou'wester. In fact, the longer that Mal looked at him, the more she felt that she might be hopelessly outmatched this weekend. However, having made out that she was happy to travel light, she now had to prove it.

When Jacques had first invited Mal, she had tentatively agreed, then looked the place up as soon as she got home. Wolf Rock was a luxury resort. They prided themselves on offering unlimited privacy and had been the venue for many individuals looking for unparalleled creature comforts. During the recent G7 conference, the Americans had hired the entire island.

Lying half a mile off the coast, it offered total privacy from drones and long-lens cameras. Private security could quickly repel any approaching boats.

All this luxury came at a cost, though, and Mal had nearly fainted when she saw the prices for the bridge weekend. She was used to charity events like this, but back when she used to attend, either work footed the bill or she earned so much that the ticket price was negligible. Now she just looked at the screen in horror. That was a month's takings for her bookshop, in summer, at the absolute height of the tourist season!

As Jacques started the engine, she looked across again, frowning.

'And you're certain your friend is happy with me tagging along?'

Jacques rolled his eyes as the engine roared into life and they made their way out of the village.

'You are not tagging along! He offered me a guest pass after I did him a favour.'

'It must have been an exceptional favour?'

'It was nothing. Besides which, I have been going for years. Maybe I have collected frequent flyer points, yes?'

'And you really are friends with Wulf Clarkson?'

'He prefers Clarksie.'

'Does he now? And what about his wife, Kira? Does she prefer K?'

'As it happens.'

Mal turned in astonishment to see Jacques openly laughing.

'I have no idea. I am neither rich enough nor famous enough or young enough for the superstar that is Kira to pay any attention to me.'

Mal scoffed. She didn't care how much of a superstar you were, Jacques still had presence. Part of the selling feature of Wolf Rock was that it was owned by Wulf Clarkson, one of the major figures of the music world in the eighties who went on from stadium to global brand, and was now an international figure in the same bracket as Elton John or Beyoncé. He had expanded beyond the music world with business interests all across the globe. And when he promised discretion and privacy, you knew he had the wherewithal to provide it.

His cachet had only improved when he married the film star and now UN ambassador, Kira. Where Clarksie had clout in the business and entertainment world, Kira had the political power.

Mal noted that Jacques had neatly side-stepped how he knew Clarkson, and what favour he had done to get a free place for Mal.

Chapter Two

Arriving in Falmouth, Mal was surprised by the size of it. Her only experience of coastal towns so far ran to large villages or small towns, like Fowey, Padstow, and Golden. Falmouth was altogether larger.

'It's been a naval base for centuries, and a dockyard. The port is huge and with the expansion of the art college, Falmouth is now a very lively venue.'

Jacques gave her a potted history as he drove through the town centre and then out toward the outskirts. As she looked at the variety of world cuisines nestled amongst the bars and restaurants, Mal felt a pulse that she had thought was missing in Cornwall. There was a busker to one side and a group of skateboarders were hanging around some barely dried graffiti. The energy was palpable as students rubbed shoulders with tourists and locals.

'Lots of foreigners in Falmouth,' said Jacques, smiling. 'Cruise liners bring them in, as do cargo vessels. Sailors and ship hands from every corner of the globe. Everyone passes through Falmouth eventually.'

He spoke so fondly of the place Mal wondered why he had chosen Golden rather than here. He looked across at her and drove slower as the street narrowed and pedestrians ambled along the road.

'You're wondering how I settled in my sleepy little village, aren't you?'

'Well, this place does seem to have more energy.'

'I wasn't looking for energy. I was looking for peace. When I want energy, I can get in my boat or car and head over here. Then, I can come home to my beautiful view and peaceful life. We are here.'

Mal had been looking out across the water as it gave way from dockyards to beaches, and now saw that they had arrived at a very large Georgian townhouse with an unimpeded view across the water. Pulling into the drive, Mal read the sign, Wolf House.

'Is this connected to the island?'

'Yes, this is their land-based arm of the hotel. You can holiday here, and they also use it as a backup if they can't land the helicopter or get a boat to the island.'

Looking at the hotel, Mal thought it was a rather impressive backstop. The red brick walls stood out from the other properties she had seen; the large columns and portico suggested a level of elegance more at home in London.

'Was this an Admiralty house?'

'I think so. Pretty grand, isn't it? Now, if we jump out, they can park the car and load our luggage onto the boat. Let's have a drink before the shuttle takes us down to the dock.'

Mal climbed out of the Land Rover and smiled at the expression of the valet as he came out to park the car. A Jaguar pulled up behind, and Mal felt certain the Land Rover would be the scruffiest car in the car park. A second valet arrived and made a beeline for Jacques, shaking his hand.

'Mal, can I introduce James? Needs to get himself off to college, but never seems to leave Falmouth.'

The young man smiled and nodded at Mal.

'Welcome to Wolf.' He had long curly brown hair, and would have looked at home hanging ten on a surfboard were it not for his smart polo shirt and chinos. He turned and grinned at Jacques. 'And as it happens, I am going to college. I got a place here at the art college. This,' he gestured to the house, 'helps pay the fees. Now give me your keys and I'll park the rust bucket round the back.'

As he left, Jacques gestured for Mal to lead the way to the main entrance.

'He'll park it next to the most expensive car back there. I think he enjoys teasing the other guests, discreetly, of course. Drivers of orange Veyrons should maybe not take life so seriously.'

As they approached the house, the doors swung open, and they were welcomed into the hotel. Mal could smell lavender and, in the distance, someone was brewing a coffee.

'Monsieur Pellofey, Madame Peck, welcome.'

A beautiful lady in her thirties seemed to materialise out of nowhere. There was certainly nothing as vulgar as a reception desk. She obviously knew Jacques on sight as she chattered to him briefly in French and then turned to Mal, addressing her initially in French.

12

'Welcome to Wolf House. I believe this is your first time?'

Mal nodded and replied in French that it was indeed her first visit, and then swapped back to English, 'And I'm very much looking forward to visiting the island.'

Claire smiled, not missing a beat, further emphasising her skill as an unflappable host.

'It is a remarkable place. Now, some of the others have already arrived if you would care to join them, or I can have drinks brought to a private table?'

Jacques thrust his hands into his pockets and smiled at their host. 'Doubtless, it will be the usual crowd.' He addressed Mal directly. 'Unless you would prefer some privacy?'

'I'm about to board a boat with them and then spend the weekend trying to beat them at cards. Let's go say hello.'

Mal and Jacques followed Claire along a carpeted corridor that led them to a light and airy room looking out over the sea. From the elevation of the hotel above the road, the view across the bay was spectacular.

Mal caught her first glimpse of what she assumed was Wolf Rock. A large, craggy island reared up from the sea. White-capped waves surrounded the island, sitting under a large blue sky. From here, she could see an impressive castle rising out of the island, seemingly the only property on the small outcrop. She nodded at the majesty of the scene and couldn't wait to explore it. Between the island

13

and the mainland, two kitesurfers flew across the waves, the wind tossing their red kites up into the air as they hung below them. Mal could imagine the hoots of delight as the surfers flew like mad gulls, twisting and looping, before bouncing back on to the water's surface and zipping along again.

The scene within the lounge was far more sedate, although as Jacques entered the room, there were some shouts of delight. One of the men sprang up from his seat and came over, his hand outstretched.

'Oh boy! Every year I hope you'll stay behind and let someone else win!'

The man turned to Mal and winked. Although his hair was white, she didn't think he was much above sixty. He was heavily tanned and a strong Texan accent betrayed his nationality.

'Let me guess, you are also a bridge demon, Madame?'

Mal held her hand out, preparing to shake, but instead he lifted her fingers and kissed the back of her hand.

She tilted her head, smiling wryly, then doubled down on her crispest British accent.

'Please, call me Mal. Malachite Peck, bridge player extraordinaire, and immune to flattery.'

'She's got you there, Teddy Bear,' drawled a woman over by one of the sofas. Her long Southern vowels indicating another Texan, though she looked several decades younger. Given the amount of stones on her fingers, Mal suspected this was a third or fourth wife.

They tended to get younger as the marriages progressed until often, if she was fool enough to have him back, the man in question would return to his first wife.

'Mal,' said Jacques, jumping in. 'May I introduce Teddy and Violet Bonderman? Also, Penny and Henry Fitzgibbon.' A couple dressed in matching knitwear raised their glasses. Her clothes could have come from Marks and Spencer's twenty years ago, but her jewellery though simple was clearly expensive. She wore a heavy gold locket with P inscribed on it, an enormous emerald engagement ring and a simple gold wedding band. They had the air of a couple who had been married for a long time and were utterly comfortable in their skins. Mal imagined they were probably loaded. Although, given the cost of this charity weekend, it was clear that everyone was loaded.

Two men sat at a corner table dealing cards to each other. They nodded at Jacques and returned their attention to the deck. Although dressed differently – one in a suit which Mal considered incredibly inappropriate for a boat; the other in a blazer and deck shoes more at home in the nineteen thirties – they were, in fact, identical.

'Morris and Laurence Barta,' continued Jacques. 'Both excellent players. Very hard to beat.'

'Amen to that,' said Ted loudly, and then insisted that Mal come and sit with him whilst Violet had already slipped her arm through Jacques' and had pulled him over to where she was sitting. Maybe she thought the writing was already on the wall and was lining up her next suitor, or maybe she and Jacques were simply old friends.

Teddy smiled after his wife and patted the seat next to him.

'You mustn't worry yourself over Violet. She simply can't bear not to be the centre of any hot-blooded man's attention. She'll release him by and by.'

Mal laughed and came over and sat beside him.

'I'm not worried.'

'Indeed,' said Teddy with a smile. 'It's nice to see Jacques with such a fitting partner.' Mal was about to disabuse him of the notion that they were together when he ploughed on and introduced the Fitzgibbons and then, taking her drink order, headed over to the bar. She watched him leave and say something to Jacques as he passed him. Jacques looked back at Mal and mouthed an apology as Violet pulled on his elbow, concerned that he wasn't displaying the appropriate amount of attention to her. Shaking her head with a smile, she returned her attention to the married couple next to her.

Penny and Henry had been watching a group of six young women over on the other side of the room, and frowning. The girls were clearly enjoying themselves and their cocktails, and Mal was pleased to see bridge appealing to a younger crowd, and said as much.

'Oh, they're not with us,' said Penny. 'They're heading over to Little Wolf for a pamper package. One of the girls is getting married next month and her maid of honour's

16

passport hasn't come through yet. Apparently, they had planned a hen party abroad, so now they are having a party here. Well, not here. Over on the island.'

Mal looked across at the beautifully groomed young women again. She was prepared to bet that every one of them skied at Verbier and spent the summer in Mustique. Their parents likely owned racehorses, estates, banks. She wondered if they knew Jasmine, her nephew's wife. An inoffensive girl that Mal had learnt to, if not love, at least appreciate. She wasn't who Mal would have chosen for her nephew, but God knows Giles did love her, and that probably was all that mattered.

These girls looked to be of an age, and if they lived in London, they probably ran in the same circles. If they didn't know each other, Mal was certain that they would have friends in common. They even laughed the same. One of the girls kept glancing out of the window over to the sea and was sipping a glass of water as quickly as some of her friends were drinking their champagne. As she stood up to let a tall girl with long blonde hair pass, she placed her hand across her stomach and Mal wondered if she might be pregnant. Catching Mal's eye, she smiled, and Mal smiled back before returning her attention to her companions.

'To have the gift of youth with the wisdom of time; wouldn't that be a joy?'

'Those girls will never have wisdom,' said Penny. 'The Botox will have addled their brains by the time they hit thirty. They're just spending their trust funds, pretending to have careers whilst they wait for a suitable husband.'

Mal was surprised by the depth of contempt and looked over at the girls again before shaking her head.

'There's no Botox there. Just generations of good fortune, health, wealth, and a stress-free existence. Do excuse me.'

Penny blinked rapidly, then reached for her glass before rolling her eyes. Dismissing Mal, she turned to her husband, who in turn had raised his eyebrows in solidarity with his wife.

Standing up, Mal smiled politely and headed over to the hallway. Jacques had his back to her, and she didn't want to interrupt him; but she didn't want to stay and listen to Penny either. She would find the loos and come back in a few minutes. She was too old to entertain idiots and bigots. She'd never done it before and she wasn't going to start now.

Chapter Three

'Well, hello missy. Why're you in such a hurry for your drink?'

Teddy headed towards her with a Bloody Mary and a big grin. 'Nemo and Lurch already sucked the joy out of your conversation, have they? Those two sure are fun sponges. They're excellent players, but oh boy, even when they win, they don't cheer up. Imagine, they've got even more money than I have, but don't have a clue how to enjoy it.'

Mal looked across at the pair in surprise.

'They seem so—'

'Dull?'

'I was going to say unassuming.'

She knew that would have been a mistake. Some people wore their wealth very lightly; some liked to splash it all around.

'How did they make their money?'

'Back in the day, he invented a piece of hardware that levered the whole internet revolution. Plus, he also has a few proprietary pieces of software. Now, who else can I dish the dirt on? The Barta twins are European nobility, lots of generational wealth, plus they're heavy gamblers. Mostly beating the odds. Mostly. When they're out of earshot, let me tell you about the time they lost a castle. The following day, they won a fighter jet. I believe they are still squabbling about whether to swap the jet for the castle.'

He held out her glass. Mal took a sniff, grinning as she smelled the celery salt. She had high expectations that this drink was going to be well-mixed. She took a sip. The kick of tabasco was powerful and her nose twitched.

'Must say your Bloody Marys look a tame affair.' He looked curiously at her. 'It looks like some sort of detox nonsense.'

Mal laughed and held the glass back to him.

'Try it.'

'No, ma'am! I like my Bloody Mary's with a bit of bite. This looks like it will actually be good for me.'

'Chicken.'

'Now, you take that back.'

He was laughing now and took the glass from Mal.

'I'm not going to let some little English lady challenge me like that. We Texans pride ourselves on having blast-proof taste buds. Your little English version holds no terror for a true born Texan.'

Taking a large gulp, he coughed explosively, as Mal winced.

'I'd have sipped it if I were you.'

He was still coughing, his face beet red against his white hairline as tears filled his eyes. Violet came running over, full of concern.

'Teddy Bear?'

He flapped his hand at her as he tried to recover his breath. By now, all eyes were on him. Even the bar staff had come into the room.

Mal knew she was going straight to hell. She'd snubbed one couple and choked another player. The boat ride would be dreadful.

Teddy wheezed and then, finally catching his breath, let out a huge bark of a laugh and turned to the server. The young girl was looking horribly alarmed at the drink she had just mixed.

'Sweetie. Will you make us two more of these?'

He turned to face the room.

'Boy, howdy! That was one hell of a drink. Violet, you have to try this. At least the Texas version has the decency to look deadly. This is the iron fist in a velvet glove!'

Having watched her husband nearly choke to death, she took the glass gingerly and sniffed it.

'Why? It's just tomato juice.'

'Well, just you knock it back then!'

Mal shook her head vigorously.

'Or maybe just a small sip?' she said quickly. 'It has a little bit of a kick in the tail.'

Violet sipped it and smiled, looking confused at her husband, and then pulled a glorious face, stretching her mouth wide and screwing her eyes closed.

'Oh my Lord, that's a Bloody Mary! Why that's positively sneaky.'

She screwed up her face again as Jacques offered her a glass of water, and the server returned with two fresh Bloody Marys. Teddy took one and passed the other to Mal.

'You got me well and proper. Think I'll sip at it this time.'

He nodded at Mal in appreciation, and this time drank slowly.

'Boy, that sure is a fine drink.'

'It certainly is. It used to be my favourite hangover cure, back in the days when I over-imbibed.'

Teddy paled.

'My Lord. You Brits are crazy. You cure a hangover with this!?'

Behind her, Jacques laughed, then stepped to her side.

'Our English hosts always keep us on our toes. Yes? This weekend we shall have to remind them of what we can achieve when France and America are united.'

Mal sighed dramatically and took the teasing in good spirits. As they chatted, a few more couples entered the room, and it was clear that most attended regularly.

'Jacques is quite popular. There will be a lot of speculation about yourself, Mal,' said Teddy as they watched the dynamics of the room. 'He's never brought a date before. He always fills in for anyone without a partner, like himself. But now…?'

'Mr Bonderman. I am not Jacques' date. I am simply new to the area and play bridge. He thought I might enjoy getting to know some new people.'

'My apologies. But now it means I can flirt with you shamelessly.'

Mal gave him an old-fashioned look.

'I think your wife would object.'

'I don't think she will. That one always keeps her cards close. She'll trade me in if a better offer comes her way.'

'Well, you seem well-matched then.'

Teddy turned and narrowed his eyes, appraising her. A smile curled around his lips.

'Betsy would like you.'

'Betsy?'

'The first Mrs Bonderman.'

'Still in touch, are you?'

Now it was Mal's turn to smirk, and Teddy blushed.

'Do be sure to send me an invitation.'

'Ah, she'd never have me back.'

'And why's that then?'

'Because Betsy has brains.' He looked forlorn for a second and then chuckled. 'You are good at seeing through people. Going to have to watch you at the table.'

Mal shook her head.

'Trust me, I'm a bit rusty. I've only been playing for fun. I can't think when I was last at a competitive event.'

'I shouldn't worry none. Some of the players here are damn fine, but mostly we play for the social occasion and to raise money for charities. We play all around the globe.'

'And Jacques goes to all of those?'

Mal hadn't pictured him as some high-flying social butterfly.

'Not a bit. This is the only one he attends. He says for the rest of the time he has to catch the fish.'

'He is a fisherman, though,' said Mal, trying to argue Jacques' position.

'And our Lord Jesus was a carpenter.'

Mal tried to reply, but wasn't certain what Teddy was getting at.

'Ladies and Gentlemen.'

Mal turned around to see Claire standing in the doorway. 'The boat is ready. When you've finished your drinks, could you make your way to the reception?'

Having spoken, she then came across to Mal.

'Madame Peck. Would you like your luggage unpacked?'

Mal nodded. It was always lovely to have everything already put away when she came into a room.

'Yes, please. And I wonder, do you have any postcards of the island? I'd like to send a little note to my great nephew.'

Claire smiled as she nodded once.

'I will bring you one now. In your luggage, do you have any clothes that need to be pressed?'

Oh, Mal did like this place.

'I have a cream silk blouse and crêpe de Chine trousers. They would benefit from a quick blitz.'

As Claire left, Mal turned to Teddy.

'This place is really top-notch, isn't it?'

'You haven't been here before?'

'Like I said, I'm new here.'

'But you'd have to be living under a rock not to have heard of it.'

She gave a friendly shrug of her shoulders and raised her palm.

'Call me a rock dweller.' She wasn't about to explain that copies of Tatler were few and far between in prison.

Claire returned with a stamped postcard and a pen, and Mal excused herself for a second. Looking at the postcard, Mal saw the hotel had chosen a glorious image of the island with a stunning sunset bleeding down onto the dark sea. It was wonderfully atmospheric and Mal immediately found herself wanting to make up a story about it.

Dear Barney,

Look where I'm going!? Apparently, the sea is infested with sharks and pirates, and there's hidden treasure in the cave. Have you read Island of Adventure by Enid Blyton? I think it's going to be like that.

Lots of Love
Yaffle.

25

Mal made her way to the front hallway and handed the postcard to Claire. Joining Jacques, she smiled up at him in excitement. This was going to be a most marvellous weekend. And she couldn't wait.

Chapter Four

The wind tugged at Mal's hair as they climbed out of the minibus. Jacques held out his hand to steady her, and she gratefully accepted his offer of help as she tried to manage her hair and handbag. She slipped her hand into her handbag for a headscarf, saw Penny and Violet doing the exact same thing, and paused. She had never been a lady that lunched, delighting in the leisure of a husband's bank account, but now she felt as if she was somehow falling into that camp; Jacques' partner, rather than a player in her own right. Stuffing the scarf back into her handbag, she pulled out a sports cap, and grabbing a bobble, pulled her hair into a ponytail and through the strap gap.

Leaving the minibus, one of the girls from the bridal party tapped her head, smiling at Mal. 'Very sporty.' Her own hair was in a sleek bob held back by a few hairpins, and Mal grinned back.

'But not quite so chic?'

'That's cute,' said her friend as she joined them, nodding at Mal's ponytail. 'My hair frizzes up the minute it gets so much as a hint of moisture.'

'Mine is in a permanent state of alarm,' said Mal in despair. 'I guess I'm just learning to live with it.'

Another girl joined them and they were soon laughing and swapping horror stories about hairstyles. The girl with the sleek hair bob introduced herself as Julia Hawkes, and as the wind blew against her dress, Mal could see clearly that the young lady was indeed pregnant. Looking at the waves, Mal hoped she wasn't suffering from morning sickness. She turned to her friend, who was rapidly tying her long blonde tresses into a hasty plait.

'Smart move, Octavia. In this wind, you'd be likely to catch seagulls if your tresses got loose.'

Octavia shuddered from head to toe. She towered over Mal, and was easily one of the most beautiful women Mal had seen in a long time, and Mal wondered if she was a model. 'I can't think of anything worse.'

'Vomit,' laughed the third girl in the trio, who announced herself as Johanna before turning back to Mal.

As Mal and the girls swapped haircare tips, Jacques made his excuses and headed over to a group of fishermen. Mal watched him walk off, smiling at his retreat, and then returned her attention to the girls. Apparently, they swore by coconut oil. It was a daft conversation, but it still made Mal grin. Being amongst such a vibrant group picked up her spirits, and she leant into their youth.

As they were chatting, Claire let them know the launch was now ready for them. That it hadn't been when the shuttle had pulled up had clearly vexed her, but Mal could see the sea was surging, and preparing the vessel had probably been an effort. The short ride across was going to be a bouncy one.

'I'll go and let Jacques know we're ready.'

'There's no rush,' said Claire politely, in a tone that suggested an immediate departure would be required. Mal smiled in acknowledgement and headed off across the quay.

Jacques was standing further along the pier, chatting with the group of fishermen. Fishing vessels were moored on the other side of the pier. In the distance, an enormous grey naval vessel dominated the skyline, and on the other side of the large harbour were several tall ships, their masts swaying back and forth. All around, the clink of yacht lines sang out in the stiffening breeze. Fishing nets hung nearby, adorned with colourful buoys and weighted with the promise of the day's catch. Seagulls circled overhead, ever watchful for any discarded bait or the opportunity to swoop down and snatch a morsel.

Jacques smiled as she approached and stepped aside to include her in the group. The men were dressed in rugged, oil-stained overalls, rubber boots, and knitted beanies, and gave off an air of experience and resilience earned through countless hours at sea. Some had beards that mirrored the salt and pepper hues of the surrounding ropes and nets, whilst others wore sunglasses to shield their eyes from the bright glare of the water. They reminded her of the fishermen back in Golden, and she smiled warmly at them as she approached.

'Gentlemen, may I present Malachite Peck, a friend.'

'Ah, Jackie boy,' said the man in the blue beanie. 'This is the first time you've brought a guest over to the island. Malachite? That's French, is it?' he asked, grinning at Mal.

'Nope. Just a father that liked daft names for his daughters. My sister is called Opal. We still don't know who got off worse.'

The men laughed.

'Londoner?' replied one of the older men gruffly. Her accent had revealed her.

'Not so much anymore. I run the bookshop in Golden. None of you coming across to play bridge, then?'

Now the men laughed harder and nudged Jacques.

'We're not made of money. Plus, Wulf doesn't owe us any favours like he does Jackie there.'

'Yes,' teased Mal. 'Exactly what is this impressive favour?'

'Oh, we don't know. He's very tight-lipped about it.'

Jacques gave the men a stern look and then smiled at Mal.

'Did you come over to let me know the launch is ready?'

Mal grinned at the fishermen. 'It looks like his secret gets to live another day,' she said, shaking her head. 'Lovely meeting you.'

As they turned and made their way back to the island group, Jacques' expression became thoughtful.

'I promise not to ask,' said Mal. If he did have a secret, then it was his to keep.

'What?' said Jacques, frowning in confusion, and then he shook his head. 'Oh, that was nothing. No, it's something they were saying that's concerning me.'

For such a reserved man, Jacques' expression was unusually serious. 'Concerning?'

'Unmarked boats.'

'Which is an issue because?'

'An unmarked boat indicates illegal activity. Smuggling, poaching.'

'Poaching? In the sea? What can be poached?'

'Lots of stuff. Stealing from lobster pots, dredging for scallops in protected zones, landing small fish, but in this case—'

'Are you ready, Monsieur Pellofey?' Claire was now walking over to them briskly. 'Only, the tide is falling.'

'My apologies. Just catching up with friends.' Ushering Mal forwards, he grimaced an apology and turned to Claire. 'Of all people, I should know better.'

'I think after last year's incident with the Hamiltons, you need never apologise again for anything. That said, let's make haste.'

He grinned at Mal and she was happy to see his troubled expression had gone. Much as she admired them, fishermen were, in her experience, superstitious doom and gloom merchants.

'What happened with the Hamiltons?' she asked, as they walked up the small gangplank.

He chuckled and shook his head. 'That is a story for a fireside and a stiff drink. I shall tell you all about them this evening.'

They stepped out of the fresh air and into a very plush cabin.

'Jacques,' trilled Violet, who had already made herself comfortable on one of the leather sofas. 'Come and tell me how to stop being seasick.'

Mal gave him a quick nudge. 'I think you have your hands full.'

He turned and gave her a mock glare. 'You're supposed to be saving my honour.'

'Oh, get on with you. I'm going to chat to the girls over here and see if I can pick up any social media tips.'

Even as she looked, three of the young women from the bridal party were all laughing into one of the camera phones, and one of them waved her way.

'Mal, come and join us.'

Making her excuses to Jacques, who was already gallantly nodding along to Violet's conversation, Mal couldn't resist a mischievous grin at his somewhat alarmed expression and headed over to the girls. She couldn't see the bride, or the girl with the red hair, or the one dressed head-to-toe in this season's Fendi. Instead, she sat down next to the pregnant girl with the smart hairstyle.

'Octavia, budge up,' said Johanna, who had waved her over. 'Julia, stay where you are.'

Julia gave Mal a pained smile as the boat hit another wave.

'I wouldn't sit too close to me. I'm liable to hurl any minute.'

'Hence why she cut off all her beautiful locks,' said Octavia sympathetically. Julia shrugged.

'She's not wrong.' She took a deep breath. 'Okay, deep breath, let's grab a selfie. I am determined to have a blast this weekend and I am not going to be responsible for spoiling things for Imogen.'

'That's the spirit,' said Mal. 'And look on the bright side; all the upholstery is leather.' The girls looked puzzled.

'Easy to wipe down,' said Mal, grinning and joining in their laughter. As the engines fired up, the boat headed out onto the choppy seas.

Chapter Five

Jordan Thatcher lowered his binoculars and spat on the rocks below his feet. Scratching his stubble, he watched the boat head towards the island. The guests were a bloody nuisance, but occasionally one of the wives would seek out a bit of rough. They took one look at his dark blue eyes, dismissive gaze, and young, athletic frame, and would suddenly declare an interest in the flora and fauna. Sex was always preferable to the tedium of their conversation. So long as he didn't get caught, it was a good way to pass an afternoon.

He turned his back and began to walk along the rocky foreshore towards the whale watch station. Tucked away from the fancier activities of Wolf Rock, the maritime observation station was co-funded by Cornwall University and Wolf Rock. A month back, a humpback had been spotted off Penzance, and all the volunteers were hoping they would spot one in their area. Funding wasn't an issue with Wulf Clarkson sponsoring the station, but the kudos would be pretty cool.

Jordan wasn't a fool. He knew his job here couldn't last forever. But whilst he was here, he wanted to make the most of it. As he trudged back, he picked up a few bits of litter and placed them in a sack. Ange whined to kingdom come if people came back without litter, and he still had a bellyache from her nagging after he ran the taps without the plug in. The island had a natural spring, but

Ange said that wasn't the point. She'd gone on and on, but Jordan pretty much switched off the minute the preaching started.

Out to sea, a flash caught his eye, and he quickly raised his binoculars. After a few minutes, he pulled out his mobile and sent a quick text. Whistling, he shoved his hands into his pockets, the rubbish bag hanging from his wrist, headed up to the grassy scrubland and trudged home. Smoke was rising from the station's aluminium chimney. The station was both his workplace and sleeping quarters. Housing ten volunteers, the dorm was mixed, but the women had pretty much dominated one end of the long bunkhouse and had vociferous opinions on how to use the toilets beyond.

Jordan spat again. If he needed a slash in the middle of the night, would they rather he turned all the lights on, or some hit the floor? There was seriously no pleasing some people.

Pushing the door open, he stepped into the main office and quickly closed it again as the wind blew in around his legs.

He nodded at Dougie, the team leader. The Glaswegian was tedious, but at least he kept to himself and didn't bore Jordan with unnecessary small talk.

Ferne Straub was working in the corner, but he ignored her. Despite her being the same age as him, she acted like someone's maiden aunt. He suspected she cut her own hair, and he'd never seen her in make-up. Even her pierced eyebrow looked ugly, and her nails tended to have mud on them as opposed to polish. If she started growing barnacles, he wouldn't be surprised. She wasn't particularly ugly, and he had tried it on with her when he first arrived, but she'd made it pretty clear that he reminded her of an unpleasant smell.

'Anything?' asked Dougie, looking up from his keyboard.

'Nothing, unless you count a bunch of rich wasters.'

Dougie stopped typing and gave a small groan.

'I'd forgotten the season starts again today. It's the bridge party, isn't it? They're not so bad.'

Ferne looked up from her keyboard and shook her head, tucking her long fringe behind her ears.

'There's a hen party coming over as well. Staying at Little Wolf.'

'Jesus,' sneered Jordan. 'Who the bloody hell books this place for a hen party?'

'Not every girl's idea of a good time is getting wasted, staggering between pubs,' said Ferne curtly.

'They aren't all frigid bitches, either.'

'Jordan!' snapped Dougie, glaring across at the younger man.

'It's alright, Dougie,' said Ferne. 'Jordan's opinions aren't high on my list of concerns. I think the idea of coming to a five-star spa with a bunch of friends sounds wonderful. If I had unlimited funds, I'd probably do the same.' She turned back to the screen and resumed typing.

Jordan rolled his eyes, then hung up his binoculars and headed towards the inner door separating the office from the living area.

'Oh, Jordan…' Ferne spoke as she carried on typing, her eyes not leaving the screen. 'Ange is looking for you. Something to do with the septic tank?'

Jordan slammed the door.

Ferne leant back and grinned over at Dougie.

'Serves him right.'

'Hmm.' Dougie was still looking in the direction of the door. 'I don't understand his sort. I'm sorry, lass. If I could fire him, I would.'

'Well, I wouldn't argue against that.'

Dougie was the Chief Ranger and dealt with hiring and firing. But Mr Clarkson had hired the younger man and had apparently asked Dougie to give Jordan a chance on more than one occasion. For whatever reason, Wulf believed in second and third chances, and felt Jordan was somehow deserving of all the chances God gave. The rest of the team had given up complaining to Dougie, and Ferne had to accept that Jordan was a hard worker when put to it. He had practically built the outpost himself, and was generally first out the door in the morning and last in at night, making his company that much easier to handle. He was also meticulous in his record keeping. It was just he was a total arse.

Ferne chided herself. She tried to think the best of everyone. That's what her therapist counselled. But honestly, Jordan Thatcher would test the patience of a saint.

'I don't like the look of these figures.'

'What's that?' said Dougie, coming over to her desk.

'Look.' She pointed at the screen. 'That pressure is beginning to drop quicker than expected and it seems to be changing direction.'

'Looks like our spot of bad weather is going to be a bit more extreme. I'll call up to the house and let them know.'

'Ha. Look,' said Ferne, gesturing at her screen.

As they had been talking, the Met Office sent out a yellow weather alert for both wind and rain coming in the following day.

'You know, girl, if you ever give up your career in oceanology, you'd make an excellent meteorologist.'

Now Ferne laughed, a rare sound, and Dougie smiled at her.

'Honestly, Dougie. What choice do we have living here? We could run rings around the Met Office.'

Dougie nodded and picked up the phone. The island was well used to stormy conditions, but preparation was the key to everything. He hoped the meteorologists were wrong, but when he had woken up this morning, the elbow he had broken on naval manoeuvres some twenty years ago was aching. A sure sign that the air pressure was beginning to drop. If a storm was brewing, he hoped it would blow through quickly.

Ferne stood up and nodded to the outside.

'I'm going to start pulling a few things into the storeroom.'

'It's only a yellow warning.'

She looked at him and shrugged.

'How's that elbow of yours?'

He grimaced and then waved her towards the front door.

'Go on, ya wee weather witch.'

Laughing at his assessment of her, she headed out into the wind.

Placing a call to the castle, he smiled as Mandy answered.

'Hello Mandy, pet. Can you let the staff know we have a storm on the way?' He paused as he listened to her questions. 'No, not until tomorrow. I tried Wulf, but the line switched to yourself.' He paused again, then nodded. 'Ah, right enough. Well, I guess the punters come first. Let him know, after he's done with them, and I'll try him again later.'

Dougie hung up and looked out the window. The sky beyond was bright blue, the pink sea thrift moving in the breeze, and it looked as pretty a picture as you could hope for. He rubbed his elbow and decided to help Ferne. Despite his reassurances, he felt this one was going to blow hard.

Chapter Six

Imogen Beasley, soon to be Lady Imogen Philips, waved to the boat below as the other half of her bridal party raced towards the island. It was only a mile offshore, but it already looked so remote. She smiled in anticipation. After all the recent press intrusion into her affairs, her fiancé Piers had offered to foot the bill on Necker Island, Richard Branson's private getaway.

She had jumped at the offer, but fate conspired against her. One of her bridesmaids was newly pregnant and whilst she had offered to stay behind, Tinks had then got in touch to say her passport was stuck in Home Office delays… and suddenly it seemed inevitable that she would be celebrating with her friends in the UK.

That's when Piers stepped into the breach again and suggested Castle Wolf. His father was receiving a lot of negative attention following some of his business deals in the Middle East. And after a rather lavish party in which one of the younger Royals was photographed in a rather compromising position, the press had been all over his family. And that included the new fiancé.

Imogen had moved from happy socialite to Disney princess to hounded villain. Losing weight for the wedding dress had been easy as her anxiety bloomed out of control. She ran everywhere to avoid the cameras and threw up all her food daily as yet another picture of herself or Piers or her friends and family turned up in the gutter press. The articles she hated the most were the ones that compared her to Piers' exes. One night he had come home to find her sobbing over the latest batch of photos and decided enough was enough.

Hence him picking up the bill for Imogen and her bridesmaids to go and escape the press and have a few wonderful days together before the big day.

She turned to the other girls and pointed to the boat below. 'As soon as they join us, the party begins!'

Francine raised her glass of champagne. 'Why wait?'

Despite it only being a five-minute crossing, Francine had insisted on opening one of the cases of champagne. She opened the bottle with a loud pop, then poured glasses for Imogen, Portia and Tinks. Imogen wanted to object as the other girls weren't there, but Francine had paid for the flight as a treat, so Imogen felt it would be churlish to complain. She looked down again at the boat.

'And the others really didn't want to come for a ride?'

Francine shook her head. 'Johanna said they wanted to experience the sea or something like that. Julia's pregnant, so obviously she can't fly.'

'That's for pressurised flights, not helicopters,' laughed Portia, but Francine just shrugged.

They watched as the boat bounced across the waves, sending up plumes of white as it hit each new wall of water.

'I think the girls on the boat might need some restoratives first,' said Theresa Campbell-Jones, also known as Tinks. She pushed her long red curls out of her eyes as she looked through the window to the choppy seas below.

She wasn't surprised that Francine had selected her over the other girls for the flight. Johanna had little time for Francine and always spoke her mind. Ever since Julia fell pregnant, Francine had viewed her as hogging all the attention. Octavia was just so bloody stunning that when she was part of the crowd, all eyes were on her. Francine was good looking, but also vain, and knew when she was outclassed.

'Honestly, Tinks, you're spoiling my present,' said Francine with an exaggerated pout.

'No, she isn't,' said Imogen reassuringly. 'This is a lovely idea. Come on, Tinks, raise your glass. You've known Francine longer than I have. You know she means well.'

'Oh, I wish I'd gone to the same school as you, too. Imagine, Tinks, I could have known you as long as Francine has. Instead, I'm just hugely grateful to have got to know Francine through you. So, cheers!'

Tinks smiled and shook her head. 'Knowing my luck, you'd have arrived right after I was shipped out again.' She lifted her glass. 'To army brats and ambassadors' kids. Long may we roam the globe in search of a home!'

They all raised a glass, Francine with more enthusiasm than Tinks. 'Okay, tell you what,' said Imogen, eager to keep the peace between the two old school friends. 'Let's make sure that everything in the house is perfect for them when they arrive. Maybe we should start with massages?'

Francine smiled and gave a cat-like stretch.

'Now that sounds like a perfect plan. And what about a facial for Julia, just in case she can't have a massage?'

Imogen raised her champagne glass in salute. This was why she liked Francine. She was good fun. And if she seemed unkind or blunt, it was often a simple case of misunderstanding.

Chapter Seven

As the boat bounced across the waves, Mal could see some of her fellow guests grimacing. Her expression matched theirs. She hadn't been on a boat since she'd been chasing a murderer who was then blown out of the water by the Royal Navy. Even though this luxurious launch was a long way from Bob's speedboat, the wind and the waves were the same. In fact, it even sounded the same, and she peered out of the window, watching as a helicopter sped past overhead.

'Well, that's one way to get there.'

She had spoken to herself, but Johanna peered out the window and shrugged.

'Yes. But then you'd have to share it with Francine.'

Julia and Octavia had moved closer to the loos. Julia was sipping on a glass of water whilst Octavia stroked her hand.

Mal studied Johanna. She was a small girl with an olive complexion, a broad mouth that turned up at the corners, and large dark brown eyes. Mal felt that pang of envy she often experienced in the presence of such youthful perfection.

'Francine?'

'Imogen's friend. Imogen's our bride-to-be. She's the sweetest girl ever, but she has an eclectic group of friends and we don't all get on as well as we should.'

'Friendships are tricky at your age,' said Mal. 'You've already made bonds that will last a lifetime, but funnily enough, you don't always know who they are with yet. On one hand, you have acquaintances who will be with you through thick and thin: and on the other hand, apparent BFFs who'll crumble under the first hint of pressure.'

'You sound pretty smart,' said Johanna.

'At my age, we have to swap our looks for our wisdom,' said Mal with a wink.

'If I look half as good as you in my fifties, I'll be delighted.'

Mal paid the younger woman more attention. Her large eyes were framed by dark, heavy eyebrows, her mouth also seemed a touch too wide for her face, and she already had deep grooves in her skin from laughing and frowning. As she ran her fingers through her hair, Mal saw a smudge of blue on her ear and wondered what it was from. She found herself drawn to the young woman, and not just because of her compliment.

'You flatter me.'

'Oh, I doubt it. If you're a day over fifty-three, I shall hold you hostage until you tell me your skincare regime. And I love your hair,' she said, giving Mal a frank appraisal. 'That's such a bold statement.'

'Are you always this forward?'

The girl laughed loudly. Two of her friends glanced over at her, then smiled at Mal before returning to their view out the window. Clearly, their friend's behaviour was nothing out of the ordinary.

'Yes. Apparently, that's one of my charms. Or drawbacks, depending who you talk to. Imogen thinks I'm charming. We met at the art studio. People say I'm too young to be a painter, but I say bollocks. I'm twenty-five. Have you seen da Vinci's sketchbook from his twenties, or Raphael's or Artemisia's?'

'That's some fine company.'

'If they were alive today, they would be dropping my name.'

Now Mal laughed loudly and a few others looked over.

Jacques cocked his eyebrow. He was firmly entrenched in a conversation with the Barta brothers. Smiling, he returned to his conversation.

'Well, it's refreshing to meet a girl so confident in her own abilities. Is that what you meant when you said some people find you less than charming?'

'Like Francine, you mean?'

Mal had forgotten about the girl in the helicopter, but she was happy to follow that line of conversation.

'You said it.'

'Yeah, it's true. Francine and Tinks went to school together, Tinks and Imogen's family are old friends, so that's how Francine got to know Imogen. Tinks is okay, I suppose. Quite a rising star in the judicial world, by all accounts. Family's filthy rich, but that hasn't stopped her establishing herself in her own right.'

'Your family isn't filthy rich, then?'

'Beyond filthy, actually. It's quite the curse.'

'Yes, having money can be quite the downer.'

'You mock, but how can I struggle?' She gave an embarrassed laugh. 'How can I find my true voice when it's muffled by all the wads of bank notes rammed into my mouth?'

Mal could see her sincerity, but what a complaint to have. Her heart seemed in the right place, but maybe her talent or her upbringing made her blind to the reality of most people's lives. Their struggles weren't inspirational for those living from hand to mouth.

'You could move out? Go travelling?'

'I did that. But I always knew that all I had to do if I ever got into trouble was to find a phone or walk into a consulate, mention my name, and I'd be evacuated back to "safety." Knowing you can always be saved removes the understanding of fear. How can I paint if I can't experience?'

She looked furious for a moment, and then a smile flashed back across her face.

'Anyway, that's why Francine can't stand me.'

'Because of your talent?'

'No. Because of my wealth. She has a few ambassadors in her family tree: I have kings and queens. It absolutely slays her.'

Mal gave her a second appraisal.

'I must have heard of you, then.'

'You know me as Johanna. But you'll never have heard of me. I fly under the radar and paint under a pseudonym. The girls know I paint, but not who I am, if you know what I mean.'

'Ah, you want your work to speak for you. Not your family ties.'

'Bingo. Francine also thinks that's very suspicious. She says – just out of earshot but always loud enough for me to hear – that I've clearly got no talent and don't want anyone to know it's me because it's rubbish.'

'Does that bother you?'

'No, it makes me laugh.' Johanna's face wrinkled up in a huge grin, her perfect teeth shining against her dark red lips. 'My art is extraordinary. I have more talent in one of my fake eyelashes than she has in her entire soul. If putting me down makes her happy, who am I to begrudge her joy?'

Mal shook her head in admiration.

'Do you know, when you get to my age, I expect you to be ruling a kingdom? Your confidence is astonishing.'

'Thank you.'

'I should love to see your work, but I fully understand why that's not possible.' Mal changed the conversation. 'So why aren't you on the helicopter?'

Now Johanna frowned and pulled back her hair, revealing her blue ear again and now Mal realised it must be paint or charcoal. The girl rolled her eyes and released her hair, shaking it over her shoulders.

'Francine said there was only room for six. And as she's paying for the tickets, I guess she can dictate the seating plan. Just another little way she likes to sow division. Octavia and Julia are livid. In fact, I'd better get back to them. They're hatching a plan to put Francine back in her box.'

With an evil grin, she got up and went to join the other three girls. Mal watched her as she left; young, boastful, and full of life. Was she arrogant or confident? Mal couldn't decide, but she decided she liked her either way, and imagined that Little Wolf was likely to see sparks over the weekend if Johanna continued to show her disdain for Francine. Friends of friends was always such a difficult relationship to navigate. She silently wished Imogen, the bride, all the luck in the world for a peaceful weekend.

Jacques wandered over and sat down beside Mal. 'Are you trying to recruit some younger players to the bridge party?'

'No. And it's just as well. I think that young woman has plans for her own games. I am so glad I'm done with that age. Everything is blinding sunlight and dark bitter shadows.'

Mal shuddered as she watched the helicopter drop out of sight onto the rear of the island.

'Bad memories?'

'Only recent ones.' Mal chuckled. The last time she had been in a boat with a helicopter flying overhead, it had been firing at the boat of a fleeing murderer.

Jacques slapped his hand on his forehead in alarm.

'I am an idiot. Are you alright with the boat ride? It hadn't even occurred to me that it might bring back bad memories.'

Mal shook her head quickly to reassure him. 'There is little here that reminds me of Bob's speedboat. For starters, I'm bone dry. No one is shooting at me and I'm not being flung from side to side. It's all good.'

In a mad attempt to stop a murderer from escaping, Mal had commandeered a boat and set out in high pursuit. She and Bob, the ship's captain, had narrowly missed being rammed by the other boat, and then dodged missiles from the Royal Navy helicopter. It was not an event she was in a hurry to revisit, but this sleek launch was a world away from Bob's high-speed RIB.

Jacques sagged in relief and changed the subject.

'So what were you girls talking about?'

'Friendships. Suffering. Art and honesty.'

'That sounds like most hen parties I have ever heard of.'

'You're not wrong.'

'Do you know in French they are called Enterrement de vie de jeune fille?'

Mal paused as she quickly tried to translate it.

'The life of a young girl? But what does Enterrement mean? I only know that as—'

'Burial. Yes. The burial of the life of a young girl.'

Mal stared at him, wide-eyed.

'And here's me thinking the French are all about the romance. That's positively Russian.'

'It is quite sombre, isn't it?'

'It's dreadful.'

The boat began to tilt as it headed towards the jetty. Looking out the window, Mal saw they had pulled up alongside a small concrete pier.

'Well,' said Mal, smiling as she rose to her feet, 'Let's hope this bride and her mourners have a jolly time before her death.'

Chapter Eight

Stepping off the boat and onto the jetty, Mal was grateful for Jacques' assistance. As the waves slapped the boat against the stone jetty, the gangplank lifted and fell. Placing her hand in his, she walked carefully down the undulating walkway. He turned and smiled at her reassuringly, then placed his hand on her arm as she joined him on dry land.

'I'm not infirm, Jacques,' said Mal, although she didn't remove her hand from his arm.

'I don't recall suggesting you were, but for me not to offer assistance would be inconceivable.' He tipped his head. 'If you'll excuse me.'

As they had been speaking, Teddy tried to make his way off the gangplank whilst Violet squealed that they would all be tipped into the ocean. The plank was all of a metre long and well attended by island staff, all wearing matching red polo shirts and cream chinos. A fleet of golf buggies waited at the end of the concrete jetty and Mal watched as the first one, laden with guests, pulled away up the drive towards the castle looming above them.

She turned back to watch Jacques lend his hand to Violet, who grabbed at it, all but jumping into his arms. Over her shoulder, Teddy mouthed a thank you as he took the last few steps off, unencumbered by his wife throwing off his balance.

By now, Mal had decided enough was enough. She and Jacques were not remotely involved, but she was beginning to get tired of Violet's behaviour.

'Was that your first time on a boat?'

She looked at Mal and giggled.

'Hardly! We spend most of our time in the Bahamas, don't we Teddy?'

'Don't they have waves in the Bahamas?' asked Mal in astonishment.

Violet giggled again.

'Of course they do, sugar. Haven't you ever been?'

'Once,' said Mal. She studied her nails, then looked at Violet again. 'But it wasn't for me.' She turned to Teddy. 'Do you sail much? I'd love to introduce you to some of my favourite spots.'

'Why, I'd be delighted,' he said as he zipped up his sailing jacket and smiled directly at Mal. 'I do love to try new things.'

The two women stared at each other, then Violet giggled nervously and quickly returned to her husband's side. Teddy clapped his hands together and suggested they make their way to the buggy.

Violet looked over her shoulder and gave Mal a worried smile, which she returned with genuine warmth. Mal had no beef with the young trophy wife; she just didn't like anyone thinking she was a pushover.

'Do you want to take a buggy or walk?' asked Jacques. His tone was even, but Mal thought she heard a laugh in his voice.

'A walk would be perfect.'

Jacques waved the buggy on and the pair of them headed uphill.

'Were you worried the fourth Mrs Bonderman might try to play footsie with you?'

He threw his head back and laughed loudly.

'No, I think poor Violet will be glued to Teddy's side for the rest of this weekend. You know, I've never been rescued by a knight in shining armour before. It's quite the thing.'

Mal grinned over her shoulder back at him.

'Well, I only do it for the most abject of subjects.'

'I am but a wretch.'

'Indeed, a wretch that adores the attention of beautiful women.'

'Was she beautiful? I hadn't noticed.'

'You just noticed the attention?'

Jacques bowed deeply and laughed again.

As they approached the castle, Mal craned her neck to take in the granite fortress. For centuries, this building had protected its inhabitants from storms and pirates. Whilst it was certainly an intimidating structure, there was also a sense of finesse in the architecture from the castellations between the turrets and a variety of levels wrapping around the stony base of the island.

Stepping in through the large double oak doors, Mal smiled in delight as she looked around the large hallway. She could fit her flat in this entrance way. A few velvet sofas were littered about the place and Mal watched as various pieces of luggage were moved up a large staircase under the supervision of an elegant lady in her fifties. She was wearing a tailored dress that whispered timeless style and understated luxury. Looking up, she walked forward to greet them.

'Welcome to Castle Wolf. I am Vivienne Chance.'

Mal knew her sort. With her sculpted black hair and graceful sophistication, she would rule the castle with a tender iron fist. On the surface, she would be all warmth and charm personified to the elite clientele for which Castle Wolf was famed. Behind the scenes, however, her steely pragmatism would take care of any messy problems for Wulf without ever chipping her polished composure: whether an influential guest overdosing on drugs, or a maid trying to blackmail her boss, Mal was certain Vivienne would fix it. The best concierges in the world aren't made, they're born, and they rise to the top very quickly.

Following their host, she and Jacques were given a brief tour, although, as Vivienne said, Jacques could probably do the tour blindfolded. As Vivienne walked them through into the ballroom, Mal gasped in delight. The windows gave an unimpeded view across the sub-tropical gardens and the sea beyond. Within, the room itself was at least eighty feet wide. Running along the interior wall were three large fireplaces, although only one was currently alight. One end of the room was laid out with bridge tables; the other end was a more informal arrangement of armchairs and sofas. Between the two and against the exterior wall was a small dais. Despite the size of the room, the heavy swagged curtains, carpet, and fireplaces lent it a welcoming air.

'This is stunning.'

Vivienne nodded in agreement.

'I've worked in a lot of fine establishments, but none of them can beat this view. Now, let me show you to your rooms.'

Mal sank down onto the bed and vowed to replace her own as soon as she got home. And the linens.

Beyond the glorious bed, her room was large enough for a sofa, a writing desk, and in a separate room, a large copper bathtub. Both rooms had views over the island and the sea beyond. Jacques had said he had a free place for her, as Wulf Clarkson owed him a favour; but this was one hell of a favour! The room was dressed in fresh flowers and had a bottle of champagne in the fridge. Checking the label, Mal was impressed with the hotel's generosity. There was also a substantial wall safe discreetly tucked behind an antique framed map of the island. She swung the picture back against the wall, leaving the safe empty. What jewels she had didn't require such elaborate protection.

Plugging in her laptop, she fired up the internet and then gaped in horror as she investigated the price of her room. She had winced when she thought it was the weekly rate. Discovering it was the day rate, she all but fainted.

She and Jacques were about to have words. Whatever favour Jacques had called in, this was exorbitant and probably shouldn't be wasted on her. That said, it was incredible and one should never look a gift horse in the mouth.

A brief note on the desk said her clothes had been put away. The plans for the afternoon were for people to settle in and unwind, then cards and dinner. It turned out that each night was, in fact, black tie. Mal ground her teeth as she found that out and winced as she tried to work out how to make her limited wardrobe work for her. Shaking out her LK Bennett evening dress. It was a long pale pink sheath dress, covered in sequins; she added a red silk bolero and red satin peep toed sandals. What she was going to do for the second night was beyond her. She'd deal with that challenge tomorrow, but trainers and jeans were figuring highly.

Sitting down, she pulled a sheet of writing paper out and drew a quick sketch of the island for Barney. She copied the image in her welcome pack and pointed out a few things to the young boy:

Dear Barney,

Here is a map of my treasure island. I am staying in the castle in the middle. It is very old and I bet it is full of hidden passages. The house below the castle is called Little Wolf. Apparently, it has a swimming pool as well as a hot tub. There is also a sauna and a plunge pool. I think that's where the pirates hide their sharks. At the other end of the island is a wildlife station. I haven't seen that yet, but I'm told it's where they keep an eye out for whales and the occasional mermaid. If I see any, I shall let you know.

Lots of Love
Yaffle.'

She put her pen down and smiled. Maybe she could write a story about this place? Over winter, she had enjoyed writing short stories and felt it might be something she could do during the long winter months. Mal yawned, realising the room was too warm for her taste.

She opened the windows, allowing an afternoon breeze to glide in and cool the place down.

Sitting on the window seat, she was about to grab a book when she heard voices drifting from another room.

'I don't think she's involved, but she's staying in the most expensive room on the entire island. Since when do ex-cons do that, unless she's on the take?'

In the silence, Mal realised the man must be talking on the phone. Was it possible that there was another ex-con on the island? She didn't want to come across as paranoid, but she wasn't about to close the window. The man started to speak again.

'Odd coincidence, I agree. What about the French guy?'

Mal's stomach turned over. Someone was investigating her, and Jacques was being pulled into it. Carefully releasing her breath, she tilted her head and tried to pick up every snippet of the one-sided conversation. It was coming from a room below hers. She wanted to lean out of the window and look down, but was anxious they may be on a balcony and catch her listening in.

'Agreed. If either of them is involved, I'll let you know. In the meantime, I'm off to play cards.'

Mal sat frozen for five minutes as the silence extended. Then, very slowly, she leant out the window and looked down. She was three floors up. There was a veranda wrapping around the ground floor. On the floor between her and the ground was an open window. She was about to look left and right when an arm shot out and pulled the window closed. It wasn't much to go on, but she knew it was a man, not old, his white shirt cuff fastened with a black cufflink that had the ace of spades on it.

With her heart racing, she sat at the writing table and wrote out all she'd heard, plus a description of the man's hand and the location of his room, then leant back in her chair and tried to digest what was going on.

Her arrival here was not of her doing. Jacques had invited her last month; he came here most years. Jacques said the owner owed him a favour, hence her free invite. What exactly did she know about Jacques?

If he was fleecing her for money, this made no sense. She wasn't destitute, but he was playing a very long con for a relatively paltry sum of money. She tutted and headed for the shower. Jacques wasn't a conman. She was certain of it. She had become so good at her previous job by seeing to the heart of an issue in record speed. Of course, that usually involved political forecasts, spreadsheets and global economics. But she did also consider herself a bloody good judge of character.

Was it possible that Jacques was involved in something, possibly unknowingly? That seemed possible. There was no denying the man in the room below was investigating someone on the island. He was struck by Mal's appearance on the island. As her only claim to fame was a financial breach, she had to assume this man was investigating a financial matter. But who? This was an island for millionaires and celebrities to come and play in total privacy. It could be anyone.

Leaving the shower, Mal saw in the mirror she had forgotten to rinse out her conditioner. Swearing to herself, she returned and chided herself for getting lost in her thoughts.

Pulling out a teal silk dress, she added a salmon stole, a single brooch, one ring, and a one-strand necklace.

Tonight would not be about ostentation. She already had one person speculating about her; she wouldn't invite anyone else.

Checking her watch, she saw she had another fifteen minutes before she met Jacques for drinks. It was time to investigate.

Chapter Nine

Heading downstairs, Mal stopped at the first floor and retraced her steps, trying to imagine she was walking back to her own room. The carpet muffled her steps as she worked out which room sat below hers. There were only a couple of doors along here, but they didn't line up with where she had judged her room to be. Of course, her room was so damn large it was unlikely the rooms here lined up. This wasn't laid out like a standard hotel, but she took note of the three room-names to her right before heading downstairs to reception.

A young man was typing into a laptop, but pushed it to one side and smiled as she approached.

'Hello,' said Mal, returning the smile. 'Can you help me? There's a baby in the room below me and it keeps crying. Is there a way you can discreetly alert the parents?'

The concierge looked puzzled and pulled his laptop towards him.

'I don't think there are any children on the island. Let me check?'

After a few minutes, he shook his head.

'No, no children or babies.'

'But I absolutely heard them. I'm in Sea Thrift. I went downstairs to see which room was below me, but I couldn't work it out.'

Tapping on the keyboard again, he shook his head.

'Absolutely no children in the room beneath you.'

'Are you certain? Maybe she's one of those mothers that carries her child around in a sling. Maybe she didn't book the child in.'

His look of incredulity was quickly smothered as he nodded along in agreement with Mal's preposterous suggestion.

'Buckthorn is occupied by a single male.'

Mal had the name of the room, now to undo her query.

'Well, what on earth did I hear? My window was open, and I heard the screaming quite loudly.'

'Could it have been the seagulls?'

Mal pretended to look outraged at such a silly idea.

'No, seriously,' he laughed. 'It catches out lots of people. You're not the first person to think they sound like crying children.'

'Do they really?'

Mal knew for a fact that they did. She herself had repeatedly misheard the gulls for distraught infants until she got used to their calls. Life in a fishing village was not the peaceful idyll she had once imagined.

'Absolutely. In fact, at the far end of the island there's a wildlife observation centre. It's manned by volunteers. If you wander over, they would be keen to show you their work. Tell you more about the birds.'

Mal looked down at her outfit and shrugged.

'Maybe not today.'

He grinned back at her.

'Good call. The birds will still be there tomorrow.'

Mal nodded, went to walk away, and then turned back.

'You won't mention this to anyone, will you? At my age, people are so quick to brand me as foolish or irrelevant. I don't want to give them any evidence that I am indeed an idiot.' She put her hand to her face. 'God, imagine if that man had opened his door. I am beyond embarrassed. Promise me you won't say anything?'

It stuck in her craw, but occasionally playing the over-the-hill card had its benefits.

'Your secret is safe with me, but I think you are wildly underestimating yourself if you think anyone would dismiss you as foolish.'

'You're too kind.'

Mal offered what she hoped was a grandmotherly smile, which was entirely spoilt by a loud wolf whistle from behind her.

Spinning round, she met the roguish gaze of Teddy Bonderman.

'My dear Malachite, you are a sight for sore eyes.'

Violet was standing next to him, her arm draped tightly over his own, and she rolled her eyes at Mal.

'Stop bothering the nice lady. You don't want to fall foul of Jacques now, do you?'

'He doesn't scare me,' blustered Teddy, winking at Mal. She, in turn, had the pleasure of watching Jacques walk towards the three of them.

'Who doesn't scare you?' asked Jacques.

Teddy jumped in the air, squawking theatrically in shock. Violet seemed unsurprised as she winked at Mal. Maybe he was very deaf.

'Hello Jacques, we were going to get a drink. Shall we?' said Mal, gesturing towards the lounge.

She turned back to the concierge and shot him a secret smile as he put his finger to his lips in a sign of solidarity. She was happy that he would keep her enquiry to himself. Now she just needed to find out who occupied Buckthorn and discover what his game was.

Just as she was preparing to leave, a movement caught her eye. To the side of the concierge desk stood a full-length mirror, now showing another couple coming downstairs. From where Teddy had been standing just now, he would have seen Jacques approaching, but had still played the cad. As she caught up with her group, Teddy grinned at her, having seen her realisation. 'You have to be pretty long in the tooth to catch me out.'

Chapter Ten

Julia's morning sickness had been overwhelmed by sea-sickness and she had spent the rest of the day vomiting. The smell of alcohol was making her queasy and, in the end, she waved the white flag and left the girls to their pampering.

The house they were staying in was beautiful. They had their own chef and a spa area. Tomorrow the plan was to sail to Falmouth, then back for lobster supper and more pampering. The entire weekend was full of fun activities and full-on relaxation, but she felt as sick as a dog. Every time she retched in misery, her thoughts towards Francine turned darker. She could easily have let her on the helicopter, but that was typical of her. Francine always played favourites and tried to keep people to herself. Imogen was marrying into a very wealthy and powerful family, as if her own weren't wealthy enough. Francine was planning to ride along on her coat-tails. Who was Julia? Just someone that had married a sailor. Neither of their families was so glorious as to merit Francine's sycophancy. And it was sycophancy. She hadn't known her long but wondered at Imogen's taste in friends. The girl was too sweet and forgiving for her own good.

There was a gentle knock on the door, and a crack of light appeared as Imogen came in with a glass of water.

'How are you doing?'

Julia struggled to sit up.

'Stay where you are,' said Imogen. 'I feel so dreadful. You should have been on the helicopter. Francine got confused about the occupancy. I should have double-checked.'

Julia bit her tongue. She had no idea why Imogen liked Francine; that woman was dreadful. She was a spiteful, self-serving slut, but Julia doubted her actions had been personal. Francine simply didn't care what effect her actions had on others.

'No one's fault. Just one of those things. I'm just so sorry I'm spoiling your party. I really wanted to be here for you.'

'And you are. And I am so honoured.'

It lay unsaid that this was Julia's fourth pregnancy, and the closest she had got to full-term so far. She and Marcus had married young, surprising all their friends and family, but his constant postings overseas made them impetuous. Sad, slow tears welled up in her eyes and tumbled over her eyelashes.

'I didn't think I would be so sick. Do you think…'

She broke off, unable to voice her fears.

'It's sea-sickness. That's all.' Imogen held her hand. 'However, if you want to go home, I will get the helicopter to fly you back to the mainland immediately. Or you can sleep now and decide in the morning. Whatever you want to do. Why don't you call Marcus and see what he says?'

Imogen suspected Marcus would probably divert the Royal Navy to come and scoop his wife up if he needed to. The pair of them had been through so much.

'I don't want to upset him. Besides, what can he do? He doesn't get back for another month.'

The life of a naval wife could be hard, especially one struggling with constant miscarriages.

'Do you want me to bring a doctor over?'

Julia sobbed and laughed weakly.

'You must think I'm overreacting. As you say, this is just sea-sickness. I am genuinely beginning to feel better, but I don't want to leave my bed right now. Not even to get on the helicopter.'

Imogen patted her hand again and asked more questions until she was comfortable that Julia was not in pain.

An hour later, when Imogen stuck her head around the door, Julia was fast asleep.

Back in the sitting room, the rest of the girls had settled in for a slumber party with a line-up of great movies.

Francine jumped up as Imogen came back in.

'Right. Let's start the shots! Party!'

Imogen shook her head.

'Let's leave them for tomorrow, yeah? I don't want it to get loud and messy.'

Johanna raised her champagne flute in acknowledgement.

'Good call. Tonight is for quiet celebrations. Tomorrow, when Julia is feeling better, we can raise the roof.'

Francine threw herself back onto her sofa and poured herself another glass.

'Honestly, Imogen, this is your weekend. Julia won't mind.'

'Well, I mind. You know what she's been through.'

'Maybe she should stop trying then.'

There was an instant roar of protest from the other girls, and Francine glared at them.

'What? I meant she needs to let her body recover. Be kind to herself. And maybe if she was this nervous, she shouldn't have come, anyway?'

'She'd have been fine without the sea-sickness,' said Johanna.

'So that's my fault, is it?'

'Of course not,' said Imogen quickly. 'No one's blaming you. I loved the helicopter ride. It was such a thoughtful gift and I am really grateful.'

Francine looked across at Johanna and smirked.

'But tonight,' said Octavia, acting the peacemaker, 'Let's just unwind. Now, DiCaprio or Hiddleston?'

There was no contest. Hiddleston won.

Chapter Eleven

It was six o'clock and the light of the day had almost disappeared. In just a few short months, the sky would still be blue and birds would drift overhead on the warm salty breezes, but for now the waves splashed on the rocks below and the occasional bird called out as it settled down for the night.

A young man sat on a slate bench looking out over the sea. His cigarette tip glowed in the dark as he took a deep drag and scratched the stubble on his chin.

'They'll kill you,' said a second man walking along the track towards him. As he approached the bench, he didn't sit down, but also looked out to sea.

'Something will kill me, certainly. At least this way I get a say in it.' He paused and dug around in his pocket. 'Want one?'

'Smoking's for losers.'

The first man shrugged and shoved his packet back into his pocket.

'So, how did today go?' asked the older of the two.

'Three sightings. All unrecorded.'

'Excellent. And what about the fisherman? Did he-?'

He broke off as the man on the bench started coughing.

'See. Bad for your health.'

'Like you care. All you want to know is how many—'

'Shut up, you fool. You don't know who else is out here.'

'I know well enough who's out here, and that's you and me. No one can creep up on me unknowing. And our friendly fisherman knows what we're doing, anyway.' He slapped his hands on his thighs and stood up. 'Was there anything else you wanted to know?'

'You let our interested parties know?'

In the darkness, the first man threw the other a look of derision, then realised his expression wasn't visible in the dark. 'Course I have. That's what you pay me for. I know what I'm doing. Mind you, there'll be nothing for the next few days. There's a proper hoolie blowing in. Reckon it'll cause some damage.'

'Nothing we haven't seen before.'

The older man's voice spoke with a confidence the youngster thought was misplaced.

'Fair enough, but I don't think we'll have seen the like of this one for a while. It's building quickly out there.'

Both men looked out to sea, and then the second man turned his collar up against the wind and walked back in the direction he had come from.

The first man stubbed out his fag, then returned it into the packet before walking to the far end of the island, away from the swanky guests, back to a cold bunk and sanctimonious conversations.

Chapter Twelve

Jacques offered Mal his arm as they headed towards the dining room, following Teddy and Violet. As Jacques' jacket pulled back slightly, she could see the whites of his cuffs, and then stared at an ace of spades cufflink. The exact same as that worn by her mysterious downstairs neighbour. She stumbled to a halt.

How could it be Jacques? The man she had overheard had no hint of an accent and had even referred to Jacques. Unless, of course, there was another French fisherman at the party. Was he involved in something, or, like her, an innocent bystander? And what the hell was this stranger investigating?

'Your cufflinks seem appropriate for the evening.'

Jacques twisted his cuffs to better display the links and then rolled his eyes.

'Not my taste, but they were a little gift from our host. They always do this. The ladies get their gifts tomorrow night.' He called ahead to Teddy. 'Which suit did you get?'

Teddy stopped and turned round, his eyes twinkling as he pulled his cuffs forward. 'Spades. I think all the men did. No doubt the ladies will get hearts tomorrow night. Me and Lady Love are always on close terms.' He squeezed Violet's waist. 'Don't you agree, dear?'

'Indeed, I do.' Smiling, she held out her hand, fluttering her fingers. 'And in your honour, I have worn this little ol' thing.'

On her finger was a massive heart-shaped ruby surrounded by diamonds. It was magnificent in its vulgarity and looked uncomfortably large on her dainty fingers. It would be better as a necklace, or sat in the diadem of a coronation crown, it was so enormous.

'That is quite the ring,' said Jacques gallantly. 'A gift from an admirer, perhaps?'

'No one admires Violet more than I do, sir. That was our one-year anniversary present.'

As Violet was still holding her hand out, Jacques held it and kissed the back of her fingers.

'It is a most charming gift and so clear how in love you two are.'

'Check the stone is still there, honey. Our Gentleman Jacques could be a renowned jewel thief!'

He roared with laughter at his own joke as Violet giggled along, pretending to look shocked, and clung to her husband.

'Like Raffles.'

'The very same. Now, shall we get some drinks before the games begin?'

As they led the way into the ballroom, Mal shook her head in astonishment.

'That damn thing looks like it came out of a Christmas cracker.'

'It is an acquired taste.'

'I suppose it is real?' Mal couldn't comprehend how that much money could be tied up in such tastelessness, but she'd been part of a financial trade deal out in the Arab states and had witnessed a solid gold bathroom suite, so there was no accounting for taste.

'Oh, I imagine it's real enough. Teddy is a billionaire, after all.'

'All that money and no taste. Imagine if he funded a cardiac wing instead?'

'I suspect he already does. His wife runs his charitable enterprises.'

Mal looked after the young woman and chided herself for her surprise. It was entirely possible to be charitable and ostentatious at the same time.

Jacques followed her gaze and laughed. 'No, not Violet. Betsy, his first wife. That's what he refers to her as, The Wife. All subsequent wives have been his queen or his princess or the love of his life.'

'Doesn't Violet object? Strikes me as very rude.'

'Did she look annoyed to you?'

Mal shrugged and decided to change the topic.

'My room is very lovely. In fact, I think it might be a bit too lovely. Are you sure it's free?'

'Please, Malachite. It's yours. Wulf owed me a favour. Maybe he threw in an upgrade as well. Who knows?'

'I'm in a suite called Sea Thrift.'

'Bof,' Jacques whistled. 'That is a very fine suite. Or so I hear. I'm in lowly Puffin.'

'Then we must swap immediately.'

74

'We must not,' he chuckled. 'Do you honestly believe that any room in this house is lowly? Besides, I like my room. It looks over the jetty. I can stare at the boats and dream I am back on the sea, with only the stars to guide my path.'

'That sounds…' Mal was going to say romantic and then changed her mind. 'Tricky.' She wasn't sure of her feelings for Jacques and felt uncomfortable mentioning romance in front of him.

'Sailing at night under a full moon is wonderful, or a new moon when the Milky Way is in its ascendancy. It can be tricky, as you say, but there's a romance to it as well.'

Uncertain how to reply, she walked in silence into the ballroom. At least now she had confirmed that Jacques wasn't staying in Buckthorn. But he was still being talked about. By whom? She had hoped that the cufflinks might prove a clue, but if every male guest had received a pair, it hardly narrowed the field. As they entered the room, she saw they were amongst the last to arrive. The tables had been set out for bridge, and people were milling about at the other end enjoying drinks and chatting with each other.

'Looks like we're the last to arrive,' said Mal. At a rough headcount, there were about forty people. 'Do you know everyone here?' she asked as they moved toward the crowd. A waiter came forward and offered them each a glass of champagne.

'No, maybe half the room? There is always a good mix of regulars and new faces. And I don't attend every year myself.'

'No, I imagine you must have to catch a lot of fish to raise the funds for an event like this?'

Jacques laughed loudly and a few heads turned their way, raising a glass in salute.

'Come on, let's join the others.'

Pursing her lips, she followed his lead. There was no way he could afford to attend charity events like this on the salary of a fisherman. She had long suspected he had a private income but had never enquired. Now she wondered what the source of his wealth might be. And apparently, she was not the only one. Somewhere in this room, a man with spade cufflinks was also wondering the same thing.

Chapter Thirteen

This evening's format consisted of a friendly game of contract bridge with new partners, followed by supper. The following day, the competition would begin in earnest.

Everyone drew a card and the person with the closest card would become their partner. Picking an eight of clubs, she then made her way to the tables as everyone attempted to find their corresponding partners. There was a lot of good humour as people hunted back and forth and existing partnerships broke up. It was a smart way to break the ice and keep everyone on their toes. She enjoyed playing in a partnership with Jacques and had become accustomed to his style of play and, between the two of them, they had agreed upon a few private conventions. If it was a risky call, Mal would always make it and because of it, they often won more than they lost. But when they lost, they did so spectacularly.

Both liked playing low twos. Mal was excellent at finessing tricks; Jacques could count every last card in no trumps. They were a good team, but she imagined this weekend they would be up against some excellent players.

Like any card game, bridge required as much luck as it did skill. Playing with a new partner would make the evening more challenging, but she was still determined to win.

Pulling out her seat, she found her opponents already seated. Penny Fitzgibbon and Teddy. She groaned inwardly with a feeling he was going to be very hard to beat.

'Dear Mal, allow me to introduce my partner, Mrs Penny Fitzgibbon. She's here with her husband and she assures me she will smite the unworthy!'

The other woman looked rather alarmed at her characterisation and shook her head firmly.

'I said no such thing.'

'I fully believe you,' said Mal warmly, dismissing her previous encounter with the woman. If she was going to have to play with her, she had best make the most of it. 'I have only known Teddy here for less than a day, but I still think I have the measure of him. And of course, we've already met back in Falmouth.' In Falmouth, Penny had been unpleasant in her attitude towards the bridal party, but Mal was prepared to give her a second chance. Smiling, she shook the woman's hand and saw like herself, she was wearing little in the way of jewellery: a simple wedding band and a large emerald ring. She had a silk blouse with a rather curious side bow, fashionable at least two decades ago, and no necklace. Her hair was cut short and was a metallic shade of dark grey. It wasn't the most becoming of looks, but Mal was only interested in her card playing abilities.

'Do you play much, Penny?'

'Twice a week. Contract only. Henry, that's my husband, plays Chicago, but I don't have time for that. I like the small gains.'

Mal nodded. What she meant was that she liked playing the margins. No grand flourishes for this lady. Mal looked at Teddy.

'I imagine you rather enjoy Chicago?'

'Indeed, I do, indeed I do. Like yourself. I can always spot a fellow gambler.'

Mal was going to protest and then laughed. How could she deny it? Contract bridge required a lot of small victories and playing the odds. But Chicago was more kindly disposed to a pair that played hell for leather and tried for slams.

'Guilty as charged. I wonder if my partner prefers contract or Chicago? Tell me Penny, have you been here before? This is my first year.'

'We come every five years or so, and this is our third time. Wulf and Kira have done an incredible job with the island. Every time we return, it just gets better.'

'Are my ears burning?'

Mal turned in her chair and looked up to see the very handsome Wulf Clarkson walking towards their table, greeting Teddy and Penny as old friends.

'Alright, gorgeous! Penny, I swear babes, you look younger every time I see you. And you, Teddy, are looking even richer, if that's possible.'

Leaning forward to shake Mal's hand, she smelled cigarette smoke and tried not to wrinkle her nose. She had always found the smell unpleasant and instead raised her glass.

'You have a wonderful place here. I know I'm going to have a very pleasant stay.'

'Ah yes, you're in Sea Thrift, aren't you? Smashing, ain't it? Kira recently refurbished that room.'

'Ah, so you got Sea Thrift, did you?' said Teddy, wagging his finger. 'Well, you beat me to the punch there. I tell you what, Wulf, if you can guarantee that room for me next year, I'll pay you double the asking price. You can put the extra money towards this weekend's charity.'

'Is it a particularly nice room?' asked Penny quietly as Teddy and Wulf shook hands and made a song and dance over how generous each other was.

'It is, but I'm not sure it's worth as much as it costs. It doesn't even have a slide into the sea.'

Penny looked at Mal with concern, then decided she was making a joke and laughed politely. Mal laughed along, but it felt strained. Penny seemed pleasant enough, but a bit Home Counties for her taste.

'Tell me, what do you do? I have a bookshop here in Cornwall.'

Penny's eyes lit up.

'I love bookshops! Where is it? We'll call in. I bet I know it. I'm always in bookshops. Henry says I could start

80

a library, but I can't imagine anything worse. What if they got returned all tattered?'

Mal was going to reply, but Penny sped on.

'I'm in two reading groups back home; The Winchester Worms and Jane's group, but that doesn't have a name. The Winchester Worms is because we're all bookworms. Isn't that clever?'

As Penny spoke, Mal decided she might not be that sharp a card player after all.

'My shop is in Golden, Yaffle Books.'

'Golden's a funny name for a village, isn't it?' said Penny. 'Everywhere in Cornwall has odd names. Do you know how Golden came about?'

'I think it's to do with the way the sunsets cause a warm glow over the village. Or it may be connected to a treasure galleon that sank off the shores. It could also be a corruption of a Cornish word.'

'Well, you have the bookshop,' laughed Penny happily. 'You'll have to look up the answer in one of them.'

'And tell me, dear ladies,' asked Teddy, now that Wulf had wandered on to meet and greet other guests. 'Have either of you passed the playing bug down to your children?'

It was a very common assumption that Mal must have children. She had once toyed with the idea, but her ex-husband had had a vasectomy and that avenue had been closed. In truth, she wasn't too appalled. Her career took up all her time, and she was surrounded by nieces and nephews and godchildren. It was a good life, and she was happy with it.

'No children, but one of the nephews is a card demon and at Christmas all the families get together and play, so the younger ones get into the swing of it as well. Although for the younger ones, we play Rummikub.'

'You'll have to tell me about Rummikub. That's not a game I'm familiar with.' He turned, smiling at Penny. 'And what of yourself? I'm sure I should know, but I have a dreadful memory. Any children? I won't ask about your grandchildren; you're far too young.'

Mal let out a playful groan at his heavy-handed flattery, but Penny's face was a stony mask. She drank from her glass and looked around the room.

'I don't have a child.' She broke off her sentence and looked around the room, her lips tight in frustration. 'Where is your partner, Mal? We're going to start soon.'

Her abrupt change of conversation and sharp words made Mal pause. She sympathised with Penny's annoyance at the assumptions and intrusions by others.

Mal joined her in looking around the room. All the tables were now occupied. Just one or two people were coming back from the bar, breaking off conversations and pulling out chairs. The games were about to start and she was sitting without a partner.

A man in his forties walked in through the double doors leading to the bar. One of the hosts walked up to him. Then, as the pair of them looked around the room, she pointed in the direction of Mal's table.

'Well, I think this is him now,' said Mal, watching him approach. He had the slim build of a cyclist or a runner. His hair was shaved down, and the shadow from his stubble suggested he was embracing his baldness before it was thrust upon him. As he walked across the room between the tables, Mal noticed how he was watching everyone. His head kept twitching left and right, and she wondered if he was looking out for his friends. Noticing her observation, he coughed, relaxed his walk and kept eye contact as he smiled and headed towards the table.

'My apologies for my delay. I believe we're going to be teammates. I'm John Markham.' He smiled at Mal. As he leant forwards to shake her hand, she saw a spade cufflink.

Listening to his soft, Scouse accent, Mal knew she had heard his voice only hours before. Was it the same man? Had he arranged this? Feeling sick, she nodded over to the host and asked for a small whisky. She needed to calm her nerves. Her hands were sweaty and she could feel her pulse racing in her throat. Sitting across from her was an unknown adversary, and she needed to gather her wits.

She sipped the drink and prepared for battle.

Chapter Fourteen

After a few words from Wulf, in which he praised Teddy for his early contribution to the charity, there were hoots and catcalls with others promising they would make his donation look like a drop in the ocean. Teddy took it in good spirit, and John grinned across the table at Mal.

'Looks like we're on a high-rollers' table, what do you say, Em?'

Mal knocked her glass down in one swig; moderation be damned. Only the people in her past trading life called her Em. Her large flourishing signature across documents was a simple capital M, indicating that Malachite Peck had executed another deal. But her family and friends didn't call her Em, and neither did anyone in her new life. For this man to do so meant he knew exactly who she was.

'My name is Mal. I don't know where you got Em from.'

She stared at him and was pleased to see him frown.

'My apologies again. I have a dreadful habit of shortening people's names. Especially when I'm nervous.'

Mal snorted, but Penny stepped into his rescue.

'Nothing to be nervous about. We're all new to each other as well. We'll have a great game.'

Mal gave a sharp nod of the head, picked up one of the packs of cards and started to shuffle.

'An extra shuffle for luck, Mal?' asked Penny. There had been no need to shuffle the cards, but she had needed to do something with her hands, and as the other option was slamming them on the table and calling this John Markham a liar, she had chosen to shuffle instead.

The games began, the tables getting the measure of their new partners and the playing style of their opponents. The room fell into silence as bids were called and cards were played. Occasionally, a loud groan would emit from a table, or a small round of applause, but quite quickly, Mal zoned them out as she focused on her own hand.

She had played three rounds so far and not had more than eight points on any deal. Given the lack of bidding from John, it seemed he didn't have the points either. After the second round of some astonishingly poor card play from him, she started to count his points as they went down. He had been the first to bid, and passed. Yet, as Mal had counted, he had sixteen points. More than enough to open the bidding. From that moment onwards, it was clear John was either not an experienced player, or the most timid partner ever.

As the deals progressed, Mal tried to guess the content of her opponents' hands as well as her partner's, and even managed to win a game or two. But it was incredibly hard work and, for the most part, she was playing defensively to frustrate her opponents' bids.

After one particularly poor play from John, the other three simply looked at his card on the table, and then Penny promptly trumped it.

Looking across at Mal, he grimaced.

'That was a bad play, wasn't it?'

'Easy mistake. It happens to all of us,' chipped in Penny. Mal could barely speak, and Teddy simply raised an eyebrow.

John looked at Mal again and screwed up his eyes.

'I have a confession. I'm new to this. I'm here at my partner's urging. She told me I would love it. Honestly, I thought I would be playing with her all weekend. I had no idea I would be inflicted on others.'

He looked so crestfallen that Penny patted him on the hand.

'We all have to start somewhere. This is just a friendly round, after all.'

'You're too kind,' said John.

You're too wet, thought Mal. It's not as if she was having to play with him.

As the games came to an end, there was general applause for the tables that had the highest scores and those with grand slams, bid and made. The highest partnership immediately offered to donate the point value of their game in cash and received another round of applause. Mal looked at her point value and wondered if it was enough to buy a first aid kit.

Rising from their table to allow the servers to clear the tables for dinner, Mal left quickly. Unwilling to spend another second in John's company, she made a beeline for Jacques at the bar.

He took one look at her and turned to the barman before returning his attention to Mal.

'I have taken the liberty of ordering an espresso martini. I think your face suggests that was the right call?'

Behind her, Mal heard laughing and hadn't realised that Teddy had kept up with her. For an old man, he sure was fast on his pins.

'Oh Jacques, your dear friend has just played the game of her life. I have never seen such skill. Quite formidable. I do hope we are not playing you tomorrow.'

Tipping his hat, he headed off in search of his wife.

'What was all that about?' he said, handing Mal's drink to her.

Taking a small sip, she sighed in relief and then wondered how much she could tell him. After all, he was also under investigation. She wanted to warn him, but what if he was involved? How well did she know Jacques, after all?

'My partner, who, by the way, referred to me as his teammate, is a rank amateur. I ended up having to try to guess his hand from inferred bids and leads from our opponents. It was quite the challenge.'

Taking another sip, she felt herself unwind.

'Do you know, on one round he opened with one no trumps and it turns out he not only had a singleton, he also had a void!'

Mal laughed at Jacques' mon Dieu and took a sip of her drink before continuing. 'Actually, I think there's more to him than meets the eye.'

'How so?' asked Jacques, still laughing from the other man's catastrophically bad bid.

'I think he knows who I am,' and she went on to explain the conversation she had overheard and the fact that he had called her Em.

Jacques' eyes narrowed as Mal recounted the events. 'And he mentioned me as well?'

'Yes, but I think he's here investigating someone else. I don't know why he's focused on you. Probably because of me. And the fact that he has focused on me suggests that he's following a financial investigation.'

'Right,' said Jacques, looking around. All sense of his previously relaxed demeanour had disappeared. He caught Wulf's eye and waved him over. 'For this evening's dinner I should like the company of Mal. Can you suggest that we sit where we choose, rather than back in our game formations?'

Wulf laughed loudly and slapped Jacques on the arm.

'Glad to see there's life in the old dog, hey?'

Then, turning away from Jacques' apoplectic expression, he tapped his knife on his glass.

'Dinner is served and please sit wherever you choose. And if, unlike some, you're tired of your lovely husband, my table is always available.'

Amongst the laughter, the crowd returned to the room and Jacques immediately choose a table in the corner. He offered Mal the seat facing the room and sat to one side so that he, too, could keep an eye on the crowd.

'Wulf's a character, isn't he?' said Mal, trying to lighten the mood.

'Old dog! Pah. He's the same age as me.'

'At least no one looks at you and wonders how much work you've had done.'

Jacques stared at Mal as his jaw dropped, then he chuckled loudly.

'I can't tell if I've been complimented or insulted.'

'Complimented, I assure you.' As a couple walked towards them, she spoke quickly. 'I thought you were going to warn Wulf of the interloper?'

'It's not my business.'

'But they named you.'

'Malachite, we are here to relax and play cards. I have done nothing wrong, and more importantly, neither have you. All will be well.'

The way he said it sounded as if he was warning the world at large not to spoil their weekend, but Mal looked around the room with a sense of foreboding.

DAY TWO Chapter Fifteen

Daybreak had announced the oncoming storm. At the far end of the island, the wildlife observers were busy securing the outdoor monitoring equipment. The wind tugged at their clothes. The occasional spray from a wave carried up on the breeze, wetting their faces.

'Is it going to rain?' asked John Markham.

Ferne looked up at the clouds but shook her head.

'No. Leastways, not yet. That's sea spray.'

John looked about him in clear disbelief.

'Really? We seem quite high up here, and inland.'

'No. I'm sure you must be right,' said Ferne in exasperation. She hated when the castle guests came over to see what was what. 'I've only worked here for three seasons. And you've been here, let me see, twelve hours?'

She smiled to take the sting out of her words, but the man instantly apologised.

'That was pretty rude of me. Here. Let me carry those sandbags.'

Offering no argument, Ferne let him take the bags from her and grinned as he grunted in surprise at their weight.

'I guess wildlife conservation is quite physical?'

Ferne nodded, picking up another two sandbags.

'It is that. We're as likely to be counting chick numbers as putting up fence posts and laying footpaths to help keep visitors off the flora.'

Which was where Ferne had found this guest, wandering around this side of the island. When she had challenged him, he had pointed to a lack of signs. Muttering under her breath, she directed him to the path and explained how certain birds tended to nest out on the scrub.

Returning to the previous conversation, John asked again about the lack of signs.

'We don't have any. Wulf doesn't want his guests to feel hampered. He wants them to treat the island as their own home. Even allowing their sodding dogs off-lead.' She picked up another sandbag and piled it up against the door of the shed. 'You don't have a dog here, do you?'

'No,' said John emphatically, glad to have finally done something right. 'So, can't you explain the issue to Wulf? I mean, doesn't the conservation charity have a say?'

'Not a word. He lets us work from here free of charge, so we have very little ground to stand on. And in fairness, he's incredibly generous. Our workstations all have satellite link-ups; the dorms are really lovely. Every time the castle or house gets an upgrade, we get the cast-offs. Anything we don't want, he sells and makes a donation to the charity. It's how we're able to employ so many high-quality researchers.'

'Like yourself?'

She stopped and stood up, stretched her back, and looked at him squarely. He was easily a decade older than her, if not two.

'I'm working on it.'

'You must see some interesting things out at sea.'

'All sorts. This year's focus is on tuna spotting.'

'What about boats? Ever see any refugees or smugglers?'

'We're a wildlife observation station.'

'Yeah, but an island off the Cornish coast; isn't that a smuggler's dream?'

'In novels, sure. The only boats I see are fishing ones.'

'No refugees either?'

'Here in Cornwall? Poor sods would have been off course to land here.'

'So, no refugees either.'

'You sound disappointed.' She cocked her head. Refugees were not an issue down here in Cornwall. France was so far away from the south-west. 'All we have are dolphins, whales, tuna, and an excess of bird life. Last week, the first swallows arrived. Quite a bit earlier than last year, which got everyone excited.'

'Did Wulf come and celebrate with you?'

'Over a bird?' She scoffed and lifted the wheelbarrow. 'He came over when he heard about the humpback whale, but of course it had gone by the time he got here.'

'So he's not a regular visitor?'

'Not really.'

'You think he'd be more interested?'

'This is more Kira's passion, but she's rarely on the island. She's an ambassador for the World Wide Fund for

Nature, amongst other things, and is always flying around the world telling us to cut our carbon footprint.'

'Seems somewhat hypocritical.'

'And then some, but what can I say? They pay my wage and I love my job. Now, I need to head back to the centre, and I suggest you head back to the castle.'

He turned and walked off.

'And stick to the paths!'

Back at the centre, Dougie had been cooking and Ferne's mouth watered. A bowl of stew was just what she needed.

'You took long enough,' said Dougie, but his tone was friendly.

'One of the guests was helping me, so it took twice as long. Plus, he could talk the hind legs off a donkey. Asking about refugees and smugglers if you can believe it?'

Ferne lifted the lid on one of the pans and inhaled deeply.

'What was his name?' asked Jordan sharply.

'How should I know? It's not like he thought I was worth exchanging names with.'

'Sodding tourists,' said Jordan, sneering. 'Always poking their noses in. Always acting better than us. I'm going to bring the quad bikes up to the door. And leave me some bloody stew this time. Last time, all I got was dumplings.'

As he left the centre, the wind caught the door, wrenching it out of his hand and slamming it against the wall. He could hear shouts of protest from indoors, as he wrestled to close it. He'd rather listen to the roar of the wind than the whine of his colleagues. Pulling out his phone, he headed for the shelter of the log store, then hit dial. This was too sensitive for a text. Three rings later, his call connected, and he shouted down the phone over the noise of the wind.

'We have a problem.'

Chapter Sixteen

Francine stretched and yawned her way into the breakfast room and saw that she was almost the last one down. Only Julia was missing.

'That is the most scrumptious bed ever. Who else slept like a log? I swear, I'm taking that bed home with me.'

Helping herself to a bowl of berry compote, she added some seed granola and a spoon of honey. Johanna was buttering a delicious brioche and Francine tutted.

'You'll never fit into your bridesmaid's dress if you keep wolfing down the carbs like that.'

Johanna grinned.

'Don't worry about me. I've decided to wear dungarees.'

'What!' Francine stared at her in horror. That was so typical of Johanna, always making it about herself with her: "I'm an artist. I'm so different." Now she was waving her brioche around as she described her outfit. Butter dripped onto her fingers and she licked it off quickly as she laughed.

'Duchess satin dungarees. I'll cut quite the figure. What do you think, Midge?'

Imogen was drinking a black coffee and smiling at her bridesmaids.

'Francine, don't panic. Everyone will look perfect in their dresses. Johanna, stop winding Francine up. No one is wearing dungarees.'

Francine huffed, uncomfortable at being the target of a joke.

'When are we off to Falmouth? What's everyone wearing? I thought jeans would be okay? Johanna will obviously be in dungarees. You can fill the pockets up with pasties.'

'Oh, God,' groaned Imogen. 'I would kill for a pasty, but the seams on my dress are already tight.'

'Rubbish,' tutted Johanna. 'Even when you wear Lycra, it looks baggy.'

Everyone laughed, but Francine thought the reason Lycra looked baggy on Imogen was because she had stretched it out of shape. She was easily a size fourteen.

'So, Falmouth?'

'Cancelled, I'm afraid. There's a storm coming in and the skipper thinks we might not be able to make it back to the island.'

'Oh, babes!' cried Francine in alarm. 'You were so looking forward to that. Shall I go and have a word? We can leave Julia behind if that's the issue?'

Imogen waved her hand dismissively.

'No, don't worry. The skipper was quite emphatic. I also had a word with Wulf, who said the forecast was looking pretty dreadful for the afternoon and evening. The staff have already removed all the loungers, and covered the pool and hot tub.'

Francine stood up and walked over to the window. Below, the waves were all topped with white, and the bushes were swaying back and forth in the wind.

'Really? You can't hear a thing, can you?'

She opened the patio door to the yells of the other girls as the wind disturbed the room. The roar of the sea filled the room as the strong breeze rushed around the girls, disturbing hairstyles and napkins. She pulled the door shut just as quickly and then laughed awkwardly as the other girls glared at her. Only Johanna returned her laugh.

'Well, that woke me up. It's already got worse since this morning.'

'So what are the plans, then?'

'Lounging and beauty treatments. It's a hard life, but someone has to do it.'

'Do you know,' said Tinks, 'I for one am looking forward to it.' She looked over at Johanna. 'I know you were keen to explore Falmouth, but I have been flat out at work. This will be a lovely reason to do nothing.'

Tinks had just completed a court case where she had successfully defended her client against a charge of industrial espionage. Whilst it had been a team effort, this was her first major case as the barrister, and at such a young age, she wanted to shine and cement a reputation for ruthlessness and success. No one rated a barrister that tried hard; they rated winners.

'Don't worry about me,' said Johanna. 'I can always do Falmouth another day.'

Imogen's phone buzzed and all the girls looked at her expectantly. Francine had a feeling she was missing something, but decided not to ask as she flicked through a copy of Tatler. Cara Delevingne was wearing the same jacket that Francine had.

'Oh look, me and Cara are BFFs.'

Everyone ignored her.

'Is it Julia?' Tinks asked Imogen.

Imogen finished reading the text and smiled as she placed her phone back on the table.

'All good. The hospital has given her the all clear, and she's on her way back to London. She sends all her love and apologises for being a ninny.' Everyone's phones buzzed. 'In fact, that's her on the group WhatsApp.'

'What did I miss?' asked Francine, aggrieved.

'Midge arranged for Julia to be flown off the island first thing this morning.'

'That's a bit selfish, isn't it?' said Francine. 'I mean, this is Imogen's party. And it's not like anything was wrong with her.'

'Come on, Francine. You know her history. I think we'd all be nervous in her position.'

'Then she shouldn't have come in the first place.'

'Really, Francine?' said Portia.

'What? I'm just saying what you're all thinking. We could have gone out yesterday except Imogen felt we should stay with Julia, absolute angel she is.'

'I'm not thinking it,' said Johanna.

'That's just because you haven't known Julia as long as some of us. There's never a drama where she isn't demanding to be the centre of attention. Remember when she cancelled the trip to the Maldives?'

'Her mother had died.'

'Her step-mother.'

'She still loved her.'

'She loved her bank balance.'

'Francine. That's unfair.'

Francine drank her orange juice and nodded her head. She felt wrong-footed and always did in this particular group of girls.

'Yes, it was. I apologise. Now, it's almost eleven. Who says we turn these orange juices into something a bit stronger? I have a case of Krug. Let's turn today into a proper occasion!'

As the other girls were keen to change the subject, they quickly agreed.

'Okay, let me just do this.' She tapped into the group chat, replying to Julia's message: 'So glad you are alright. You made the right call, but it won't be the same without you. Lots of love and take care of yourself and your precious cargo.'

She smiled at the others.

'See, I'm not a total monster.'

As she headed out of the room to the kitchen, Johanna rolled her eyes but decided not to comment. She was the newest in the group, but Francine was very hard work. Imogen wouldn't hear a word against her, but then she was the most forgiving soul Johanna had ever met and wouldn't spot a manipulative social climber even if she bit her. Johanna wondered if maybe Francine was blackmailing her, or guilt-tripping her. She seemed the sort.

Chapter Seventeen

Mal had slept poorly and blamed the mysterious John Markham. All night long, she kept worrying about Jacques. His story about Wulf owing him a favour rang alarm bells and now, with John referring to him as well, she didn't know what to think. She wanted to confront him, but she didn't know how to ask without offending him. What was the nature of the favour? She'd bet all she had that Jacques wasn't crooked, but what was the relationship between the two men? It certainly didn't seem friendly, so why would Wulf give Mal such a generous suite?

Every time she woke, she felt Mack's absence and hoped the cat was doing well without her. She'd left plenty of food and water and he had his own secure route in and out of her flat, but if he decided to move on to a new, more reliable member of staff, she would miss his company.

Deciding there was nothing she could do about Mack, she also resolved to let go of any temptations to interrogate Jacques whilst on the island. Should it go awry, she didn't want to be marooned on an island with him, trying to play bridge. Which reminded her; breakfast, then cards. Today was the first of two full days of cards. Tomorrow night would be a gala dinner and then the following day it would be back to reality. Looking out of the window, she was glad not to be travelling today; the waves looked quite bouncy. Overhead, a helicopter tipped in the wind and then headed back towards the mainland. Checking her watch, she wondered if it was a crew change or if a guest had bailed. Losing a bridge player would be annoying, as the tables were set up for four players, not three. Three-handed bridge was not impossible, but it definitely wasn't as much fun.

After slipping into a pair of purple tartan trousers and a cream silk blouse, she made her way down to the breakfast room and found herself smiling. Jacques stood up as she walked in.

Mal and Jacques were in the middle of swapping notes about their opponents' playing styles from the night before when Wulf entered the ballroom and started walking around the tables, chatting to each of the guests and acting like the perfect host. As he travelled, he left a wake of smiles and chatter behind him. The great man was seeing to their needs as though that was his only concern. Mal never failed to be amazed by how easily people fell for the allure of fame and glamour. When it was their turn to be blessed, Mal picked up her coffee cup, giving her the excuse for silence.

'Well, Jackie boy, how did you sleep? If you got any, that is?' he laughed and tipped his head Mal's way. Mal's cup clattered in her saucer.

'I beg your pardon?'

He stepped back in mock alarm, raising his hands.

'You misunderstand me. Jacques' room faces west. The brunt of the winds today is coming from that direction. I simply worried that his room would be too noisy.'

Mal picked up her cup again and stared at him. She knew what he had meant.

'I slept perfectly, Wulf,' said Jacques, a new frostiness in his voice. 'I'm used to storms back in Golden.'

'Alright! That's what I like to hear. And tonight we have some rather special wines on the menu, that I think you will appreciate.'

He smiled and Mal wondered if he thought that grin ingratiated himself to people or if he just couldn't stop playing at the genial host. It all felt so forced.

'Tell me,' said Mal, putting her cup down more carefully this time. 'The helicopter this morning. Have we lost a guest? Will the bridge be disrupted?'

'A guest, yes, but not from this party. We have a group of young ladies celebrating an engagement down at the house. One of the lasses is pregnant and has a few concerns, so she's on her way home. But nothing to worry about.'

Mal thought back to the young woman with the blonde hair and green face. She hoped everything was going to be alright. She wasn't a believer, but at times like this, she always sent a little message upwards, hoping that someone would take care of things.

'The forecast is poor for this afternoon,' said Jacques, changing the subject.

'It is, but nothing untoward.'

'We have an amber weather warning.'

'Ah, you fishermen, always looking to the skies. It will be fine, trust me.'

Clapping Jacques on the shoulder, he hurried away.

'An amber warning is pretty severe, isn't it?' said Mal. 'That's what hit Golden a few months back, wasn't it?'

'It was, yes.'

'Well, we all weathered that one.'

'We did, but I think this is going to be worse. I was online studying the charts. I haven't seen a low-pressure front dropping so fast in decades. I think this is going to be a big blow.'

Mal put her spoon down.

'Is this serious?' She looked out the window in alarm. She was stuck on an island. Would they be safe?

'We'll be fine. This castle was built in the fifteenth century. It has no doubt seen worse. Wulf is a bit of an arse, but he's right; we'll be fine. And if you don't trust him, trust me.'

Mal let out a small sigh of relief. If Jacques wasn't concerned, she would follow his lead.

An hour later, the games had begun, and they were sitting opposite each other, playing against a pair of sisters. Both women sat down and introduced themselves.

Then, having instructed Mal and Jacques that they hoped the game would be played in silence, they cut the deck and play commenced.

After half an hour, Mal could barely look at Jacques as the sisters continued to hiss and tut at each other as mistakes were made or opportunities missed. Jacques had taken to staring at the ceiling to avoid catching Mal's eye. Both were fit to start giggling as the sisters continued to admonish each other.

No one spoke a word until the game came to an end. The two women stood up, shook hands with Mal and Jacques, and then turned and walked away in opposite directions, blaming the other for their loss.

As other tables were still playing, Mal had to choke down her laugh. But as she and Jacques leant across the table, their foreheads almost touched.

'That was mad!'

'When you trumped her Jack of spades?'

'I know! I thought she was going to crown her sister.'

'I wonder who we'll get next? Hopefully, the next pair won't be so scary.'

The next pair were indeed friendlier. Two men who were here with their wives, but in order to preserve marital harmony, they had chosen to play boys versus girls.

'The memsahib gets shirty when I make a stupid move,' said the chap in a pair of russet trousers and with a glorious moustache. 'I have to say, the girls are far better players than us. They'll have much more fun playing together. And so, by default, will we.'

Cyril's playing partner was an older gentleman called Andrew, who, despite his assurances that he was hopeless at the game, nicely finessed Mal's ace and all of Jacques' hearts. It was touch and go, but in the end, Mal and Jacques just about scraped a win.

'Let's hope we don't meet the memsahibs. They'll wipe the floor with us,' said Jacques, and Mal fervently agreed. Although secretly she hoped they did. There was nothing more enjoyable than playing against a better opponent and winning.

They were just about to meet their third couple when Wulf took to the small dais and called for everyone's attention. No doubt Teddy had managed to donate another thousand pounds for something or other. Maybe the Swiss couple had decided to accept the challenge and match his bid? Mal had overheard them at breakfast chatting away in German, determined to outshine the American's largesse.

Wulf cleared his throat and everyone turned attentively.

'Lords and Ladies, Ladies and Gentlemen. Just a little weather update. The Met Office have now changed their advisory notice to red for this section of the coastline. The storm should reach its peak intensity by this afternoon and early evening. By tomorrow morning, all danger should have passed.'

Chapter Eighteen

The room instantly broke into mutterings, and one of the men stood up.

'Major Cartwright, ex-Fusiliers.'

Oh, God, thought Mal, one of those types. Eager to put themselves forward and make sure everyone knew they were someone important.

'Is it too late to evacuate the island?'

'But, of course,' muttered Jacques under his breath.

'No need for that, Major Cartwright,' said Wulf, smiling reassuringly around the room. 'Absolutely the safest place for you all is in here, enjoying cards, tucked up warm and dry. Now we will be making a few changes in light of the warning for the safety of all on the island.'

'First, for tonight only, we are asking all guests to keep their windows closed. And smokers, we are setting the Buttery aside for you, should you wish to smoke. No need to battle nature. I will probably join you.'

This was met by warm laughter.

'We will also be welcoming a few extra souls this evening. As you may know, we have a wildlife observation centre at the far end of the island. They will stay here tonight in the west dormitories. So if you see a few unfamiliar faces, that's who they'll be.'

'What about the young ladies down at the beach house?' demanded the major, who hadn't yet sat down.

'They are staying put, as they're on the sheltered side and that house has stood for two hundred years. They have, of course, been offered the shelter of the castle, but they are perfectly happy where they are. Young girls these days are quite the warriors, Major. Besides, they'd find us very dull company. A hen party versus a bunch of bridge players.'

There was more laughter and Jacques leant across the table.

'He has a point. But I have to say, I know whose company I prefer.' He gave Mal a wolfish smile and wiggled his eyebrows. Mal had just taken a sip of water and now spluttered her drink in surprise, scowling as everyone looked her way.

'Did you do that deliberately?' she hissed. As he nodded, she laughed back at him and promised to get her revenge later.

As Wulf stepped off the podium, a few people approached him. Mal turned back to Jacques.

'We will be okay, won't we?'

'Completely. It will probably be quite noisy in a bit, but these windows are all triple glazed and the walls have withstood cannon fire. We'll be perfectly fine. Now, according to the timetable, it's time for us to move to table five. Let's see who awaits.'

Sitting at the next table were a young couple, possibly the youngest in the room, and Mal made the fatal mistake of underestimating them.

They were a particularly good looking couple. Each could have featured on the cover of Vogue. He was dark-haired, with a firm jawline and a long fringe that was brushed back from his forehead. She had long brown hair falling in waves down her back, clipped back with two diamond encrusted combs. She was wearing very little make-up, but her eyes were full of mischief and she was smiling widely. The two were clearly having an excellent time.

As the husband introduced himself as Seb and his wife as Ariana, she confessed to having played since childhood with her parents and sisters. Mal quickly revised her opinions. Children who grew up around cards were the fiercest of all competitors and soon they were off to a lively round of bidding, with the young couple bidding to slam.

Mal looked at her own hand. She had length in clubs, a singleton King and three trumps. If she could ditch the singleton, she stood a chance of trumping early.

Of course, she didn't get a chance to derail the game. Jacques and Mal looked at each other in alarm, as neither could do anything to arrest the march of the young couple. As the thirteenth trick was played and made, Mal and Jacques applauded them and Ariana beamed in delight. They were the last table to finish their hand, so disturbing the other players wasn't an issue.

Seb groaned and muttered to his wife as Wulf headed their way.

'Sorry Ari, looks like you are about to lose the new rose garden.'

'Countess Hiverton, Sir Sebastian. Did I hear a grand slam being made?'

Seb stood up and bowed graciously to the room.

'All down to my dear wife, but I believe we shall now have to add £5,000 to the charity pot.'

Ariana bent her head towards Mal.

'Sod the rose garden. We need new gutters. Seb's always so easy about money.'

Mal thought it was an odd line from a countess, but clearly someone had to watch the purse strings. She had always thought the titled classes were pretty rubbish with financial accountability, but she knew a few that had worked out money wasn't a dirty word. Maybe Countess Hiverton was one of them. That said, she was smiling fondly at her husband, so at least she was prepared to forgive his generosity.

'It's a charity dear to us. So I guess the gutters will have to wait.'

'Are you on holiday?' asked Mal, warming to the younger woman.

'We are. My sister lives down here and so the children are with her for the weekend. I just wish, with this storm, I was with them.'

Seb sat down and squeezed his wife's hand.

'Let's FaceTime the children at lunch. Put your mind at rest.'

'What if Paddy is staying at the beach house?'

Her fingers were white as she gripped her coffee cup.

'Not a chance. She'll have made a duvet fort in front of the telly up at the house and they'll all be watching Shrek.'

Mal wondered if Ariana was a nervous mother, or one that just didn't want to be separated from her children during a red weather event.

Looking at the sheet, it was their turn to move again. Mal felt her spirits plummet as she saw John Markham and his partner sitting at the table. It took all her willpower not to turn to Jacques and warn him that this man was investigating them. Instead, she paused, pretending that her necklace was caught. As Jacques bent down to help her, she muttered quickly.

'Don't ask me why, but I very much dislike that man.'

Jacques' fingers paused on the clasp momentarily, and then, acting as if nothing had happened, freed her hair and stepped back. With a small bow, he kissed her hand and then guided her towards their table. It was these small acts of solidarity that made Mal appreciate Jacques.

John Markham stood up as they approached.

'We meet again! I hope I prove to be better opposition than I was a partner,' he said, somewhat gallantly. 'May I introduce my partner, Susie? She's the brains between us.'

'Indeed,' said Mal, and sat down. 'I saw you were in late again this morning.' She smiled sympathetically at Susie. If this woman was his partner, Mal was a drunken sailor. But if they were playing games, she would keep them on their toes. 'You must have a very busy job that keeps you engaged? Do you work in the same line of business?'

She kept her tone disinterested, but she saw his jaw clench and he ground his teeth. He took the seat to her right and looked at his cards.

'I was out for a walk over at the wildlife station and got waylaid helping them prepare for the storm. They are an interesting bunch over there. Do you know any of them?'

How neatly he had side-stepped her inquiry into his job. Mal had counted the points in her hand and decided she was going to annihilate this so-called John Markham and his partner. Now she looked at him, his face bland with casual enquiry.

'Do I know a bunch of strangers living on an island off the Cornish coast?'

'Yes.'

'What a strange question. To the best of my knowledge, no.'

'To the best of your knowledge?'

'Well yes, until I meet them, how would I possibly know if I know them? Jacques, what about you? To the best of your knowledge, do you know anyone at the wildlife post?'

Jacques stroked his chin. 'That is quite the question. How do I answer it without perjuring myself? What if I were to say no, only to walk over and discover Hortense Picard? I would exclaim in delight, "Hortense, I haven't seen you since school and yet here you are on an island off the Cornish coast." What a liar I would be, had I said I knew no one.'

'What was Hortense like at school?' asked Mal.

'A terror. Mon Dieu, that girl, I would pull her plaits and she would break my pencil leads. I was forever having to sharpen them.'

'Young love.'

'I know, and yet here we are reunited on an island off the Cornish coast, all thanks to Mr John Markham here.'

Smiling at each other, they turned back to John.

'There we are then. I hope that answers your question. Neither of us are knowingly aware of anyone living at the wildlife station.'

John's smile was tight and barely made it past his cheeks. His eyes were angry.

'Oh dear,' said Susie, 'I'm afraid my husband is sometimes overly inquisitive. Anyway, it's the nature of our jobs. We own an accountancy business.'

'Fascinating,' said Mal, cutting her off. 'Shall we play?'

If these two were married, Mal would eat her black patent leather boots. But the fact that they were claiming to be accountants had confirmed Mal's suspicions: they were here on a financial investigation. They may even be accountants, but Mal didn't believe for one second, they were self-employed. Her best guess was that these two worked for His Majesty. Serious Fraud or Customs and Excise. They were British, which probably ruled out an overseas authority, and to be investigating someone on this island, it probably involved some serious financial breach. Determined not to be dragged into a case that had nothing to do with her, she started bidding.

Twenty minutes later, they were the first table to finish as Mal and Jacques obliterated them. Rising to her feet, she and Jacques immediately left the room rather than make small talk.

'I think I agree with you,' said Jacques, as he returned with two coffees. 'They are not card players. So why are they here?'

Mal shrugged and placed her coffee cup on the table. 'I am determined to ignore them. Nothing is going to spoil this wonderful treat.'

'I'm glad to hear that,' said Jacques in relief. 'I know you like a good puzzle but I agree with you, this weekend is about having fun.'

A gust of rain slammed into the windows, causing both of them to look up in alarm.

'Has the storm arrived early?'

Jacques shook his head. 'I fear this is the opening act only.'

'Hell!' Mal stood up. 'I think I'm going to check on my window. I know I closed it this morning, but I just want to check I got the latch secured.'

As she headed back towards the entrance hall, she interrupted Wulf and a young man dressed in outside work gear. They were engaged in an intense conversation and Mal paused, uncertain if she should return to the lounge or interrupt them. Wulf was stabbing the younger man in the chest with his finger, and Mal thought the younger man was one jab away from decking Wulf. Coughing loudly, she approached, and the pair sprang apart. The young man glared at her and barged past, heading towards the back of the house.

'Is everything alright?' asked Mal.

Wulf's expression remained furious as he stared after the departing man. Then he shook himself and smiled at Mal.

'It's true what they say. You just can't get the staff these days. Now tell me, have you had good cards?'

Accepting his change of direction, she complimented him on a marvellous weekend so far and then, excusing herself, headed upstairs.

The way Wulf had behaved towards the young man suggested something other than a staff dispute. She wondered who he was and what was going on between them.

Back in her bedroom, she was relieved to see the window was firmly closed. Looking out over the island, she could see the waves crash over the shore. Plumes of white spray flew into the air, dwarfing the large manor house closer to the shore. She shuddered and wondered what it was like staying in there. She knew the waves weren't actually crashing on the house, but it still looked spectacular. She took a few photos, then uploaded her favourite to Instagram. Flicking through various photos, a brief message popped up.

Jasmine had liked her photo and a moment later, she saw a little comment pop up.

- *Friends are staying there right now! WOW! SCARY!!*

Mal replied quickly that her friends were perfectly safe, then closed the app. She had suspected that Jasmine might know the girls, but now she'd be inundated with messages. Something to bond over. Although, of course, they weren't friends; they were acquaintances. Why had that word fallen out of usage? Now everyone was besties, best friends forever, even frenemies, for heaven's sake. If Jasmine was actually a friend, she would be with Imogen at the wedding party.

'Well, maybe she is friends with one of the girls, just not the bride. I shouldn't be so uncharitable.'

Mal looked over to Mac for agreement and then remembered he was many miles away. She winced and wondered when she had become so used to talking aloud to herself. Maybe there was a seagull nearby and she could pretend that she was talking to the bird instead. She stopped still and shook her head. As if talking to animals was any better.

Tutting, she left the room and made her way back to Jacques. She smiled, already preparing to share her folly with him, thinking of ways to craft the conversation, and decided that chatting to Jacques was infinitely more pleasurable than an imaginary seagull or an absent cat.

Chapter Nineteen

Outside, the storm ramped up power. Some of the most savage weather systems crashed into the UK mainland in March. Lured by the warmth of spring and the promise of summer, people thought that the worst of the winter weather was behind them. These storms boiled up in the Atlantic and roared across the water, gaining ferocity until they smashed into the British Isles.

Small boats had long since fled for the safety of harbour. Large cargo vessels rode out the monstrous waves far out to sea, and the sailors swore they would find a new job as soon as they made it home. If they made it home.

Up and down the west coast, people brought their bins in, weighed down the trampolines, and explained to the dogs that today was not one for walks. Fires were lit, candles made ready, radiators switched on, and the country braced for impact as the afternoon slipped into darkness.

As the wind and rain relentlessly battered against the sturdy walls of Little Wolf, the wedding party found comfort within its cosy confines. They gathered around the crackling log fire, revelling in its warmth and the delightful company they shared. Francine delicately removed the pins from Imogen's hair, allowing a cascade of luscious curls to tumble down her back. Excitement filled the air as the girls experimented with TikTok beauty tips. The room was now a vibrant tableau of tousled curls, cat-like eyeliners, and daring contouring.

Imogen, unable to contain her excitement, sprang from the sofa and hurried to the mirror on the wall above the fireplace. Her wedding dress, adorned with ethereal ostrich feathers, lent an air of whimsy to her every movement. The feathers swayed in harmony with her graceful steps, creating an enchanting aura around her. It wasn't her actual wedding gown, but like the rest of the girls, she had dressed up in bridal attire for the afternoon's entertainment.

They had planned to wear wedding dresses on their trip to Falmouth. It was going to be huge fun, and the girls had had a blast choosing gowns to wear out and about. Just because they could no longer go to Falmouth, they wouldn't be denied the fun of their extravagant dresses.

Johanna, resplendent in her own elaborate ensemble of hoops and frills, couldn't help but feel reminiscent of the legendary Scarlett O'Hara. She brushed off Francine's snide remark about a loo roll cover, choosing to bask in the glamour and indulgence of the moment. Francine, on her part, had donned a figure-hugging sheath of satin, a dress that left little to the imagination and ensured all eyes would be on her; not only the groom, but also the entire congregation.

Imogen's laughter echoed through the room as she admired her reflection in the mirror, playing with her new

119

curls. 'Francine, this is absolutely brilliant!' she exclaimed, her eyes sparkling with joy. She turned to her friends, eager for their input. 'Girls, what do you think? Should I style my hair like this for the wedding?' The room erupted in excited chatter, each girl voicing her opinion amidst peals of laughter.

Francine stood proudly beside Imogen, capturing a photograph of the two of them, freezing their happiness in a timeless frame.

'Group shot!' Imogen called out.

'I'm not going anywhere near that fire,' said Johanna. 'Come onto the sofa. There's loads of room.'

Giggling, the girls eagerly piled on, limbs interlocked amongst the plush feather cushions. Champagne glasses were raised in celebration as they took turns immortalising the moment with countless selfies. Engulfed by a sea of billowing tulle and satin, it became challenging to distinguish one sun-kissed limb from another. Creams and ivories mingled together, creating a confectionery palette that only accentuated their youthful radiance. Their faces glowed with energy, their laughter filling the room as they gathered around their beloved friend.

Johanna, filled with artistic inspiration, struggled to her feet to fetch more champagne, her heart brimming with admiration for her companions. Grabbing her camera, she took more shots.

'I'm going to paint this! We look magnificent!' After pouring fresh glasses for everyone, she settled back onto the sofa, draping her legs across Francine's lap.

'Francine, this champagne is exquisite. I am grateful for your generous spirit,' said Johanna with a contented sigh. For a brief moment, Francine was taken aback by the heartfelt compliment, a flicker of surprise dancing across her features. She quickly regained her composure.

'Only the best for dear Imogen,' she replied, a subtle warmth tingeing her words.

Suddenly, the air exploded in a deafening roar, causing the girls to shriek in alarm. The rain and wind intensified, assaulting the windows with relentless fury. The very foundations of the house trembled as the storm unleashed its full force. Flickering lampshades cast eerie shadows across the room, compelling the girls to huddle closer together.

Thunder reverberated through the house, rendering them all momentarily speechless. Faced with Mother Nature's raw power, they couldn't help but feel small and insignificant. Imogen's voice trembled as she broke the silence, her words punctuated by a mix of awe and fear.

'Bloody hell, that was incredible. Are anyone's ears still ringing?' Her query was met with nods of agreement, and Tinks burst into tears. Apologetically, she wiped her eyes and let out a groan.

'I'm sorry, I'm fine. It was just a bit intense,' she managed to say between sobs. 'And look, TikTok got it wrong. Turns out Vaseline doesn't make mascara waterproof after all.'

The tension dissolved as laughter filled the room once more, a shared moment of relief. With a collective curiosity, the girls turned their gaze towards the window. 'I can't even see the beach now,' said Portia, her voice shaded with awe. 'It's like a cauldron out there.'

'So much for a night-time dip,' drawled Francine.

Imogen stuck her tongue out playfully. 'You'd have enjoyed it.'

'Darling, I love you greatly but if the sea temperature is not above twenty-five, this body is staying by the pool.'

'Well, hopefully when this storm has passed, they'll take the covers off the pool and we can sit out there tomorrow.'

Another flash of lightning illuminated the room, blinding everyone as a crash of thunder detonated overhead. The girls all recoiled as the wind picked up in intensity. At that minute, a tree fell and smashed into the patio doors. The frame shattered and shards of glass exploded inwards, slicing through satin and skin alike. The branches of the tree whipped into the room, filling it with wind and rain as the girls screamed in alarm, their voices drowned in the roar of the storm.

In a panic of cloth and limbs, they ran to the far door, hitching up their long gowns and large skirts as they sprinted for the exit. They spilled out into the corridor, panting as they leant against the door, bracing against the wind howling behind them, the chandelier swinging wildly above their heads. Beyond the door, they could hear furniture falling over and glasses and vases breaking into smithereens as they were hurled against the walls. Something heavy smashed into the door, making the girls flinch.

Johanna was already on her phone as Imogen tried to calm the other girls down. Tinks was still screaming. Francine was tending to Portia, whose arm was bleeding.

'Hello!' shouted Johanna into the phone. The noise from the storm beyond drowning out her voice. 'This is Johanna at Little Wolf. The patio doors have given way. We need to get out of here.'

She listened to the response and turned to the girls.

'Five minutes. They're coming in the Range Rovers.'

Francine ran for the staircase to grab a few things when a large gust of wind roared downstairs and doors started slamming as the storm tore into the house.

'Right,' shouted Imogen over the sound of wind from upstairs. 'We go as we are. No one is going upstairs.'

No one argued.

Chapter Twenty

Mal was heading back to the dining room for the afternoon's final hand of bridge. She wasn't sure where she and Jacques were on the leaderboard, but they had lost very few games and racked up a lot of points. Her head was buzzing, trying to figure out who may be ahead. Her worries about John Markham were slowly receding. She refused to let his presence spoil the weekend.

As she came down the stairs and into the foyer, she met a scene of feverish activity. The front hall was covered in tatty bags and heavy-duty plastic boxes. People were milling around and Mal sensed an air of busy calm as people were ticking lists and piling the boxes into neat stacks. Dressed in sou'westers, serious boots and waterproofs, Mal decided that these must be the scientists staying at the far end of the island. Wulf had said they would be staying here this evening, and it looked as if they had brought their work with them.

Picking her way through the equipment and trying not to get in anyone's way, she saw two Range Rovers heading up the drive, their headlights on against the rain and poor light. Although the sun hadn't set, the storm had darkened the sky to night, and Mal wondered what possessed anyone to be outside driving. Even as she watched, a bucket flew through the air, followed by a small bush. From the warmth of the hall, the conditions outside looked dreadful.

'Here come the brides,' murmured a voice beside her, and Mal turned to look at a tall, middle-aged man. He was wearing a wax jacket and robust leather boots, the sort with tabs on the side to help pull on and off.

'The brides?'

'Aye, we've had to evacuate the wedding party from Little Wolf. The castle will be full tonight.'

Mal looked him up and down. 'You must be from the observations station.'

Introducing himself as Dougie McDonald, Mal caught a Glaswegian accent and wondered what brought him so far south.

'I do hope your workstation doesn't get too damaged,' she said as the first car turned up the drive.

'So do I, but we've backed up all the data. And we've brought all the physical samples with us. Much to Wulf's disgust.' The man chuckled.

'Young Jordan over there suggested we put the guano samples in the main kitchen fridge.'

Mal looked at him blankly.

'Guano is bird excrement,' said Dougie, and Mal screwed up her face in disgust. He laughed. 'I'm fairly certain Jordan was joking. He's always needling Wulf. But then, he always needles everyone.'

Mal looked across at the younger man and recognised him as the one with whom Wulf had been arguing earlier in the day. Maybe that was what they had been fighting over? Wulf ran an exclusive resort here. Jokes about bird crap in the kitchens wouldn't go down well.

'So where has this guano gone now, then?'

'Cold storage shed down in the cellars.'

'He can chuck it down the oubliette for all I care,' said Wulf, joining them. 'Dougie, can you and your team get your stuff stored out of the way of the guests? They're hardly going to be wanting a welcoming committee of grubby environmentalists, are they?'

A flash of disgust crossed Dougie's face and then settled into a sneer as he turned away. The two cars now pulled up and the drivers hopped out and opened the passenger doors as a few members of staff joined Wulf at the front door.

Mal watched in surprise as the first woman scrambled out of the car, wearing a wedding gown. The wind grabbed at her skirts as she tried to handle the train whipping around her legs. She turned around and shouted into the car as another girl climbed out, also in a white wedding gown, and helped her friend run to the front door. As more of the women emerged from the two cars, they created a massive cloud of white gowns being battered in the wind and rain. Leaning against each other, their hair whipped into the air as the drivers tried to shelter them with the jackets. In an explosion of wind and rain, they all tumbled into the hallway.

'Bloody hell,' muttered Mal as she stepped out of the way of the chaos. All seven women were in wedding dresses and had no doubt been playing dress-up when the storm crashed into the house. There was no luggage. As she watched them shivering and laughing, she saw a few had cuts and were bleeding. She recognised Johanna and gave her a small wave. The young woman grinned back at her, fizzing with energy.

White towels and dressing gowns were being handed out as Wulf welcomed them.

'Ladies, I've opened the President's Suite for you. There are four emperor beds in there and four singles.'

'We have a row of eight bunk beds in the same dormitory,' murmured Dougie, who had come back to collect some more baggage. 'They don't even have suitcases. Had to evacuate in what they're wearing. I bet old Wulf there is sweating buckets they don't sue him. I reckon that would be the final straw for him.'

Heaving one of the bags onto his shoulder, Dougie turned and headed away from the ballroom. Mal watched as he passed one of his colleagues, who seemed transfixed by the brides. She was about the same age as the bridal party, but couldn't look more different. Her eyebrow was pierced, her hair cut in an unflattering bob, and she was wearing cargo pants and Doc Martens, but it was her expression that set her apart. She was staring at the girls in shock. Her mouth hung open as she blinked constantly. Mal had never seen such an expression of distress in real life and she took a step towards her.

'Tinks,' shouted a girl with her long diaphanous veil currently tangled in the door handle, tugging at her hair. 'Can you help me?'

'Hang on,' Tinks shouted back. She was down on her hands and knees, trying to pull another girl's long train out of the door, as staff darted in, trying to help. As she stood up, she turned to one of the other girls and Mal heard a strangled gasp from her left.

The young conservationist took a step towards the girls, then turned and fled down the corridor. The others didn't notice her departure as the door was pulled open again. As the dress was released, the wind and rain surged in.

'Close those bloody doors,' roared Wulf. Then silence reigned as the girls caught their breath and laughed nervously.

'Now, if you ladies will follow me. We'll get you settled in and then you can join us for dinner.'

Mal considered following the young conservationist, but decided to mind her own business. Besides which, she was hungry and Jacques was waiting for her.

DAY THREE Chapter Twenty-One

Mal stretched and smiled at another delightful night's sleep. Five years in prison and seven months in Golden meant she could now sleep through a hurricane without so much as a tousled pillow. Plus, this really was a fabulous bed.

Getting up, she opened her curtains. The sea beyond was still pretty wild-looking; a maelstrom of white water and black seas reflecting the dark clouds overhead. She cracked the window open slightly and heard the roar of the winds as a flush of cold air swept into the room. Checking her watch, she was surprised to discover it was already seven-thirty. She had arranged to meet Jacques for breakfast at eight.

Grumbling that she wouldn't have time to dry her hair, she had a quick shower and attempted to keep her hair dry. It was an exercise in futility, but Mal was determined that she would master her locks one day. Removing the towel from her hair, she grinned back at herself in the mirror; she loved how undisciplined her curls were. They were so far removed from her old corporate image and she wouldn't be without them. But damn it, some mornings it was like wrestling with Medusa. She pulled her skin back and peered at her lines. If Medusa could oblige with an alabaster face as well, she'd be grateful. Sighing, she released her skin back to gravity and popped on some day cream, ran a comb through her hair and got dressed, dabbing on some lipstick.

Today she was in long red chinos and a white linen blouse. Just the ticket for another day of bridge in the company of Jacques. Deciding that her hair was not going to oblige, she thrust two hair combs in and pulled the curls away from her face, then nodded at her reflection and tapped her finger on the dressing table. She looked good. No private investigator was going to spoil her day. If the worst came to the worst, Mal had decided last night that she would approach him and ask him what his game was. Having made that decision, she had slept like a baby.

Entering the breakfast room, she smiled at a few familiar faces, but Jacques wasn't one of them. The room was almost empty. No doubt the storm had caused many a restless night. Taking a window overlooking the sea, she wondered if he too had overslept? She didn't know him well, but she had him pegged as the sort of man who rose at dawn, exercised, prepared for the day ahead, read the morning papers and then set out to meet the world. She knew she was over-romanticising him, but it was hard not to. He was a very romantic figure. And a late one.

'Good morning. Is it Mrs Peck?' A young girl standing by the table pulled Mal's attention away from the view. According to her name badge, her name was Anna. She looked nervous and kept smiling and then pausing, as though she was overdoing it. Her eyes were also red-raw, and Mal was certain that she had been crying.

'Yes, can I help?'

'I have a message from Mr Pellofey. He says he will be a bit late.' She broke off, and Mal could see her hands shaking before she composed herself and carried on. 'Can I get you some tea or coffee?'

'Where is Mr Pellofey?'

'He's down at the jetty. What's left of it. But the management has asked if everyone can stay inside for now. There's a lot of storm damage outside.'

Mal watched the young server. None of her behaviour seemed adequate for some damaged infrastructure. However, the right thing to do was to wait for Jacques' return and he would let her know what was going on. Smiling, she requested a cafetière and watched the teenager leave. As soon as she had left the room, Mal stood up and headed towards the garden exit. If guests were being asked to stay inside, there would definitely be someone on the front door. Staying inside was clearly the right thing to do for most people but rightly or wrongly, she had never been most people.

In the service corridor by the garden exit were a variety of wellingtons and waterproofs for guest use. Mal slipped out of her shoes, tucked her trousers into the boots and slung a long, waxed raincoat onto herself. The coat was damp and had recently been worn, and the sleeve was covered in scratches. Mal felt something small and hard in the pocket and quickly retracted her hand. She was not averse to wearing something that someone else had

131

recently worn, but the horror of touching something touched by them made her flinch. She was about to shrug the coat off when she heard a door slam nearby. Not wanting to cause a scene, she slipped out of the building.

Making her way down to the harbour was an effort in itself as she stepped over branches and benches. Large stone planters had toppled from their plinths. Statues were draped in foliage and seaweed. It was a sorry sight.

Mal pulled her hair into a plait and pinned it up on her head with a comb. Looking like the wild woman of Borneo wasn't the style choice she had been going for when she met Jacques, but it would have to do.

As she zigzagged along the path winding down from the house to the jetty, she could see the house the bridal party had been staying in appeared to be in one piece, but a tree had fallen onto the helipad. After her next turn on the path, she walked down towards the sea. It was more exposed here and the sea spray was already wetting her face now and then. Ahead, on the hardstanding by the water's edge, she could see a group of men looking at something by their feet. Jacques crouched down, but the item was obscured from view. To their left, Mal could see that the jetty had been mostly washed away. All that remained were lumps of concrete with metal bars jutting upwards. Mal stared in dismay. It would be impossible to climb along that to board a boat. It might even be impossible for a boat to come alongside. What if some of that concrete was in the water, twisted and bent out of

132

shape, metal prongs waiting to tear at any vessel? Was this what had concerned the waitress and why Jacques was down here? She felt a little foolish. What help could she offer? But at least Jacques was safe. For a moment, Mal had been concerned he was hurt, and that was the cause of the girl's distress.

As she approached the men, the occasional wave slapped the rocks, sending up a spray, but the tide was falling and she kept to the edge of the landing bay, stepping carefully through the debris of seaweed. A gull was tangled in the flotsam, as was a large eel, both dead. One of the men spotted her and called to her to remain where she was. She recognised Wulf Clarkson and continued heading towards him.

'Stay back,' he shouted, waving his hands at her.

She wondered if he thought that was going to stop her. She waved back and carried on. Over the wind, she heard Jacques' voice. Wulf turned around, then shrugged and beckoned her forwards.

'Can I lend you my arm? It's very slippery.' Mal was going to decline but at that moment trod on a patch of weed and lunged forwards, snatching at Wulf's arm.

'Thank you. I thought Jacques had been hurt, and was coming to see if I could help. Seems like it's your jetty that's hurt instead.'

Wulf looked over at the wreckage and grimaced.

'That cost two million to build ten years ago. Christ knows what it will cost now.'

133

'How will we get off the island?'

'God knows. But that's not my greatest problem right now.'

They had just approached the two men: Jacques and a man she recognised as the head of the wildlife centre whom she had met yesterday. They stood up. A large bundle of fishing nets were at their feet.

'Mrs Peck,' said Dougie, looking worried. 'Can I suggest you wait here? This is not a suitable site for a lady.'

Mal raised her eyebrow and stepped towards Jacques.

'Good morning, Jacques.'

He nodded but didn't smile, which surprised her. Mal followed his glance to the bundle of rubbish by his feet. The fishing nets were a mess of orange and blue ropes. Mal could see scraps of pink amongst the weed, and it took a second for her brain to process what she was looking at.

Five polished toenails and a mottled foot stuck out of the nets.

Stepping to one side, she could now see the bundle side-on.

It was one of the girls from the night before, the white wedding gown a grim contrast to the orange fishing nets and ropes. Her face was cut and bruised but any blood had been washed away. Her lipstick was still in place, making her lips unnaturally red against her grey skin. Mal was grateful the poor girl's eyes were closed, although the bruising on one eye had removed some of her eyelash

134

extensions, giving her a grotesque, unbalanced look. Mal was reminded of A Clockwork Orange. It was such a ridiculous analogy that she laughed, then turned sharply and threw up.

A second later, Jacques was by her side, supporting her as she heaved again, and then stood up, embarrassed.

'Here,' he offered her a handkerchief, and she gratefully dabbed at her mouth, then shoved it in the other pocket. She was aware of more stuff in the pocket but decided the time for squeamishness was past.

Secateurs lay to one side of the debris and it was clear that the men had been cutting the body free of the nets.

'Have her friends been informed?' asked Mal.

'Not yet. We haven't identified her yet.'

'Her name's Francine,' said Mal, recognising her from the evening before.

Wulf groaned. 'Francine Blake. Her father's a fucking billionaire who throws down lawsuits like a brickie on double-rate. Fuck me.'

'Did you know her, Mal?' said Jacques, concern colouring his voice.

'No, only from yesterday. Although I think my niece does. Well, my niece-in-law.' She broke off. She was rambling. 'How did it happen? Does anyone know what she was doing down here in the storm?'

'Maybe she came down to watch the waves, silly maid,' said Dougie sadly as he returned to cutting her free of the tangle. Mal watched in sorrow as he and Jacques released her arm and laid it gently to the side. Beside her, Wulf continued to swear and mutter.

'Would you like me to come with you when you inform the girls?' said Mal quietly.

'Christ, yes.' He paused and looked at her reflectively. 'Could you do that for me? And call her dad. I'm going to have to call my lawyers.'

Mal blinked. He was in shock, no doubt, but she wasn't going to be calling anyone's father.

'I'll talk to the girls, but I am not informing the next of kin. Besides, how would that look to her father if you called your lawyers whilst a guest informed him his daughter was dead?'

Wulf was about to disagree, then exhaled deeply.

'You have a point. If you can tell her friends, I will tell her father.'

Walking away, he pulled his phone out and Mal assumed he was still going to call his lawyer first and then, presumably, his insurance agent.

Mal was going to say more when she noticed Francine's right arm was now free and one of her long, pale pink fingernails had snapped off. She stepped closer and crouched down by the dead girl, gently lifting her head. Pulling Jacques' handkerchief from her pocket, she rubbed it underneath one of the dead girl's nails.

'What is it, Mal?' asked Jacques, watching her carefully. Mal lifted the cloth to her face, looked at the smudge on it, and then sniffed. She could smell her own vomit, the sea, and a faint whiff of something familiar. Her suspicions were mounting. 'Hang on.' She passed the handkerchief to Jacques. 'What does that smell of to you? Ignore the vomit.'

He raised his eyebrows, but he took the cloth and sniffed it. 'Smells like dubbin? Why would she have wax under her nails?'

Dougie waved for the cloth and sniffed, then nodded. 'Yep, that's dubbin, right enough! Is that some sort of nail treatment? I thought it was just used to waterproof fabric.'

Mal looked at the long scratches on the sleeve of her coat and put her hand back in her pocket, then pulled out the small, hard object she had felt earlier. She opened her palm and showed it to the two men, one finger holding it in place against the wind. Jacques and Dougie looked at it and she saw the same conclusion forming on their faces. In the palm of her hand lay a single pink nail; a perfect match for the broken nail on Francine's hand.

'Wulf,' shouted Jacques. 'You need to get off the phone.'

Wulf turned and walked towards the others, and placed the call on mute.

'What? I know I sound callous, but I'm trying to save my business. An accident like this is never good news.'

'It wasn't an accident,' said Mal, watching as his face broke out into a smile.

'Suicide? Can you prove it? Oh bloody hell,'

137

He let out a huge sigh of relief as he choked back a laugh. 'Fuck me! I thought I was ruined.'

'No, Wulf,' said Mal again, 'This wasn't suicide. This was a murder.'

Chapter Twenty-Two

Wulf tapped the phone, telling whoever he was speaking to that he would call them back, then glared at Mal.

'Are you joking?'

Mal was carefully removing her long waxed-coat, folding it inside out, and wrapping it into a ball. In terms of preserving evidence, it wasn't much, but she hoped it helped. Jacques had already removed his jacket and handed it to Mal. He, at least, was wearing a jumper, and she accepted it gratefully. Her linen blouse offered no protection from the wind chill.

'It's hardly a joking matter. Look at her hand. Her missing fingernail was in the pocket of this coat. There are gouges along the sleeve. And if you smell the jacket, you'll notice the smell matches the substance under Francine's fingernails.'

Wulf stared at her as if she had sprouted a second head. 'Are you mad? She clearly came down to watch the waves. Got a few snaps for her social media and slipped in. Tragic accident, but we warned all guests not to go outside. Deeply regrettable.' As he spoke, his voice fell into a solemn register. 'My heart goes out to her family. A beautiful young woman—'

'Who was murdered,' said Mal, finishing his sentence.

'Stop saying that! And say nothing at the house either. Remember the NDA you signed when you completed your registration?'

Mal looked at Jacques in surprise, but he shrugged unhelpfully. 'I didn't sign anything. Maybe Jacques did, but under law you can't sign that sort of thing on behalf of someone else.'

As she spoke, she saw Dougie cut through one of the ropes lying across the body's torso. As it released, her white silky gown slithered off her body, leaving her exposed. Dougie flinched and looked up at Mal in horror. Crouching by his side, she pulled the fabric to maintain the girl's modesty.

'I'm being ridiculous,' he muttered, his voice breaking. 'Sorry.'

Mal didn't know what to say, but she knew any murder investigation would want the scene preserved. Sophie would be roaring at him right now.

'I think you are being incredible. Why don't you pause a second?'

Mal didn't want to tell him to stop. She didn't know how SOCO would handle this crime scene or this body, but she felt confident that they would be happier if Francine remained fully entombed in the nets until they could take it apart. Jacques had been talking quietly to Wulf, who stepped away and started shouting and pointing at Mal.

'Rubbish. The privacy of our guests is paramount. Everyone signs.'

'I didn't,' said Mal, getting up to her feet and stepping away from Francine's corpse. 'Besides which, in this case, who are we protecting? The victim? She's dead, but if she had a say, I suspect she'd be shouting about this from the rooftop.'

'Don't be ridiculous,' spluttered Wulf.

'So who are you protecting, then? Your reputation? Your business? Or maybe you're protecting the murderer?'

Now Wulf turned to Jacques, ignoring Mal's questions.

'Jacques. Can you make your guest see sense? She's raving.'

Jacques stepped to Mal's side and shook his head.

'She's not wrong. Even if this was an accident. That's not your decision. You have to call the police.'

'Jesus!' Wulf shouted at the top of his voice, strode away from them and started tapping on his phone. Jacques and Mal shared a look and then turned to Dougie, who had been listening to the developing row.

'All he bloody cares about is his bottom line. Wulf swans in and out via helicopter and shouts at the rest of us if we so much as turn the lights on. This season, he wanted me to ask the weight of my volunteers because he said heavier passengers cost more boat fuel.'

141

'That's outrageous,' exclaimed Mal. This guy was a lawsuit waiting to happen.

'What do you think?' asked Dougie. 'Should we stop this? Don't they always say not to touch the body?'

Mal was relieved he had come to this decision on his own. He was trembling and clearly wanted to continue to free her, but it was probably a mistake. Whilst it seemed so unlikely that any evidence remained on the body, having been tossed around in the sea, Mal had been paying enough attention to various investigations and a bit of online research to know that those forensic boffins could find evidence in the most unlikely of scenarios.

'You're probably right, but it just seems so disrespectful for her to be laying in all this rubbish. At least keep all the netting. Maybe evidence would have fallen into the nets?'

'The sea would have washed it away.'

Mal considered Jacques' words. 'I think you're right, but again, I don't think we can make that call. It feels sacrilegious, but I think we should now preserve her as she is. Her face and hands are free. That feels appropriate.'

'So, should we stop?'

Mal studied Dougie as he paused, looking at her beseechingly. If she had to guess, she'd say he was in his mid-forties. He may even have a daughter this age, and he was clearly struggling mentally to hold it together. She needed to decide on his behalf.

'Yes. The police will be here soon enough. They can take care of her when they arrive.'

Dougie shook his head emphatically, and Mal rushed to reassure him.

'Oh, they will. I know a few police officers and they really do care. She will be treated with total respect. They won't rest until they get her killer.'

He shook his head again.

'I'm sure they will, but how will they get here?'

Mal glanced at Jacques in alarm and saw him scowling at Dougie.

'Jacques?'

He seemed reluctant to talk and then sighed, glaring at the other man.

'The issue is, the jetty is damaged, and the sea is still really big. They need the wind to drop or turn, and even then, they'll only be able to land a boat on a high tide on the beach by the house. Dougie here thinks it will be at least a day before anyone can get to us.'

'What about the helicopter?'

'Stuck on the mainland. And there's a fallen tree on the helipad. We were just getting ready to take the chainsaws to it when I found—'

His voice petered away as he looked over towards the body. Scraps of seaweed caught in the debris fluttered in the breeze, slapping against the white satin. For a brief moment, he had forgotten about her and was now battling the reality of the situation.

'Mal,' said Jacques. 'I think you should go back up to the house. Dougie and I are going to move the body to the boat shed. Protect her from the elements.'

Mal looked around at the bleak scene. She had wanted to spend a weekend with Jacques, get to know him better, play cards, drink wine, laugh and chat. Now the rain had started again, the wind was whipping up the waves, and a dead body lay at her feet. There was a killer on the island and no one could get off.

Chapter Twenty-Three

Agreeing with Jacques, Mal turned and trudged back up the footpath, with the coat rolled up under her arm. It was her intention to lock it in her bedroom. Only herself, Jacques, Wulf, and Dougie understood its significance. So long as none of them mentioned it, they had an upper hand over the killer. As she headed back uphill, she leant into the wind.

Pulling her phone out of her pocket, there was only one person she wanted to speak to right now.

'Sophie? It's me, Malachite Peck.'

The wind pulled at her words and she tucked herself into the lee of a garage as she heard Sophie laugh in reply.

'I know who you are, Mal. And even if I didn't, my phone displays your name. What's up?'

Sophie's breezy manner was a tonic, and Mal felt some of the tension release. Without wasting any time, she explained the situation to Sophie.

'And has the owner called the police?'

'He says there's no point, as no one can get on or off the island. I think he's in shock and trying to cover his arse.'

'Do you suspect him?'

Mal thought about it. She hadn't taken to him and she was convinced there was more to him than met the eye. But murder?

'I don't think so. This island is one of his crown jewels. He's freaking out that this will ruin its reputation.'

'If she was pushed into the sea, he could have thought her body would never be recovered.'

'True.' Sophie had a point. Maybe this would be an open and shut case. 'What do I do now?'

'Nothing. You have a murderer on the loose with no way of escape. They will be very dangerous. I'm going to make a call and get the ball rolling. Keep your phone by you. And do not investigate!'

Sliding her phone back into her pocket, Mal left the shelter of the garage. Leaning into the wind, she headed back to the front door of the castle.

From the foyer, Wulf was waiting for her and waved at her to come and join him. He had clearly overtaken her coming back up the hill. He was looking around surreptitiously and, if anything, drawing attention to himself by trying to appear discreet.

'I've spoken to the Chief Commissioner. He says we need to inform her friends she has died, but not to mention foul play. Can you do that?'

She stepped away from him and stared at him coldly.

'Can I do what?'

'Tell the girls.' He stared at Mal. 'I'll be with you, but it will sound better coming from you.'

She was about to protest when he carried on. 'And I need to check her room. If you are with me, no one can claim foul play.'

146

'Are you looking for clues?'

'What? No. That's for the police. I'm making sure there's no incriminating evidence. Her parents will thank me for protecting her reputation.'

'What will you do if you find something?' Mal imagined hoteliers were used to covering up indiscretions, but tampering with evidence in a murder investigation could rebound badly.

'Depends what I find. Drugs, sex toys, stuff like that, we obviously tidy away.'

Mal disagreed but realised she wanted to have a look inside Francine's room as well, and held her tongue. Wulf was going in that room, with or without Mal. If he hid anything, Mal would at least know. And Wulf clearly didn't know of Mal's friendship with Sophie or her previous experience of law and order. For now, she would go along with Wulf's wishes, but she couldn't help but wonder if Wulf was worried that he may have left evidence in her room.

Following Wulf upstairs, Sophie's warnings to not investigate were still ringing in her ear. But this wasn't really investigating; this was helping out whilst keeping her eyes open. They walked along a corridor that Mal hadn't visited. This was the presidential wing that had been opened for the girls following the storm. Francine had insisted on her own room, and Wulf now unlocked the door and they walked inside. Wulf switched the light on to reveal an undisturbed bed and a tidy bathroom. Mal

147

drew open the heavy curtains, letting in the daylight, and looked around.

'She was barely in here,' said Mal thoughtfully. Looking around, she felt certain that Francine had never returned to her room after dinner.

'Agreed. Not what I'd call a party animal.' He laughed, but Mal thought he sounded disappointed. Would signs of an orgy and rampant drug use have somehow made her responsible for her own death? 'I'll check out Little Wolf later on. Let's go and talk to the girls.'

Turning to leave, Mal spotted a sheet of writing paper which had fallen off the back of the dresser. She stooped down to pick it up and read the short message in surprise. Was there any chance that Clarkson hadn't seen what she had found?

'What you got there?'

Mal straightened up and held out the sheet of paper. Two words were written at the top, as though Francine were starting a letter.

"Naughty Wulfie."

Clarkson's face paled as he read the brief note in Francine's large, flowing hand. And then gave an embarrassed laugh as Mal folded her arms.

'Was this the sort of evidence that you were trying to keep from the parents?'

'What? You can't think… Look, gorgeous, I didn't, that is to say we didn't. Look, nothing happened. Last night, she was coming on to me. She was pretty drunk, but that's all it was. I mean, look.'

He stopped and took a deep breath, then snatched the paper out of Mal's hand and screwed it up.

'Nothing happened. Alright?'

He gave a ragged laugh.

'Look, I get girls throwing themselves at me all the time. You know the score. Multimillionaire rock star, it goes with the territory, love. But since I got hitched, those days are behind me. I don't know what that silly kid was thinking.'

He rubbed his face, then sighed.

'Come on, let's go tell the bride she's one short on the wedding list.'

As he walked out of the room, Mal had no option but to follow as he locked the door behind them. Did she believe his story, that Francine was simply flirting with him? Johanna had said she was always pursuing money or power. Maybe this was what she was doing here. Wulf Clarkson was a revolting piece of work and Mal was determined to soften the blow of the news by being the one to tell the girls they had just lost a best friend. Especially if Clarkson was the architect of their misfortune.

Five minutes later, the women were all gathered in Imogen's suite. As the bride-to-be, she had been given the largest suite of rooms. They were now sitting on the sofas, wrapped up in dressing gowns and nursing hangovers.

'I can't get Francine to open her door,' said Octavia, the only one dressed. According to Imogen, Octavia was an early bird and was currently wearing a set of hotel lounge pants and a cashmere hoodie. Several of the others wore the same and Mal was reminded that they had dashed into the castle in wedding gowns with a storm at their backs.

Wulf was about to speak when Mal realised she hadn't asked how the parents had reacted. Turning her back on the small group, she muttered to Wulf, getting him to confirm the next of kin had been informed. When he shook his head, she swore.

'Are you mad? We can't tell them. What if they call Francine's parents?'

His lack of forethought appalled her. Or was it cowardice? He looked at her and shrugged.

'We tell them not to.'

'Don't be ridiculous,' she hissed, annoyed by his stupidity and craven attitude. No doubt he had hoped that one of them would break the news to the parents. 'Imagine the headlines.' Mal could see this got through to him as he stood up.

'What's going on?' said Imogen. 'Why are you whispering?'

'Dear ladies. I'm afraid I need to make a phone call. I will leave Mrs Peck here to explain what has happened.'

With that, he all but sprinted out of the room. Mal watched his fleeing back, then turned to the girls who were now looking either confused or alarmed. She took a deep breath.

'Sit down girls, I have some bad news.'

Imogen grasped Tinks' hand and squeezed it tightly. Johanna slid down onto the sofa and snuggled up to Octavia and Imogen.

'I'm very sorry to tell you that sometime last night Francine died.'

There were gasps all round and Imogen started to cry, shortly followed by the others.

But not Johanna. Instead of denying Mal's words, she watched her closely and then looked at the other girls before returning her attention to Mal.

'How did she die?'

Mal thought about what Sophie had said. She couldn't say the death was suspicious, but Francine was young. Any sudden death was suspicious.

'It's uncertain.'

'What does that mean?' sobbed Imogen. 'Can we see her?'

Tinks shook her head, appalled at the idea.

'I'm afraid not,' said Mal. 'The police have asked that we leave her body alone.'

'The police?' said Johanna sharply.

'Any death of a young person has to be investigated.'

Imogen cried again. 'Where is she? Oh God, her poor parents. Will I have to tell them?'

Mal shook her head. 'No, that's being taken care of. I have no doubt that Wulf will be back to talk to you all soon about arrangements to leave the island.'

Now Octavia gathered her senses, her hangover a distant memory, and looked at Mal, the barrister in her coming to the fore.

'Where was her body found?'

Mal paused.

'If you won't say, I'm simply going to walk until I find the cordon.'

'Why does it matter?' asked Imogen.

'Because that's what Octavia does,' said Johanna. 'She asks questions.'

The girls looked at Mal and she studied their faces. In all likelihood, the murderer was staring back at her. Mal didn't believe a random murderer killed Francine. This wasn't a street mugging, and she'd be amazed if there was a random serial killer on holiday here. Francine had either seen or done something she shouldn't, or her killer already knew her. And that meant she was in this room. And if she was, then she was a very cool customer.

'Francine was found down by the harbour.'

'Outside! In that storm? Francine!'

The voices came in a slew of astonishment.

'Was it possible that she was taking photos?' asked Mal.

'No way!' said Octavia fiercely.

'What about for her Instagram page?' said Mal cautiously.

Octavia had been about to deny Mal again when she paused and the others frowned.

'She was always on her social media feeds,' said Johanna. 'I would spend all my time trying to avoid being in her photos. Last night, she was taking loads.'

'I know,' said Mal, and then explained to the girls that her niece knew Francine from uni and had spotted Mal in one of Francine's photos of last night's gathering. Once the girls established who Jasmine was, there was a subtle shift in the atmosphere. Mal had moved from being a friendly stranger to someone they could trust. Or at least relate to.

'Can't you tell us how she died, Mrs Peck?' asked Octavia, the one girl that Mal hadn't spent any time with.

'Malachite or Mal, please.' She took a deep breath. 'I'm afraid it looks like she drowned, but that will be confirmed after an autopsy.'

'Oh God,' sobbed Imogen, grabbing her phone. 'She must have gone down to look at the waves. I said they would be spectacular. We all did.' She turned to Johanna. 'Remember, you said you loved painting stormy seas?'

Now Johanna looked appalled. 'I didn't say we should go and look at the waves, though.'

'Ladies. No one is to blame if she chose to go and look at the sea. You are all adults. If Francine went to watch

153

the storm, that was her choice. The winds had died down after dinner. Maybe she thought it was safe.'

'Maybe she wanted some fresh air after that girl started shouting at her,' said Octavia. 'You knew what that was about, Tinks. Who was she?'

Mal watched the blood seep out of Tinks' cheeks as she stood up and walked over to the cafetière.

'She was drunk.'

'She threatened you, Tinks,' said Imogen. 'She said you were dead. She said you were dead, and that Francine was a bitch.'

Tinks shook her head and shrugged, but Mal saw her hand was shaking as she popped a pod in the coffeemaker.

'Like I said. She was drunk.'

'Who was she?' asked Mal. She could only think of two women that could be called girls. There was that quiet conservationist who had been bringing in the samples; and there was the one she had played bridge with last night, whose children were on holiday in Cornwall. It could be one of the staff, but she thought that Imogen and Tinks would have known who they were and said so.

'It was some girl in camouflage trousers and a pierced eyebrow,' said Imogen. 'Are you sure you didn't know her? You and Francine had quite a little huddle afterwards?'

Tinks sipped her coffee and shrugged again. 'I've already said we didn't know her. Look, can we go? I need to pack.'

Mal stood up. It was time to leave these young ladies to it, and she had a volunteer to track down. However, she had one final piece of news.

'At the moment, none of us can leave the island. The jetty has been washed away, the helipad has a fallen tree on it, and the storm is still blowing.'

As she headed out, she saw Octavia was the first to reach for her phone, quickly followed by Johanna.

Mal cleared her throat. 'I know this is hard, but until her next of kin has been informed, could you delay mentioning this?'

Chapter Twenty-Four

Leaving the bridal party to their frantic attempts to get off the island, Mal headed down to the ground floor and bumped into the Bondermans and Penny Fitzgibbon.

'A fourth!' declared Teddy as he spotted her heading across the foyer. 'Have you heard? We're stranded. Clarksie is going to make an announcement soon, but we thought we'd play a quick game beforehand. Just friendly.' He beamed at her. 'What do you say?'

'I'm afraid—'

'Oh, come on,' said Penny with a laugh. 'Henry's nursing a bit of a hangover, so I'm on my own.'

Their jollity grated, but clearly the word hadn't got out yet. That would likely end once the girls emerged from upstairs and started demanding answers, but for now, Mal wanted to find the young conservationist. Leaving the buoyant trio behind, she headed off in the direction of the staff quarters after getting instructions from the front desk. The receptionist was looking shell-shocked, so the news was clearly spreading. As Mal headed down a functional corridor, she could hear a conversation taking place further on.

Looking into a large storeroom, she could see the woman she was after, a man Wulf had been arguing with the day before, and an older woman.

'Hello,' she said, smiling at the trio, and then looked at the young woman. Sophie would kill her for doing this, but the chance to speak to people before the news broke would be invaluable and she could tell the police her impressions. 'Could I have a word?'

The man looked her up and down and then sneered. 'What about?'

She ignored him and looked at the younger woman. 'I'm sorry, my name is Mal. I saw you last night bringing some logbooks in. I just wanted to ask you about your observations. Dougie said you were well informed.'

'I do the observations,' said the man again, interrupting her.

'And my niece is around your age and interested in marine oceanography. I'd love to hear how you got into it?'

'Is your niece dull as well?'

Now Mal turned and looked at him directly. She cocked her head, looking him up and down, and then gave a little snort before returning to the girl.

'I'm sorry, I didn't catch your name.'

'It's Ferne,' said the girl, rising to her feet. 'Ange, do you mind carrying on without me? When Dougie gets back, give me a shout.' She turned back to Mal. 'Come on, we can chat elsewhere.'

As they left the room, Ferne turned and smiled at Mal.

'Sorry about Jordan. He's the world's greatest arse.'

Agreeing with her assessment, Mal followed her into a laundry room and pulled out a pair of hard plastic chairs. They sat opposite one another.

'So what does your niece study at the moment? There are lots of ways into this career.'

She was leaning forward and smiling, although the smile wasn't quite reaching her eyes, and Mal noticed she'd been crying recently.

'Are you okay?'

Ferne blinked quickly and looked away.

Mal needed to talk to her before the news about Francine was revealed. If she was guilty, Mal hoped she might spot something in her manner. Certainly, looking at her now, she seemed to be holding herself together by a wire.

'It's just I couldn't help but notice your reaction when those young ladies from the bridal party came into the house. And then there was that big row later.'

Mal hadn't witnessed the shouting match that Octavia had mentioned, but if she suggested she had, Ferne may be prepared to say more.

'It was just a shock.'

'All those girls dressed as brides. It was quite the scene. Are you married? You seem quite young? But what do I know? My nephew is your age, and he's married.'

Mal wittered on, trying to sound like a gossipy old aunt. Someone that Ferne might confide in. She was finding it hard work, but often this sort of inane burbling encouraged a greater level of intimacy. She didn't expect Ferne to confess to murder, but she might reveal more than she meant to if she thought Mal was just a harmless chatterbox.

'He's married to a lovely girl,' Mal continued. 'Well, I say lovely. She can be a little thoughtless. Maybe only thinks of herself. A girl's girl, if you know what I mean?'

'Oh, I do.'

Ferne wasn't looking at Mal, which gave her time to study the younger woman. Her face had twisted in pain and her breathing had increased.

'Ah. Like those girls last night. Do you know them? Imagine that, bumping into old friends?'

'Not friends. Just girls I went to school with.'

'And you weren't invited to the bridal party. Oh, my dear. How distressing.'

'Yes. Well, no. I only went to school with two of them. Well, one. The other—' Her breath hitched, and she gave an ugly sob. 'I killed the other one.'

Mal sat still, then stood up and grabbed some paper towels from the side of the sink and passed them to Ferne, who was now crying freely. She patted her on her back before choosing a seat by the door. She didn't think Ferne would attack her, but she wanted to be as close to an exit as possible. The rest of the wildlife conservationists were just down the corridor; they should hear her call for help.

'When you say killed her…?' Mal kept her voice quiet.

'That's what I thought. That's what Francine said.' She started crying again. Mal bit her lip. The girl was making no sense. If she could stop sobbing for a second, this would be much easier.

'Francine said you killed her?'

'Yes.'

'And how did you kill Francine?'

Mal didn't want to crow, but sometimes she was convinced being a detective was easier than they made out. Certainly, this was the easiest confession she had ever encountered. Ferne didn't even seem dangerous. Just utterly remorseful.

'Not Francine. Tinks.'

'You killed Tinks?'

Oh, this was dreadful. For some reason, she had killed Francine by mistake. Mal wondered if she should tell her, but she had a confession. It really would be best at this point to withdraw and let Wulf Clarkson know. As owner of the island, he presumably had somewhere the girl could be detained until the police could make it.

'Yes, that's what Francine said. But yesterday she ran into the foyer, laughing her head off and absolutely one hundred per cent full of life.'

Mal recalled the scene. She had witnessed Ferne staring at the girls with an expression that she couldn't place at the time. Now she knew it to be horror, but her words made no sense.

'I don't understand.'

Mal stood up again and poured Ferne a glass of water.

'When you say Tinks was alive, why do you think you had killed her? Did you know she was on the island already?'

She passed Ferne the glass and sat back by the door, this time opening it. The situation had changed, and she felt uncertain. Maybe Ferne was more unstable than Mal had realised. An easy escape route might be required.

Ferne's tears had dried up as she sipped her water. She looked across at Mal and smiled weakly.

'It was a long time ago. I should have done more, but I was so scared. My counsellor said I should have confessed to the family. That it would help me with my guilt. But I was such a coward.' She hiccoughed and then gave a bleak laugh. 'If I had...' she trailed off.

'You thought you killed Tinks before?' asked Mal slowly.

'At school. Francine, Tinks, and I were all at school together. Or rather, they went to the nearby boarding school. I was at the local comp, but we shared a few lessons. It was a partnership initiative. You know the sort of thing; look how inclusive our school is! Don't remove our tax breaks, sort of thing.'

'And you became friends?'

'Yes. The three amigos. Tinks was really good fun and Francine was so cool. I just don't think you can understand how much in awe of them I was. It wasn't just the money. I mean, they were so rich, but it was the air around them. They walked in a cloud of confidence.

161

When they spoke, they just expected to be listened to. They had no concept of denial. It was astonishing. All the girls I had grown up with felt stunted in comparison.'

She looked over at Mal, who nodded.

'Extreme wealth and privilege lend a certain sort of gloss, don't they?'

'Aye. Gloss. That's exactly the word. Underneath, they're no different from the rest of us.'

'True. Money divides in ways we often don't understand.'

Ferne was nodding again.

'But in some ways, they are worse than us. They do things they think are funny just because we don't matter. I thought I was their friend, but apparently, I was just an experiment. Or at least, that's what I was to Francine.'

'Did you fall out?'

Mal didn't believe for a second that Ferne fell out with these girls. They would have been like goddesses to Ferne. She was grateful to be part of their little group, padding after the lionesses as they swayed through the school halls.

'Killing Tinks put an end to our friendship. Although Francine was terribly supportive.'

She laughed again, and it was beginning to sound really ugly. Mal listened out for the murmur of voices down the corridor. It wasn't much, but she thought Jordan and Ange were still in the equipment room.

'Why did you think you had killed Tinks?'

'The three of us had been playing by the cliffs. Tinks stumbled, and I tried to grab her, but my hand was too slippery and she fell. She was just lying there. I was so scared that I ran home.'

'What happened next?'

'At first, I stayed at home. Told my mum I was sick. I spent days in bed shaking and crying. I've never been very brave, but I was terrified I was going to be in trouble. A week later, Francine came to see me and said Tinks had died. But she told the authorities it was an accident. She said she and Tinks had been on their own. She made me believe she was covering for me.'

'But surely you saw Tinks after school, when you returned?'

'No. She wasn't there. And it wasn't long after that I had a nervous breakdown and finished my education from home and hospital.' Ferne's voice was quiet, and she spoke without inflection. She could have been reading someone else's words off a page. Mal wondered just how traumatised she had been. She sounded in a state of complete shock, reliving those days. She picked the skin around her fingernail as she continued: 'Francine kept in touch, though. Always so concerned. Always reminding me not to say anything because then we'd both go to jail. Me for pushing Tinks off a cliff, and her for covering for me.'

'But you didn't push her?' Mal asked gently.

163

'No, but Francine convinced me that as I was the last person to touch her, it was sort of my fault. I know it doesn't make sense, but I was fifteen and terrified. When I went to university, I stopped answering Francine's letters. I felt so ashamed, abandoning her like that.'

She started crying again and Mal watched on, trying to put herself in Ferne's shoes. If Mal had been in her position she would have asked questions, gone to the hospital, visited the parents. She would have tried to make amends. Atone. But Mal was not Ferne, and had never been a shy, vulnerable, insecure teenage, caught under the thrall of a rich powerful girl. Ferne took a sip of water and continued through her tears.

'I just wanted to rebuild my life. Start anew. I stopped talking to my friends, my family. I reinvented myself at university. I built a perfect glass wall around myself. I could see out, but no one could get in.'

'And last night that wall broke,' said Mal.

Ferne cried again. Her tears ran miserably down her face. Mal stared at her in the silence and wondered what had happened. Francine had played a cruel trick and then doubled down on it, but was Tinks involved?

She could hear footsteps moving down the corridor from the main house and a girl's voice called out Ferne's name.

Ferne looked up as Tinks burst into the room.

164

'There you are,' said Tinks breathlessly. 'Ferne, something dreadful has happened. You need to come with me.'

She turned and saw Mal sitting behind her.

'Have you told her?' she asked Ferne before turning to Mal. 'Why are you here? Ferne, what have you said?'

'I was telling her about what Francine did—'

Tinks held up her hand.

'Stop. Don't say another word.' She narrowed her eyes as she stared at Mal. 'What? Were you hoping for a confession?'

Clearly, Tinks had already jumped to the conclusion that Mal was already considering. That Ferne had taken revenge for a dreadful lie that had been suffocating her for years. But how did Tinks know if, according to Ferne, she never saw her again? Had she been in on Francine's wicked prank?

Mal was about to speak when there was a static buzz and then the house Tannoy burst into life as the voice of Wulf Clarkson spoke through the airwaves.

'Attention all. Please will everyone, staff and guests, all gather in the dining room now. This is an emergency broadcast. Everyone must attend. Please make your way to the dining room now.'

Chapter Twenty-Five

'What's happening?' said Ferne, confusion colouring her voice.

'Not a word!' warned Tinks, although it wasn't certain who she was talking to. Mal grabbed her opportunity to shock a response out of Ferne.

'Francine is dead. She died last night.'

Tinks glared at Mal, then spun around and grabbed Ferne's hand. 'You're fine. Say nothing.'

Ferne was blinking in confusion.

'What does she mean, dead?'

'I'll explain on the way. Don't speak to anyone.'

Still furious at Mal, Tinks pulled Ferne to her feet and dragged her out of the room.

Mal stood up and followed slowly. Ferne's face when she had heard Francine was dead was one of total bewilderment, but Mal had never heard of a better motive for murder. Francine had effectively tortured her for years. From the age of fifteen, Ferne had turned her back on her friends and family, believing she had killed her friend, and she could never confess what had happened because she would effectively send her other friend or herself to jail. Francine certainly had done a number on her.

Had Ferne then done a number on Francine in revenge? God knows, she had cause. Was Tinks in on it? Why was she protecting Ferne? If Ferne had killed

Francine, Tinks could be in real danger. Mal had to speak to her quickly. Galvanised, she sped up. What if Ferne convinced Tinks to step outside for a moment? Was her surprise all an act?

It was easy to see Ferne as a victim, tortured for years. But when she suddenly came face-to-face with the reality of that abuse, how would she react? Mal breathed a sigh of relief as she entered the room and saw Tinks and Ferne sitting with the other girls.

The room was filling up as everyone sat down around the small tables. Mal looked around, but couldn't see Jacques and instead sat down at a table with three of the conservationists.

'Do you know what this is about?' asked Mal, feigning ignorance. Someone had killed Francine, and she wanted to gauge people's reactions without them knowing they were being studied.

'Storm damaged the jetty,' said the woman whom Mal had seen earlier down in the boot room. 'Reckon with that and the damage to Little Wolf and the conservation centre, we're all stuck together for a bit.'

'No more bridge parties for you, eh?' mocked Jordan, and the other two volunteers rolled their eyes.

'Ignore Jordan. He's always this pleasant. I'm Angela Davis, deputy warden, and this here's Freddie.'

Mal smiled at the two. Ignoring Jordan, she spoke to Freddie as he shredded a piece of paper.

'Do you play bridge? Maybe we could widen the party?'

'Not us,' he said morosely. 'We'll be out there in the rain making repairs whilst you sit around in here.'

'Still, those lassies over there don't seem happy about spending the weekend with you lot, do they?' said Jordan, looking across at the bridal party. 'All that sobbing. Maybe they've run out of champagne, hey. What a tragedy.'

'Going to offer them more comfort?' muttered Freddie.

'Jealous, much?'

'No. You know the rules,' said Freddie, now starting on another scoring sheet. 'No mucking around with the guests. Mr Clarkson is very clear about that.'

'Who says I was mucking around? Last night I was Mr Serious. The ladies love a bit of that.'

'For Christ's sake,' said Ange in exasperation. Shaking her head, she rolled her eyes at Mal. 'I play bridge. As it happens, so does Dougie. But I suspect we'll have to sing for our supper, as young Freddie put it so nicely.'

Snorting, Freddie picked up his phone and started scrolling. Jordan continued to watch the wedding party thoughtfully. Which girl had Jordan spent last night with? wondered Mal. None of the girls were looking his way. Had he been with Francine?

The room quietened down and Wulf walked over to the dais. Mal spotted Jacques walk in behind him as he moved to the side, leaving Wulf alone on the platform. She didn't care for Wulf and couldn't understand Jacques' relationship with him. From what she had observed, Jacques didn't seem overly friendly with Wulf either, especially not to the tune of a very expensive gifted suite. What tied the two men together? Looking around, there was no sign of Dougie, and she imagined he had remained with Francine's body.

'Ladies and gentlemen,' began Wulf. 'As you are no doubt aware, we suffered a considerable amount of storm damage last night.'

'I'll say,' called out a voice from the other side of the room. 'I opened my window and suddenly my vodka was on the rocks! If you know what I mean.'

This was met with some light-hearted laughter, but Wulf didn't join in and the atmosphere in the room quietened down. If their most gregarious of hosts wasn't joining in, maybe things were more serious than first thought. Wulf continued to speak.

'Unfortunately, several of the buildings on the island have suffered structural damage and we are going to have to ask everyone to stay in the castle for the foreseeable future.'

'I just want to go home,' sobbed one of the girls. Mal wasn't certain, but she thought it was Imogen. A moment later, Ferne burst into a manic laugh that Tinks quickly covered with a louder sob. She hauled Ferne onto her feet and dragged her out of the ballroom. The rest of the room

169

glanced over at the crying girls, surprised at their reaction. Mal saw at least one set of eyes rolling. No doubt words were being muttered about younger generations being made of weaker stuff.

'This leads to another issue,' said Wulf. 'The jetty has been damaged. At the moment, it is not possible to leave the island as we won't be able to get a boat to dock.'

'Hang on a minute,' shouted a male voice. 'You can't keep us stuck here. Get the helicopter over!'

More voices shouted in accord, and Wulf had to raise his voice over the general hubbub.

'If you will just hear me out.' He wiped his forehead with the back of his hand and carried on. 'A tree landed on the helipad. As soon as the weather permits, we'll be out with the chainsaws removing it.'

'Aye, we will, will we?' muttered Jordan, and Freddie sighed as Wulf continued.

'When the waves calm down, we should be able to land a RIB on the beach. But we need to wait for the winds to die down, which, according to the Met Office, should be in a few more hours.'

'But this leads me on to my last point.' He paused and closed his eyes for a second. Soon, what little conversation there was had died away until all that could be heard were a few girls crying.

'Last night a guest lost her life.'

Gasps broke out around the room as people looked about to see if they could tell who was missing.

170

'I'm deeply heartbroken to say that one of the ladies from the bridal party must have gone wave-watching last night, and drowned.'

He paused again to let people see how distraught he was before carrying on.

'Now, this will mean the police are going to need to come over to the island.'

A man from the bridge party shot to his feet in alarm.

'What for? Didn't you say she drowned?'

'Unexpected death. Isn't it?' called out Major Cartright. 'Police always get involved.'

As the room began to call back and forth, Wulf shouted to regain attention.

'It's exactly as the major suggests. An unexpected death always requires a police presence.'

'Bloody hell!' muttered Jordan, and Freddie smirked at him.

'Whatever you and Clarksie are up to is about to come to light.'

'Shut up. We're not up to anything.'

'Like hell you're not.'

'Boys,' snapped Ange. 'For the love of God. Stop bickering. Someone has drowned. Freddie, stop stirring the pot.'

'They won't be talking to us,' said Jordan, looking around the room. 'What's some girl drowning got to do with us, anyway?'

171

Mal listened to the exchange and wondered when they would remember she wasn't one of them. So far everyone seemed to accept a verdict of accidental drowning, but it was curious how alarmed Jordan was by the idea of police on the island. He was still looking around the room, almost as if he expected them to burst in.

'Mr Clarkson! Wulf, Major Cartwright here. I have experience in this sort of thing. I was in Iraq. No need to go into details, but the police will want someone with some experience in these matters. Happy to volunteer.'

'Bloody do-gooder,' grumbled Jordan.

Freddie was smiling now, revelling in Jordan's discomfort. Mal made a note to talk to Freddie later. If there was any dirt on Jordan, Freddie looked all too happy to spill it.

'Agreed,' said Ange, 'I bet Dougie is with the body. I wonder which of the girls it was? I do hope it wasn't the bride. That would be so tragic.'

Mal pictured Francine lying there in her long white wedding dress and shuddered.

'It wasn't the bride,' she said. 'And yes, Dougie is with the body.'

The other three looked at her, their expressions ranging from sullen to curious. Mal had wanted them to forget about her, but now she wanted to know more about Jordan and Wulf's relationship. Mal remained convinced that one of the girls was responsible for Francine's murder, but Jordan's response to the police had been curious. Could there be another explanation for Francine's death? Had she stumbled into something? As the three conservationists stared at her, she figured that if she gave them some news now, they might be more inclined to talk to her later on.

'And how do you know that?' said Jordan.

'Because I was there. I was trying to find my friend this morning and found him with Mr Clarkson and Dougie down by the dock. That's where Dougie had found Francine. That was her name.'

She knew that strictly speaking she shouldn't be saying anything, but also knew the girls wouldn't be keeping this secret. In fact, looking over, she could already see them being consoled by various other people from the hotel staff and bridge party. The headline details were already seeping into public knowledge. She would keep the important parts to herself. Maybe later, if she could chat to Ange and Freddie on their own, they might let a few details slip out. And find out why Jordan was looking quite so worried.

'In light of all this, we will have to postpone the charity event. But if individuals wish to carry on playing bridge, please do so.'

Henry Fitzgibbon stood up.

'This weekend raises a lot of money for charity. I propose we carry on as before, so long as we are flexible to the needs of the staff and any police investigation.'

173

The vast majority of the room murmured in agreement, and Wulf declared that seemed a fine compromise. Mal's table muttered scornfully about not allowing the death of a young girl to spoil their fun and Mal nodded in agreement. She had no intention of playing bridge unless it provided her with an opportunity to ask questions.

'If you'll excuse me, I think I'm going back to my room.' Standing up, she caught Jacques' eye, nodded, and watched as he walked through the room towards her. As he passed, several couples called out to him, asking whether he was still playing. Each time he shrugged politely until he reached Mal, and they walked out in silence towards the lobby.

'It's like a scene from the Rue Morgue,' grumbled Jacques when they were out of earshot. Mal agreed, but tried to be charitable.

'I imagine they would feel differently if they had seen the body. But look, I had the most interesting conversation just now with one of the scientists. It turns out she knew Francine and Tinks from school.'

Mal relayed her conversation and Jacques' expression became sombre.

'What a dreadful thing to do! Young girls can be vicious. You will tell the police when they arrive, yes?'

'Of course,' said Mal, and Jacques stared at her suspiciously.

174

'And that's all you're going to do, yes? No more questions?'

'There are a lot of unanswered questions. Wouldn't it be helpful if they were all resolved by the time the police arrived?'

'Malachite. This wasn't an accident. There is a murderer amongst us and they can't get off the island. They probably thought her body wasn't going to be recovered. They will be desperate. All that's working for them right now is that they believe it's being viewed as an accident. If you start asking questions, you could alarm them. If it is Ferne, tell the police what she told you. Otherwise, leave it to them.'

Mal frowned and shook her head. 'I suppose you're right. But I want to know what John Markham is up to. If there's a financial investigator here and he knows who I am, I think I have the right to know if I'm being investigated.'

Jacques looked exasperated.

'He is clearly here for someone else. Don't draw attention to yourself. Please.'

'I shall be perfectly fine.' Mal wanted to end the conversation before she got shirty. She very much enjoyed Jacques' company, but if he was about to tell her what she should and shouldn't do, then they were going to experience some turbulence.

'If you'll excuse me,' Mal said curtly, and headed back to her room. She'd wanted to discuss Ferne's story more,

175

and also the fact that Jordan and Wulf seemed to have something going on, according to Freddie, but obviously Jacques would not indulge her curiosity.

Resisting the temptation to slam her bedroom door, she kicked off her shoes and headed over to her desk and wrote down all the questions she had. As the words flowed, the tension released, and she was able to recall Francine's body without flinching. Eventually, she knew she was ready and called Sophie.

'Hi, Mal. Are you okay?'

Mal smiled.

'All fine, but I have some observations and want to share them with you.'

'Mal…'

'So that you can pass them up the chain. There are no police here and, apparently, they won't be here for hours because of the weather. Plus, no one here knows it's a murder yet, so their defences are down. Surely it makes sense for me to keep my eyes and ears open?'

Mal took a breath and listened to the silence from the other end.

'Are you still there?'

'Yes, Mal, I'm still here.' Mal could hear the laughter in Sophie's voice and relaxed. 'Tell me what you've got.'

Mal started to tell Sophie about Ferne's relationship with Francine.

'Oh boy, that's nasty. What about this Tinks? Was she in on it?'

'How could she not be? Otherwise, why would she suddenly ghost Ferne?'

'And yet she came and found Ferne and told her to not say anything. If Tinks was involved, wouldn't she assume Ferne had killed Francine, and that she was next? She should have been shouting from the top of her lungs that Ferne was the murderer.'

'Except no one knows Francine was murdered yet.'

'But, Mal, if Tinks was involved in that trick on Ferne, then she must have wondered how much of an accident the drowning was.'

Mal sighed.

'So why did she rush to find her when she heard Francine had died? And why did she tell her not to talk to me?'

'Covering her arse?'

The two women paused, considering all the angles.

'What does your gut say, Mal?'

'I don't know. All that is clear is that Tinks was genuinely protecting Ferne, not herself.'

'Okay. Let's look at the other suspects for a minute. Tell me about the other girls.'

Mal consulted her notes and read them out.

'Julia Hawkes, pregnant, left on the first morning. Imogen Beasley. She's the bride and the focus of the group. Johanna Schwartz, artist. She has a secret identity, paints under another name. According to her, no one knows it. Portia Tunbridge has a line in dogs' clothes.

Apparently, no dog is properly dressed without a Fitzy. Finally Octavia Winthrop, refers to herself as a yoga influencer. Not entirely sure what that meant, so I looked her up on Instagram. Basically, she seems to be young, slim and beautiful, and travels the world posting about how fabulous life is.'

Sophie laughed. 'I've seen those sorts of posts. Is she dreadful?'

Mal thought about it and shook her head. 'No, she seems nice, if utterly unaware of how the other half live. In fact, none of them strikes me as a killer. And they all alibi each other.'

'Right,' said Sophie. 'I've made a note of all that, plus Ferne's relationship with Tinks and Francine. Chances are that one of them is guilty. Stranger killings are far rarer.' She paused, no doubt finishing her notes. 'Anything else?'

'There's a young man called Jordan who works at the wildlife centre. Last night, he was hitting on the girls. Don't know who yet. He's also involved in something with Wulf Clarkson, according to his colleagues. So I wondered—'

'Okay, stop right there, Mal. I'll pass that information on as well, but no more "wondering." You need to stop asking questions.'

Mal took a deep breath.

'Mal, do you hear me?'

'I hear you. You sound like Jacques.'

'Glad to hear he's making sense. I hope you didn't give him a hard time?'

'No.'

Sophie laughed.

'Mal, you go and apologise to him!'

Now Mal laughed as well.

'I just wanted to talk things through.'

'And now you have. I'll pass your intel on, and in the meantime, you keep your head down. Is the raincoat still in your safe?'

'It is. I was going to move it to the hotel's safe, but honestly, what if the murderer is one of the hotel's staff and can access the safe?'

Mal heard Sophie click her tongue as she thought it through.

'Makes sense. Who knows you have it?'

'Jacques, Dougie, and Wulf.'

'Okay, let's hope it stays that way. Don't worry, the police will be with you as soon as possible. Just don't take any risks.'

Agreeing, Mal hung up and gave a massive sigh of relief. She had felt paralysed, but now she had done something useful. Brushing her hair, she touched up her make-up. Checking her watch, she saw lunch would be served soon.

Chapter Twenty-Six

When she came downstairs, there was no sign of Jacques. Lunch wasn't ready, and Malachite Peck found herself in a dangerous situation; she had unanswered questions and time on her hands.

Grabbing a coat, she opened the front door and went off in search of answers.

Although it was raining heavily, the wind had finally died down, but looking out to sea, Mal could see the police wouldn't be coming by boat yet. Heading along the main track between the castle and the wildlife centre, Mal hunched herself up against the rain and wondered why Tinks was so keen to get Ferne to remain silent. Only a few people knew Francine was murdered, so why was Tinks so keen to keep their relationship secret? Was she protecting Ferne or herself? If Tinks had killed Francine, then Ferne was the perfect fall guy. But why would Tinks kill Francine? Mal tutted. Instead of answers, each question just exploded into more; a fungal bloom of confusion.

Ahead of her, she could see the wildlife observation centre and quickened her pace. She thought the girls would all close ranks. And she was curious about Jordan; who had he been with last night, and what was he involved in with Wulf? If she couldn't investigate who killed Francine, she could at least see what Wulf was up to.

Banging on the door to the wildlife centre, she opened it up and walked in. The door opened into a boot room with various ropes and coats hanging above rows of wellies and walking boots. There was another wooden door. Repeating herself, she knocked and entered. This was a much larger room with a stove to the side, some sofas, a long table, and a rudimentary kitchen. A rough breeze disturbed the papers on the table and Mal wondered if a door was open around the other side. There were no voices within, so she called out. A minute later, a tall woman popped her head out from behind a door. In her hand, she was holding a bucket, and Mal noted her knuckles were red and her skin was calloused. She was wearing a fleece top over utility trousers and walking boots, and Mal recognised her as the deputy manager she had met earlier back at the castle. She stared at Mal in surprise.

'Oh, hello again. We're not doing tours today.'

She spoke sharply and frowned at Mal.

'No, of course not,' said Mal quickly. 'I just thought I would volunteer. I can't imagine how much there must be to do, and what with Dougie being involved with the body, I thought you might be short-staffed.'

The other woman relaxed and nodded.

'Short-staffed doesn't even begin to cover it. We're down four members of staff this season.' She sighed deeply, then waved her through. 'I could use a hand! Come on.'

Mal followed her into another room to a scene of chaos. Rain and daylight were pouring in from a hole in the roof, soaking the computers below. The walls were lined with Admiralty charts, but many of these were flapping about in the breeze. The floor was covered in ledgers that had been blown off the worktables. At the far end was a stack of journals that the woman had clearly been retrieving from the floor. Mal surveyed the damage.

'My name's Mal, by the way,' said Mal, looking around for somewhere to start.

'Ange, and thanks. Sorry if I sounded sharp back there, but today has just been... Well, you know.' She trailed off, and Mal decided to put her investigations aside for a moment to help.

'Is the electricity switched off?'

'Yes.'

'Did you back up your files?'

'We back up remotely every night.'

Mal nodded. At least this wasn't a total disaster. She imagined scientists, like financiers, lived for their data. Power cuts and damaged IT networks could range from frustration to ruin.

'What are all these journals?' asked Mal, as she and Ange continued to stack them up on the table.

'Personal reports, diaries, sketch books. Each ranger keeps a handwritten journal.'

'Even the youngsters? That's nice,' said Mal.

'Jordan's the most prolific of all of us. Always scribbling away. I don't much care for him, but these journals are important in their own way.'

The two women moved around the room, dodging the hole in the roof as they picked up the maps and journals.

'Still, his girlfriend must be a good influence on him.'

'His what now?'

'Girlfriend. The young woman I saw last night helping with the bags?'

Ange placed a pile of books on the table and paused, her brow furrowed in concentration.

'You don't mean Ferne, do you? Short brown hair, pierced eyebrow?' She laughed when Mal agreed, and carried on. 'She is definitely not his girlfriend. I wouldn't wish him on my worst enemy, let alone Ferne.'

Mal raised an eyebrow. 'You're really not a fan of Jordan, then?'

'I am not. Plus, Ferne is such a special girl. Vulnerable sort, if you know what I mean. Flinches a lot. Chews her fingernails. Always apologising. Not that she ever has to. She's such a hard worker and clever with it.'

'Unlike Jordan?'

Ange tutted and pulled a journal out from the pile on the table.

'Well. Much as I don't like the lad, I can't fault his diligence. He is always recording his observations. Look…'

183

She opened up one of the ledgers, displaying a large double spread of handwritten notes and beautiful illustrations of birds and plants.

'He's diligent about recording everything. Look, these numbers are for the air pressure.' When Mal stared at her blankly, she flipped a few pages. 'Here we go. Three days ago, the air pressure was normal for this time of year. Yesterday, he measured every hour. He knew a storm was coming. As the numbers drop, that indicates lowering pressure. And it's that falling pressure that shows a storm is coming.'

'Is that what the phrase "the mercury is falling" is about?'

'Indeed. Old barometers used mercury to measure the air pressure. For all his faults, Jordan is meticulous about his observations. Not that he ever lets us read his journal.'

'How can you read it? His scrawl is almost illegible.'

She had been peering at the ledger and was only capable of picking up one word in three.

'Dreadful, isn't it? But you get used to it. Besides, it's his artistry that's particularly wonderful.' She started flicking through the journal again. Mal pointed to the sketch of a large tail breaking out of water.

'Is that a whale?'

'Indeed, it is. That's a humpback.'

'I didn't know we had humpback whales in Cornwall.'

'We didn't use to, but that's global warming for you. And that's what we're doing here. Monitoring and

184

recording. We log the gains and losses so that we can understand the bigger picture. Last year a walrus came south. And we're seeing a rise in numbers of tuna.'

'Cold water and warm water animals?'

'Exactly. The tuna is noteworthy. But the numbers seem low.'

She flicked through the journal until she paused on the image of a large fish leaping out of the water; a few flicks of the paintbrush and Jordan had conjured a sense of speed and strength. Its silvery torso bent in the air as water fell from its flank.

'He's talented, isn't he?'

'As much as it irks me to give him credit, he is. Anyway, here is his record for that day.'

She began to read and then broke off, muttering.

'Is everything okay?' asked Mal. The other woman was frowning and looking over at the computers.

'My memory is letting me down. I could have sworn Jordan said he only saw two on that day, but here he's referred to an entire shoal with plenty of breaches.'

'Check another record,' said Mal. 'Some days I can barely remember if I'm about to make a tea or if I've just drunk it. It's the mundane things that trip us up. One gull, ten gulls, fifteen gulls. I bet they all blur into one.'

'Don't. I'm only forty and yet half the time I wonder what the hell I'm doing in the kitchen with a fork in my hand.' She laughed as she turned the pages in Jordan's ledger. 'Let's start from yesterday. Jordan said the storm was scaring them away as he hadn't made a sighting in over a week.'

She started from the blank page, turning the pages backwards, but stopped immediately. 'Hang on. He has a tuna sighting here.' She stabbed her finger on the page. 'And another here.' For a moment she stood staring at the page in silence and then slammed the journal closed, standing up abruptly. Grabbing the journal, she tucked it under her arm. 'Come on, let me see you back to the castle. Guests shouldn't be helping like this.'

'What's the problem?'

'Nothing. But look…' She glanced at Mal and then over her shoulder. 'Don't mention this to anyone, will you? It's just a silly admin error. A big deal for us boffins, but nothing to bother a guest about. But I'd hate for anyone to question our record keeping. Just a silly error. It's like I said, Jordan is more trouble than he's worth.'

As she sped on, ushering Mal towards the rear door, Mal nodded her agreement.

'As you say. Just an admin error.'

Ange sagged in relief. 'Exactly. Oh, and don't mention this to Jordan. He's quite prickly about his stuff.'

I'll bet he is, thought Mal, as she walked away into the fresh air. The rain had stopped and, as the clouds scudded past overhead, she saw the odd glimpse of blue skies and gulls flying overhead. Mal looked out across the waves to the mainland. There was nothing to see. No whales, no fins, no tuna. Just white-capped waves racing towards the shore. What was Jordan up to? Ange had said that he was an excellent record keeper. Why would he be falsifying the numbers of tuna? Mal knew little about wildlife observation, but she knew double accounting when she saw it.

She'd ask Jacques. If there was any significance to Jordan's strange record keeping, he would understand it. Saying goodbye to Ange, she walked against the wind back to the castle. Instead of finding answers, she'd found more questions. But at least now she knew Jordan hadn't been with Ferne last night.

Chapter Twenty-Seven

As she approached the house, her prayers were answered when Wulf stepped out, followed by Jacques. They were standing under the covered walkway that wrapped around this side of the castle; the slate tiles sheltering them from the worst of the weather. Standing exposed on the track, Mal envied them their shelter.

Wulf hadn't seen her, but Jacques had. Mal watched as he shifted position, causing Wulf to fully turn his back on Mal.

They were a good team, she thought to herself. The last thing she wanted to do was explain her actions to Wulf. He had told everyone to stay in the house and no doubt would have something to say about her disregard for his orders. Wulf was hiding something, she was sure of it; but was it murder? And what exactly was his connection to Jacques? Even now, the two of them were standing outside, talking privately.

From this distance, she couldn't hear any words, but the body language suggested an argument. She had to find out the nature of their relationship. She couldn't believe Jacques was involved in anything illegal, at least not deliberately. Had he done Wulf a favour and was now being blackmailed or implicated in something? Her frustration mounted until Wulf threw his hands in the air and stormed off around the side of the building.

Mal hurried towards the house, smiling at Jacques as she approached.

'What the hell do you think you are doing?' he snapped. 'How could you be so stupid?'

As Jacques glared at Mal, the words fell heavily in the space between them. Her smile slipped as she blinked rapidly.

'Stupid?'

'Yes. Stupid. The storm hasn't passed yet. You weigh less than a mackerel, you could easily be blown over and, in case you have forgotten, there's a killer on the loose. If they discover you are asking questions and peeking behind the scenes, you might also have an "accident."'

'I'm a mackerel?' asked Mal in astonished fury. She hadn't expected Jacques to be so cross with her, and his anger lit a spark in her own temper.

'That is what bothers you? How stupid are you?'

All the time he scolded her, her hackles rose until she was about to spit back at him. However, just as she was about to tell him what she thought of his instructions, he turned his back on her.

'Come on. Get inside before anyone notices your absence.'

Mal snapped.

'God forbid anyone should wonder what I'm up to. What about yourself?'

Jacques turned quickly and glared at Mal.

'What's that supposed to mean?'

189

'You and Wulf. There's clearly something going on around this island, and I want to know if you are part of it. The room I'm staying in is ridiculously expensive. Exactly what sort of favour does Wulf owe you? And what were the two of you arguing about just now?'

Jacques stared at Mal and was about to speak when he sighed deeply and shook his head, swearing softly to himself.

'There is nothing between me and Wulf. Mon Dieu. I am a fool.'

Leaving her gaping, he turned and opened the back door. She was about to turn and head to the other entrance when Teddy saw her from the open door and called out.

'You two lovebirds catching a bit of fresh air,' he said, oblivious to any tension. 'Can't say I blame you. No, sir. It's stuffier than a henhouse in a hurricane in there.'

Mal walked inside reluctantly, Jacques trailing behind.

'Well, what say we all play some bridge?' Teddy asked brightly. Mal was about to turn him down when he cut her off. 'I know the event has been cancelled officially, but hell, we can still play unofficially. It would be a damn shame if the charity lost out just because of a tragic accident. Don't you agree?'

'What a pity,' said Mal quickly. 'I'm afraid Jacques has a headache and isn't up for a game. Maybe another time?'

She smiled sweetly at the two men. Teddy raised an eyebrow, but Jacques simply stared at her, his expression blank.

'Not at all. Actually, I feel fine.' He gave Mal a thin smile. 'A hand of cards is an excellent idea. Shall we?'

Frustrated, Mal tried not to bite her lip. The last thing she wanted to do was sit still and play nice.

'Silly me. I completely forgot. It's me that has the headache. Please excuse me.'

With a quick nod of her head, she turned away and walked along the corridor until she turned the corner and was out of sight. She had behaved like a bad-tempered fool and she knew it. Still, what right had Jacques to speak to her like that? Did he think that because she was his guest, he could treat her like a vassal? No wonder he was single, if that was how he spoke to women when he thought they owed him something. And as for comparing her to a mackerel, what was he thinking? She'd been insulted many times in her life, but to be called an oily fish… No, not that, less than an oily fish! It was incredible. For a second, all thoughts of finding Francine's killer flew out of her mind. The minute they could get off this island she would, and then arrange for a taxi to drive her home. She would have no more to do with Jacques and his high-handed attitude.

As she strode across the main hallway, she spotted Henry Fitzgibbon approaching her. Deciding not to alienate anyone else, she paused.

'Mal, Penny and I are looking for a fourth member for our table. We thought as we're here anyway we may as well play. What do you say?'

Reading her expression, he hurried on.

'I'll partner John Markham if that helps. Or Penny will.'

'Markham's your third seat?'

That changed things. Mal was in a bloody foul mood, which just happened to be the perfect temperament to spend time with a man that was running a covert investigation and had already turned his attention on her. 'I think that's an excellent idea. I may have been harsh with him last time. I didn't know he was a beginner.'

Following Henry into the main dining room, she could see several tables were already playing informal hands. Death was not the deterrent it used to be. It all felt in very poor taste. But then, Mal knew Francine had been murdered. Did that make a difference? A volley of laughter came from a table in the corner and Mal winced inwardly. However she had died, a young woman had lost her life. This felt inappropriate, and she was glad to see none of the bridal party were present. Looking around the room, she couldn't see Jordan either, although that wasn't surprising. She imagined most of the staff were busy trying to make the island accessible. As her mind drifted towards his illustrated notebook, she gazed vacantly until she felt someone's gaze resting on her. Snapping to attention, she saw Jacques watching her across the room.

He was playing with Morris and Laurence Barta, as well as a woman she didn't recognise. The woman tapped Jacques on the hand. He looked away and smiled at his companion.

Mal bit her lip and turned away. Walking towards her own table, she saw John Markham already seated opposite Penny Fitzgibbon. Henry pulled a chair out for Mal and she sat down. John was to her right and Penny to her left. At least she would be spared having to play with him. She would toy with him instead.

'Shall we keep this friendly? I think if we play for money, poor Mr Markham here will bankrupt his partner.'

This was met with a light-hearted laughter and Penny chided Mal, saying that John wasn't so bad as all that. Mal suggested they play one round and decide after that.

Penny opened the bidding with a two no-trump which John immediately passed despite having fourteen points in his hand. It was all Mal and Henry could do to not snigger as their opponents won all thirteen tricks, but as they had failed to bid them, their score was derisory.

'Was that very bad of me?' asked John, wincing as Penny broke the lead of her pencil, writing up her score pad.

'Not at all,' said Penny. 'We were all beginners once. However, if your partner opens at the two-level you really, really ought to respond, if only to show your longest suit.'

'So…' Mal grinned. 'Are we playing cash for points?'

Penny swallowed visibly, then sighed in relief as her husband came to her rescue.

'What about £200 per game? Win or lose? And the proceeds go to the charity. No reason they should lose out because some silly drunken girl fell in the harbour.'

'Per table or per player?' asked Mal quickly, revolted at Henry's attitude but determined to stay and try to see what John Markham was up to. Besides which, she simply didn't have the funds to play at this level. She winced inwardly, knowing these stakes weren't even that high. She'd have been quite happy to gamble, knowing she could beat John and Penny with her eyes closed. But an all-in, win or lose, meant she had no hope of dodging the kitty.

'Per table,' suggested John quickly. Clearly, he also wasn't keen on the stakes either. 'Shall I deal?' Given that the system of dealing was already prearranged and only a total amateur would ask, Penny groaned deeply and cut the deck to Mal.

'So, John,' she asked as she dealt out the pack, 'Besides catching up with Wulf, why did you come here?'

He had been picking his cards up as she dealt them, much to her annoyance, but now he stopped and looked at her.

'I don't know Mr Clarkson.'

'Are you sure?' said Mal. 'I thought I heard you mention him to your partner. Where is she, by the way? Catching up with Wulf?'

194

John looked rattled now as Mal continued to deal.

'She doesn't know him either.'

'Really? I could have sworn I heard you say Wulf was playing his cards close to his chest, but he'd met his match?' She dealt the last card and smiled brightly at him. 'I assumed you must have played together in the past?'

'I think you must have been mistaken.'

'Like when you called me Em instead of Mal?'

Mal didn't take her eyes off him and was gratified to see him swallow. Whoever he was, his skills were not in subterfuge. Mal was onto him, and now he knew it. She picked up her cards.

'One spade.'

'I have never met Mr—'

Mal held her hand up.

'No chitchat during the game.' She smiled sweetly and was pleased to see him frown and then drop his cards as he tried to rearrange his hand. Mal and Henry won the next game with ease.

'Bid and made. Well done, partner,' said Henry, as a roar of laughter burst out from another table. Clearly, they were having even greater success, but again, it struck Mal as distasteful.

'Are you okay?' asked John, surprising her with his concern.

'Yes. It all just feels wrong. Here we are, playing cards, and yet out there a young woman is lying dead.'

'I understand.'

Mal looked at him and was surprised to see a genuine expression of disgust on his face.

Henry shook his head. 'Not at all. This isn't wrong. It's the most natural response in the world. Do you know the phrase memento mori?'

Mal nodded, but he ploughed on, regardless. 'It means death is all around us; life is for the living. We should celebrate what time we have on the planet because soon we too will be dead.'

'Hear, hear,' said Penny and raised her arm for a waitress, who quickly came over. 'Four glasses of champagne, please.'

Mal shuddered.

'Not for me. I'm sorry. I'm sure you're right, but seeing her body has made me feel less like celebrating my existence and more like mourning the loss of hers.'

Her words fell like heavy weights as the other three stared at her. Penny clasped her hand over her mouth and waved the waitress away, dismissing her order.

'I'm so sorry. I had no idea. Where did you find her?'

'Was it clear she had drowned?' asked Henry.

John simply stared at her, his eyes narrowed, before interrupting.

'I doubt Mal wants to talk about it.'

'You're right, I don't.'

The fact that Francine had been murdered and not the tragic victim of an accidental drowning was not known, but she still felt wrong discussing her death in front of others. Who knew who was listening in on their conversation? So far, the killer thought they had got away with it, and she intended to keep it that way. Talking about it may inadvertently let something slip.

Mal pushed her cards away from her.

'Would you excuse me? I'm so sorry, I think I would like to lie down for a bit.' John and Henry stood as she rose from the table.

'You do look pale,' said John. 'May I accompany you to your room?'

The sound of laughter was getting to her. The angry look on Jacques' face was haunting her. And now this man, that she knew had been investigating her, was suggesting he follow her to her room. Mal took a deep breath.

'Certainly not.'

Moving quickly away from the table, she walked across the room and headed upstairs. She wanted to run, but that would just draw attention. Instead, she moved slowly, stopping to chat to one or two other guests, before closing her bedroom door behind her and falling onto the sofa in despair. A young woman had been murdered and her killer was walking the castle as if nothing had happened. She trusted Wulf as far as she could throw him, but why would he murder a guest? She also hated his relationship with Jacques. Jacques was her friend; she was trying to protect him. But how could she help him if he wouldn't tell her what was going on?

Chapter Twenty-Eight

Half an hour later, there was a tap on the door and she wearily got up from her bed and headed across the room to open the door. A young woman was standing outside carrying a tray with a plate under a cloche. Beside the cloche was an envelope.

'Room service.'

'I didn't order any.'

'I know. Mr Pellofey thought you might be hungry.'

Mal choked back a laugh. Why was that damned man always feeding her? Waving for the girl to place the tray on the table, Mal wondered what he had ordered.

'He also asked me to hand you this note.'

Handing the letter to Mal, she left the room, closing the door softly. Mal wandered back to the table, looking suspiciously at the cloche before sitting down in the armchair overlooking the sea. Untucking the envelope, she removed the sheet of paper.

My Dearest Mal,

A mackerel is one of the most beautiful fish in the sea. Its silver body shimmers in the water as it races through the oceans. It is fast and graceful, as beautiful as you are clever. It is I who is stupid. With all my heart, I apologise for my stupid words prompted by fear.

Please eat.

Yours. Always yours.

Jacques.

Mal slumped back into the chair and stared at the letter. It was possibly the most eloquent apology she had ever received, and suddenly she didn't feel worthy of it. Of course, he was just concerned. She had overreacted and should apologise to him, but wasn't sure why she had allowed her emotions to impede her better judgement. Perhaps because she had just seen a dead body. And because there were questions about Jacques' relationship with Wulf that she didn't fully understand. Sighing deeply, she headed towards the table and removed the cloche, laughing at the plate of grilled mackerel with gooseberry sauce and a slice of homemade bread and butter. Her stomach grumbled. Sitting down, she tucked into the light lunch, blessing Jacques for his forethought.

There was a knock at the door and for a second her heart beat faster, and then she dismissed the idea. She knew instinctively that Jacques would not call on her. He would view that as intrusive. He had apologised, and would not belabour the point, but wait for Mal to accept it and search him out.

She was about to call out that the door was open, then remembered that a killer was in the castle and she was all by herself. She headed to the door and opened it carefully.

Standing in front of her were Tinks Campbell-Jones and the one person who had more than sufficient grounds to want to kill Francine, Ferne Straub.

Mal studied the two young women. They were the same age, the same height, the same colour and size, and yet everything about them screamed their differences. It wasn't just their start in life; it was how they then lived that life. Tinks radiated confidence. Mal saw a lot of herself in the young woman. Her whole world was ahead of her and she was going to conquer it. In contrast, Ferne already looked beaten. Her eyes were bloodshot, her skin had a pale waxy shine to it, making a few red spots around her temple stand out like angry sores. Mal wanted to snap at her and tell her to stand up straight, but she thought Ferne was well beyond tough love right now. She looked like a dog that was used to being kicked by its owner. Mal wondered if she had finally turned and bitten that same owner.

Tinks cleared her throat.

'May we come in?'

Mal stepped aside and Tinks ushered Ferne into the room. The three of them sat down facing each other on the two sofas. Mal sat quietly and waited for them to begin. Ferne stared into her lap, picking at the skin on her fingers whilst Tinks looked around the suite. Finally, when she realised Mal wasn't going to speak, she inclined her head slightly and gave Mal a tight smile.

'Please don't let us interrupt your lunch.' Mal moved her plate to one side. As if she was going to eat in front of people who weren't!

'No, that's okay. How may I help you?'

'We'd like to ask about Francine.'

Mal shrugged, but remained quiet. Only a few people knew Francine's death was not an accident, and one of those people was her murderer. Mal didn't know what Tinks was up to, but she knew Ferne was certainly a person of interest.

'Did someone kill Francine?' asked Tinks, all smiles gone.

'How should I know?'

'Because I understand you saw her dead body.'

That news travelled fast. Then she remembered she had mentioned it herself. And of course Jacques, Wulf, and Dougie knew. Dougie, who worked with Ferne.

'Ferne, did Dougie tell you I was at the harbour?'

The girl nodded.

'And does he know your relationship to Francine?'

She jerked her head up, staring at Mal, then turned to Tinks for support.

'No, he doesn't,' said Tinks. 'And we'd be grateful if it could stay that way.'

Mal fell back into silence. Tinks clearly wanted to control the narrative. But if she thought Mal was going to be a pushover, she was about to be re-educated.

'I've looked you up, Malachite Peck.' Seeing that Mal was going to do nothing more than raise an eyebrow, she ploughed on. 'Here's what I discovered. You are very clever. Ruthless even, but tempered by a moral code that effectively ended your career as one of the City's leading traders. Which makes me wonder why, on hearing about a row between Ferne and Francine, you made a beeline to speak to Ferne about the details? You don't strike me as the grandmotherly type, comforting the bereaved.'

The silence stretched out until Tinks snapped.

'Well?'

'Well what? If you would like to ask a question, please do so. But if I can remind you, Miss Campbell-Jones, we are not in a courtroom but in my suite. Maybe you would like to adjust your tone?'

'Very well. Why would you approach Ferne, if Francine's death was an accident? Do you think she killed Francine?'

Mal was going to reply, but Ferne gave a deep moan and burst into ugly sobs. Immediately, Tinks morphed from ruthless barrister to caring companion, throwing her arms around her friend and telling her not to worry. Mal got up and grabbed a box of tissues, passed them to Tinks, then called down to reception and asked for a tea tray for three to be brought up. When she sat down again, she sighed deeply, staring at the two friends sitting on the sofa opposite her.

'Francine died. That really is all I can say.'

'But foul play is suspected. Otherwise, why would you have dashed off to interview Ferne?'

'Call it curiosity. It's how I'm hardwired. I see something out of place and I investigate.'

'And now, having spoken to Ferne without a lawyer present, you believe her to be guilty of Francine's murder?'

'I didn't interview her. Did I, Ferne? We were just having a chat. Isn't that right?'

Ferne blew her nose and then wiped her eyes with another hanky.

'That's right.' She looked at Tinks. 'It wasn't anything as formal as an interview. We were just chatting.'

Tinks raised an eyebrow.

'Just chatting. And did you record this chat, Malachite? Or later write up any notes?'

'How formal you make it sound.'

'Indeed. But maybe less formally, do you keep a diary? Maybe record the day's events?'

Mal's eyes twinkled, and she smiled brightly. 'Why, yes. And I write letters. And I update my Instagram feed daily.'

Ferne groaned and Mal took pity on her.

'But a private conversation remains just that in my eyes.'

Tinks sagged in relief. Mal didn't feel the need to tell her she had already told the police everything she knew.

'She didn't do it, you know.'

'Do what?'

'Kill Francine.'

'No one is saying that Francine's death was anything other than a dreadful accident.'

Tinks flung herself back on the sofa.

'That's rubbish and you know it. None of us have been allowed to see Francine's body. You dash off to interrogate someone that Francine was seen arguing with. Wulf Clarkson is acting like a man possessed. We have a financial investigator from the Treasury jumping at shadows. And somehow, they are all connected.'

'The Treasury?'

There was a knock at the door and all three flinched before Mal remembered her request for tea. Taking the tray from the waitress, she placed it on the small table between the two sofas and poured three cups. Ferne's hand shook as she took hers and the cup rattled in its saucer. Mal and Tinks abstained.

'You said there's an investigator from the Treasury here?'

'Yes. Surprised you haven't clocked him: dressed in supermarket clothes, with not the first clue about how to play cards. And yet he's here on an island of millionaires pretending he belongs. I assumed he was here investigating you. With Francine's death, I'm not so sure.'

'How do you know he's from the Treasury?'

'I took a photo of him and sent it to my clerk. Asked her if his face rang a bell and it did. He's an investigator for the Treasury, works alongside Customs and Excise and the Inland Revenue.'

Mal blew out her lips. Whoever he was after, this was clearly a major investigation.

'John Markham is not looking into me.' Tinks smiled as Mal showed that she too had clocked him. 'But if he is, he won't find anything.'

'So why is he here? And what does he have to do with Francine's death?'

'Can I ask why you care?' said Mal. She knew it was a provocative question and hoped it would unsettle Tinks. The young woman was quick-witted, and if she was trying to cover up Ferne's crime, Mal needed to act with caution. Mal was no match for the two younger women if they overpowered her. At least by having the tea brought up, she had a witness.

Tinks blanched as Mal asked her question.

'Of course I care. Francine is my friend… was my friend. And so was Ferne. So is Ferne.'

She reached forward for her tea and took a deep gulp before continuing.

'Look. I know Ferne has told you about what Francine did to her. It was dreadful.' She paused and shook her head. 'Actually, dreadful doesn't come close. I have never heard of anything so cruel. I knew Francine had a mean streak, but I never realised how deep that ran. I had no idea. And when I found out last night, I exploded.'

Mal remained quiet. Tinks appeared to be manoeuvring herself into prime suspect. 'It was inconceivable. And yet when Ferne told me, I believed her immediately. What, you don't believe me?'

Mal pursed her lips.

'And yet all you had to do to relieve Ferne's suffering was to let her know you weren't dead. You didn't have to play along.'

'My God. You think I knew anything about this? That day when we were all playing at the cliffs, I said goodbye to Ferne. We were moving again. A crisis in the Middle East meant my father was reassigned to Oman. Usually ambassadors get plenty of prior warning; sometimes it's an overnight departure. I fell off the cliff before I got to say goodbye. I was stuck in hospital for a few days, and then I flew out. It was years before I returned to the UK. I got my first degree in the Sorbonne and returned to London to study law.'

'And you never thought to look up Ferne?' asked Mal, eating a biscuit and wishing she'd had a chance to eat her lunch before the girls came in. She was starving. Even now that her mackerel was cold, she could still smell the sharp tang of the gooseberries against the sweet, oily fish. The homemade bread was sitting there, tempting her as she nibbled on the shortbread.

'Like I said. When my family moved away, it was years before I came back to the UK. I've always had just one goal; to be a High Court judge. I didn't have time to look up old friends.'

'And yet here you are on a bridal weekend with Francine.'

'Believe me, I had no desire to resume our friendship. She could be cruel and spiteful. She was also not above blackmailing people at school. It wasn't the sort of behaviour I wanted to be associated with. And yet London is tiny. People move in the same circles and soon I discovered that Francine and I were in the same small orbit. Had I had an inkling of what she had done to Ferne, I would have called her out publicly. But Ferne has done nothing wrong.'

She took a deeper gulp of tea and, as she put her cup down, Mal refilled it.

'But no one has accused Ferne of doing anything.'

Tinks waved her hand in dismissal.

'Ack, don't you see? I am not in the least bit surprised that Francine is dead or that someone may have murdered her. She could be deeply unpleasant. But if she was murdered, then Ferne didn't do it. She was with me all night.'

Mal picked up her cup and sipped carefully.

'Can you prove that?'

'Yes! After dinner that night, we were all drinking and dancing. It was getting late and a lot of the hotel guests had turned in.' Mal nodded. She and Jacques had had a few dances early on, laughing along to ABBA, but he called it an early night when Boney M came on. And whilst Mal had stayed up a little longer, chatting with Teddy, she too had turned in, leaving the youngsters to it. 'We were just starting on whisky sours when Ferne came in and started screaming at Francine. I didn't recognise Ferne at first, but when I did, I was staggered. She was so angry. So, anyway, I pulled her away, and we went up to my suite and she told me the whole sordid story. The other girls saw her when they came up.'

'And was Francine with them?' asked Mal.

'No, Octavia said she was distraught and wanted to be left alone.'

'Did anyone stay with her?'

'No, everyone came back and then that was it for the night. No one left. They didn't know why she was there or how we knew each other, but they all saw her in our wing of the castle.'

'And when you slept; how do you know she didn't leave the room, or any of the others?'

'Slept?' Tinks stared at Mal and laughed. 'I had just been reunited with an old school friend and, in that moment, discovered the most heinous of acts that I had been implicated in. Do you really think for a moment that either of us could sleep?'

Mal looked at the pair of them. Ferne's exhaustion was obvious, but Tinks looked like she could go another ten rounds with a grizzly. The joys of good make-up and youth. Even listening to their sorry tale made Mal tired.

'Very well. But this changes nothing. Francine's death was an accident until the police say otherwise.'

'And you won't mention Ferne's connection?'

Mal shook her head. 'I can't promise you that. The police need all the facts. But I won't mention it to anyone else on this island.'

Tinks scowled at her, but Mal shook her head.

'It's the best I can offer you, besides this piece of advice. Hypothetically, if Francine was murdered, then her killer is on the island. Ferne here is the perfect scapegoat. And you are her main alibi. I wouldn't let her out of my sight until the police arrive. And I'd also watch my back, if I were you.'

'I don't understand,' said Ferne.

'I do,' said Tinks darkly. 'I'll explain later.' She patted her lap, and Mal forestalled her departure.

'You said she used to blackmail people in school. Tell me more about that.'

'Oh, that was Francine's little game. If you had a secret crush, a late period, if you'd copied your homework, stolen from someone else's locker, she would find out.'

'And what did she do with that knowledge?' asked Mal. What did a wealthy young schoolgirl really need?

'She just used the knowledge to make her victims react.'

'She never asked for money?'

'No. That didn't bother her. She saw people as experiments. She enjoyed making them twitch.'

'A strange sort of friend for you to have?'

Tinks sighed. 'I know. I wish I had woken up to her sooner. But in the beginning, all I saw was the funny Francine. She befriended me as soon as I arrived, and then we met Ferne and we became a little gang.'

Mal nodded her head. Teenage girls and their friendships were a Gordian knot of angst and emotions. The young women standing in front of her were no longer teenagers. But were their emotions still driving their actions?

Chapter Twenty-Nine

When Ferne and Tinks left, Mal sat down and started to scribble. She didn't give two figs for Tinks' concerns about a paper trail. She was a barrister; it was her role to protect her client. It was Mal's instinct to get to the truth and the way she was going to do that was by writing things down until she saw patterns. It was easier with numbers; those she could see in her head. But thoughts and motives, they required a pencil. As she wrote, she made light work of her cold lunch and was pleased when her stomach stopped rumbling.

She was increasingly convinced that Ferne was innocent. The coincidence was unfortunate, but no more than that. However, without Tinks' alibi, Ferne was still the prime suspect. The police would immediately home in on that. And if the killer knew about Francine's treatment of Ferne all those years ago, and how traumatised Ferne had been by it, then Ferne made the perfect fall guy. Had the killer known? Mal paused and put her pencil down.

According to Ferne, she had told no one what had happened. And she had refused to open up during therapy, despite her increasing mental health problems. Which left Francine. Had she mentioned it to someone? From the sounds of the woman, she would have found it funny enough to pass on. The only other person was

Tinks herself. She claimed to know nothing about it, but could she be lying?

Picking up her pen again, she scribbled down Jordan's name, and then John's. One was falsifying records, the other was investigating under an assumed identity. How did either of them connect to Francine? Tapping her pencil on the paper, she knew she had to find some answers.

Grabbing her phone from the charging point, she saw a slew of missed text messages from Jasmine. No doubt news had somehow leaked out, and indeed, the first message simply said *'OMG.'* And then in an outpouring of digital guff, Jasmine portrayed shock, horror, and grief via a range of GIFs, emojis, and just occasionally, the written word. Given the tsunami of messaging, Mal was amazed Jasmine hadn't simply rung. Sure enough, no sooner had Mal thought it than the phone rang and Jasmine's caller ID showed up.

Taking a deep breath, Mal answered the phone.

'Oh my God, you're alive! I was so worried. I told Giles we should call the police. He agreed. If you hadn't answered the phone, we would have called Scotland Yard immediately. Are you hurt? You're not hurt, are you? Oh my God, are you alright? When I heard the news, I panicked. Julia told me and I all but passed out there and then. Mal? Mal, are you there? You haven't said a word.'

'You haven't let me get a word in edgeways.'

Jasmine gave an embarrassed laugh.

212

'Whoopsie. My bad. I swear I talk even more when I'm nervous, and when I'm worried, I'm even worse.' She took a deep breath. 'But you're okay?'

Mal sat in the armchair. The girl was a ninny, but deserved kindness. If this was going to be a long call, she may as well make herself comfortable.

'Yes, I'm fine. And please tell Giles I'm fine as well.'

In the background, Mal heard Giles ask to speak to Mal, but Jasmine cut him off.

'Giles sends his love. He was going to chat, but men don't have the sensitivity for this sort of thing, do they?'

'I think you'd be surprised what men can handle,' said Mal.

'Oh, emotions are definitely a pink task. Paperwork's a blue task, and you're so clever at that, aren't you, Mr Snookums?'

Mal pinched her nose and hoped Jasmine was talking to her cat rather than her husband.

Jasmine continued, 'Giles is nodding his head. Oh Mal, I was so upset. What a tragic thing to happen to poor Imogen.'

'Don't you mean Francine?'

'Oh well, yes, her too, I suppose. Although she's dead now, so it won't affect her. But this was Imogen's special weekend.'

'Do you know Imogen well? How did you find out?' asked Mal, trying not to laugh at Jasmine's wonderful insouciance regarding the short life of Francine Blake.

'Through Julia. I don't know Imogen terribly well. But Julia and I have been spending quite a bit of time together, and she told me. She knew you were on the island.'

'And do you know any of the other girls?'

'Julia, obviously. When she told me, I just died. The thought of you alone on an island, cut off from the mainland. A storm cutting you off from the rest of the world with—'

'Jasmine. I'm fine. This is an absolutely beautiful establishment. There are loads of people here. And I'm with Jacques, so there really is nothing to worry about.'

'Oh, thank God. He's wonderful, isn't he? Giles says so. Are you on a date?'

'Absolutely not,' said Mal with more edge than necessary. It galled her that her family were clearly discussing her private life. Even so, Jasmine wasn't to blame, and she modified her tone. 'But you see, I'm perfectly safe. What happened to Francine was a dreadful accident. Nothing more. Did you know her?'

'Not really, although we went to the same university. But we weren't friends as such.'

'Really?' That surprised Mal. Jasmine was friends with everyone.

'Oh, we went to a few of the same parties. But after a while, well, she could be a bit mean.'

Her voice got a bit quieter and Mal suddenly felt a flush of second-hand embarrassment.

'I know I'm not the brightest girl, but Francine used to enjoy asking me questions in front of everyone and then we'd all have a good old laugh when I got it wrong. Like the time I thought Belgium was just a type of chocolate. I didn't know they'd named a country after it as well.'

Mal bit her knuckle before replying.

'An easy mistake, I'm sure. But not a very kind thing of Francine to do.'

'I know. But that was just her thing. She was always the life and soul of the party. That's partly why I dropped out. I realised the uni life wasn't for me.'

'Oh Jasmine—' Mal suddenly felt sorry for the poor girl, hounded out of university.

'No, Malachite. I don't regret it in the slightest. Uni wasn't for me. Francine was mean, but she wasn't wrong. Uni is no place for dunces like me. Besides, I had a blast at the catering school and then got to travel all over the place. I would never have met Giles.'

Mal smiled. 'And what a lovely thing that was.'

'Yes, it was!'

'But it must have been hard to be singled out like that by Francine?'

'Oh, it wasn't personal. If it wasn't me, it was someone else. Too fat, too ugly, too poor, too thick. Anyone with any chink of weakness was rich pickings for Francine Blake. I tell you Mal, it's dreadful that she died, but it couldn't have happened to a more deserving person.

215

There was some scandal about her in her final year; can't remember the details. I know it was all hushed up, but I'm pretty sure the police were involved.'

Mal's ears pricked up.

'The police?'

'Yes. I wasn't there, remember? But I heard it on the grapevine. Was it her grades?' Jasmine mused.

'It would be very interesting to know, Jasmine, if you can remember.'

There was silence, and then Jasmine spoke quickly.

'Nope. It's gone. And Giles is waving. It's our turn. If I remember, I'll call you. Got to go and I'm so glad you're okay. Lots of love. Oh, Giles sends his love as well. Toodles.'

And with that, the girl was gone.

Mal sat in silence and thought of how she had dismissed and derided her irritating niece-in-law over the years, and felt a sense of shame. When push came to shove, Jasmine was a nice girl and didn't deserve to be bullied for her woeful intellect. That said, Mal would never be able to eat a Belgian chocolate again without grinning.

Her revelation about Francine backed up Ferne's story, and Mal wondered what had happened in her final year at uni. The girl was clearly a nasty piece of work. Mal ran the conversation back over in her mind and smiled when she remembered telling Jasmine that she was with Jacques. Somehow, it had made her feel reassured.

216

Looking across at her empty plate, she knew she had some humble pie to eat first.

Chapter Thirty

Her first stop in her search for Jacques was the kitchens, where she dropped off her tray. The atmosphere was subdued, and Mal wondered if the staff felt as trapped as she did. When she asked if there were any updates about getting off the island, a woman chopping onions laughed and said she was sure they'd be the last to know.

'We're bloody lucky if we get paid on time, let alone kept up to date.'

Mal withdrew as the others joined in their general level of disgust with the workplace conditions. Heading towards the dining room, she peeked around the corner and saw Jacques was no longer sitting at any of the tables, and so she began to explore the castle properly.

He wasn't in the library, his room, the solar, the games room, or any of the reception rooms. Eventually, she headed downstairs to see if he was in any of the workspaces, but it didn't take long before she discovered she was hopelessly lost. The corridors down here were a maze; doors in rooms led to other smaller corridors and staircases. If upstairs the castle was a scene of gracious living, down here it was chaos. Peeling paint and piles of boxes.

'Alright, gorgeous! Are you lost?'

Mal spun around. Wulf was standing behind her with a couple of bottles of wine in a carry container.

'Or have you come to raid the wine cellar?' His tone was light, and Mal saw a twinkle in his eye.

'Now there's an idea! But no I'm looking for Jacques. This place is a warren.'

'You think this is bad? Try the level below. Lots of storage rooms and then some tunnels leading out to caves and the sea.'

'You should do tours down here.'

'I think the insurance costs to cover the health and safety concerns would bankrupt me. Do you know we even have an oubliette? It's a place where they used to throw prisoners and then forget about them.'

'I thought they only existed in France. Imagine spending your final days in one of them.'

'It's tidal, so your final days would only last about twelve hours. Unless they could swim.' He grinned at Mal. 'Maybe I should make a tour of it and feature it as a deterrent to those that don't pay their bills!'

'I think a tour of the wine cellar would be more appealing.'

Wulf gestured for Mal to walk ahead towards a small staircase that Mal had missed.

'Tell me. Do you really think guests would enjoy a tour of the lower quarters?'

Mal thought about it.

'Why not? This place must have so many historical stories to tell. You could make it a specialised weekend, like this bridge one, but for historians.'

219

He laughed. 'As if they have any money. I'm always getting letters from the local history societies asking for permission to visit the archives.'

'Target the Americans. No end to their resources. And maybe once a year, you can have an open day for locals?'

Wulf shook his head. 'I'm not a charity. If they want to visit, they pay like everyone else. You have no idea what my bills look like. And after this morning, God knows what will happen to my bookings.'

'Run a true crime event then,' said Mal ironically, and was appalled when Wulf appeared to take her suggestion seriously.

'Is there much money in that sort of thing, do you think?' Then he paused and shook his head. 'Probably too soon.'

Mal nodded faintly and agreed with him. What was wrong with this man? A young woman had been murdered on his island and he was swanning around replenishing the wine bar and thinking of ways to make more money.

She shook her head. Who was she to judge? Running a business at this level was all about the margins.

'Still, you seem remarkably upbeat. Have you been able to get the helipad cleared?'

'Tomorrow morning, I've been told. The forecast for tomorrow is that the winds will drop sufficiently so a chopper can land. If needs be, we'll evacuate everyone by air. The insurance covers that.'

'Aren't you worried the killer will escape?'

Mal had dropped her voice. Although the staircase had come out into an empty corridor, she had no idea where she was. It could be easy to overhear conversations here, and so far, they still had the element of surprise.

'Not my problem, dear lady. Not my problem.'

Mal frowned. His behaviour seemed out of place. Following Francine's drowning, he had spent all morning freaking out about lawsuits and snapping at everyone. Now he was back to being the amiable host.

As far as she was concerned, Wulf was a definite suspect. But she wasn't going to let him know that. She didn't know why he would have killed Francine, but Mal suspected Francine was blackmailing him. The note in her bedroom suggested a relationship between them beyond host and guest. 'Naughty Wulfie' - was she flirting with him? Or threatening him?

'Did you find anything on the tapes?'

'What?'

'You just seem a little more optimistic this afternoon?'

Optimistic seemed an understatement.

'Oh, the tapes were a waste of time. But you know what, darling? Sometimes you just have to go with the flow. And I, dear lady, am going with the flow.'

Throwing open a door, she found they had walked into the far end of the dining room. She looked back at the door in surprise and saw that it was cleverly disguised in the panelling. Wulf looked at her and winked.

'What did I say? This place is full of surprises. Now, I must return to the role of dutiful host, and you must return to the role of estranged lover. I believe Jacques is down by the harbour with Dougie, seeing how bad the damage is. Toodles.'

With that, he crossed the floor and made his way around the table, leaving Mal staring after him in astonishment. This morning he had been all for covering up the incident. A man facing ruin. This afternoon, he was Mr Conviviality himself. Frowning, she left the room and headed to the front door. She needed to speak to Jacques and find out what his relationship with Wulf was. As she entered the reception hall, she saw Markham coming downstairs, talking on the phone. He looked at Mal and quickly ended his call.

Just you try it, thought Mal. I bloody dare you to come over here and question me. Whatever he was up to on this island had nothing to do with her. But could it possibly involve their host?

Chapter Thirty-One

Jacques was on his way up from the harbour. He'd offered his expertise to Wulf, but the harbour was going to be impossible to use until an angle grinder removed all the jutting pieces of rebar. And even then, access along the damaged jetty would be tricky. The top granite step was missing. Along the jetty itself, several stones were missing, causing the surface to be pocked and difficult to navigate. It was useable, but barely. Especially not by some of the guests on the island. Infirmity was less an issue than sheer inconvenience. These were people who were used to having every whim indulged, and every bump smoothed over. They were not people that slummed it. He tutted to himself. A beach landing would work, but my God, who would risk getting their wet feet?

He looked up and spotted Mal walking down through the pine trees as the path snaked back and forth. Here was a woman who didn't care about wet feet, although he admired how she always paid attention to her appearance when it mattered, and paid it no care when it didn't. A proper lady in his eyes; and one he had insulted. He hoped his apology had been accepted. The very last thing he wanted was to fall out. All would be well, so long as he could steer her away from any questions about Wulf.

'Hello, Jacques. Can I ask you about Wulf?'

Mal looked Jacques straight in the eye. She had meant to apologise first, but after Wulf's bizarre behaviour, she just needed to understand the situation. Jacques took a deep breath and flexed his shoulders.

'Did you like the mackerel?'

'Yes, I did. But I wanted—'

'And did you get my note?'

Now it was Mal's turn to sigh. She was being rude. She had overreacted. He had offered a fulsome apology, and yet she was continuing to be a bore.

'Yes. I want to apologise as well. I was a prickly fool.'

'Not at all. I was so rude.'

'A little.'

'Hmm. And maybe you also overreacted?'

She glared at him and then laughed. 'Possibly.'

'So, we are good?' he asked, offering her his arm as she turned and began to walk back uphill.

'We are. Which is just as well, because I need to ask you about Wulf.'

Her arm jerked as Jacques stopped walking and he turned to look down at her.

'Why are you so keen to talk about him?'

'And why are you so keen not to? Jacques, he's up to something. This morning he wanted nothing to do with the police; now he couldn't care less. I know he's your friend, but honestly. I think he's up to his eyeballs in this.'

The wind blew through the trees and Mal looked around. They were completely on their own. At the far side of the path, the trees gave way to the edge of the island and the rocks below. She wished Jacques would confide in her.

'I am certain that Wulf is not involved,' grumbled Jacques. 'But let's go inside and you can tell me about your suspicions, and I'll hear you out. If I think you are onto something, then I will keep an eye on him until the police arrive. How does that sound?'

Mal was about to reply when her phone rang. Pulling it out, she looked at it and showed Sophie's details to him.

'Take the call,' he said. 'I'll be up in my room.'

With a nod, he walked off.

Mal stepped away from the house and tapped her screen.

'Hello Sophie. Any news on when the police are going to get over?'

'Has anything else happened?'

Mal laughed.

'No. I think one dead body and one decimated island are enough. But I wonder if you could do me a favour?'

'What do you need? I swear to God, if you make me come over there, you will regret it.'

Mal paused and then grinned to herself.

'Was that for me or one of the children?'

Sophie was a brilliant police officer, but an even better mother. Mal had no idea how she juggled both roles. She put the fear of God into Mal, but sometimes her children seemed totally oblivious to her impressiveness.

'For the children. Trust me. If I could run away to an island, I would be on the first boat out there. Now, Mal, what do you need?'

'There's a man on the island going by the name John Markham. One of the other guests says he is a Treasury investigator. I'm sending you his photo.'

Mal tapped the screen, then returned to the call.

'Have you got it?'

'I have. But Mal, why are you asking?'

'He knows all about me. I'd just like to balance things up.'

'Please tell me you aren't investigating?'

'I'm not.'

'You know lying to an officer is an offence.'

'Are you talking to me as an officer?'

'Are you asking me as an officer for a favour?'

Mal held her tongue. Sophie was in the right, of course, and there was no point in trying to deceive her. But the less she knew, the less she had to worry about.

'I am not investigating. I just want to know who's investigating me.'

In the background, one of Sophie's children screamed in protest at some sibling infraction. Mal knew for all the tea in China, she'd rather be out here in the wind and rain than trying to navigate motherhood.

'Very well. I'll see what I can find out. In the meantime, stay close to Jacques. And don't ask questions.'

Tutting, Mal hung up before she could say something she might regret and headed inside. For a young, liberated woman, Sophie had some old-fashioned views about Jacques. Right now, it was Mal trying to protect him in case he had become caught up in something beyond his control.

Chapter Thirty-Two

Heading upstairs, she knocked on the door and was surprised when he called out for her to come in. Opening the door, she saw Jacques under the small desk against the side wall. Around him lay the debris of two teacups and a teapot. The window was open, and the curtains were flapping wildly in the breeze.

'I've had a small mishap.'

Mal slipped off her jacket and got down on her hands and knees, and began to pick up the broken pieces of crockery.

'My window latch is broken. So I have been repairing it with a sock holding it in place.'

Mal held up a green and black striped sock.

'This one?'

Jacques frowned and grabbed it from her.

'What's wrong?'

'It has a hole in it,' he muttered, his head down as he tried to sweep up the sugar from the carpet.

Mal looked at the chaos and laughed.

'Are you embarrassed about a holey sock? You should see my knickers.'

Jacques' face was such a picture that Mal roared in delight.

'Are you blushing?'

'I am not. I...' Speechless, he crawled back out from the table as Mal continued to sit on the floor laughing.

'Jacques, I apologise. I apologise for not listening to you. I apologise for embarrassing you. I apologise for worrying you. But, Jacques. This is who I am.'

He walked across the room and held out his hand to her.

'And you must never change.'

As he pulled her to her feet, she patted down her knees and then, taking a step back, smiled up at him.

'Good. Now let's call for more tea. And let's clear this mess up before the girl arrives. God knows, they have enough on their hands today. A gallic Heath Robinson is more than anyone can handle.'

Half an hour later, Mal had told Jacques all about her conversations with Sophie, and with Tinks and Ferne, and then the one with Wulf. It was so good to have someone to bounce ideas off.

Jacques had listened to her in silence until she came to an end, and then shrugged his shoulders, his palms held out.

'What were Sophie's last words to you?'

'Don't investigate.'

'And?'

'Tinks and Ferne came to me!' protested Mal.

'And Wulf?'

'That's not to do with the murder. At least I didn't think it was. Now I'm not so sure. I was in Francine's room with Wulf, helping him make sure there was

229

nothing that would embarrass her parents. There wasn't, but I did find a note saying "Naughty Wulfie". '

Jacques pinched his nose and then rubbed his face. 'Did he see it?'

Mal nodded. 'He said it was a silly crush. But I've been thinking; what if she was blackmailing him?'

'Okay. Let's go through everything you've got.' He tutted. 'Mon Dieu, you will kill me. So we start at the beginning. These two girls said Francine used to blackmail girls at school. This is the act of a child. Children grow up.'

'I don't think they always do. I think when their behaviour is this pronounced, it is pretty clear the sort of person they will become. She made Ferne believe she was a murderer for years.'

Jacques rubbed his face with his hands. 'That was incredibly cruel. But Mal, I think this makes her the more likely killer.'

'Agreed, but Tinks is providing her alibi.'

'Have you considered that Tinks is the killer instead?'

Mal smiled and screwed up her face in delight. She loved how quick Jacques was, how he kept pace with her.

'I have, but honestly, my gut says no. My brain says maybe. But when my gut talks, I listen.'

Jacques shook his head. 'You British, you always talk about your stomach but always feed it rubbish.'

Mal put down the biscuit she had just picked up and gave him a quick pout.

230

'And you French think food is the most important thing there is.'

'Ridiculous.' Mal raised an eyebrow as he continued. 'What about wine?'

He laughed, and Mal swatted him on the arm.

'We shall go downstairs soon and you can educate me all over again about which wine with which fish. But for now, I think Wulf is up to something, and I think our John Markham is here investigating him. Remember, this morning he wanted the police well away from here, but suddenly he had a change of heart. Maybe Francine was blackmailing him, and maybe with her dead, he'd suddenly let out a sigh of relief? At first, he was appalled the body had resurfaced, but then he realised there was nothing he could do about it and it didn't matter. She was dead and he couldn't be blackmailed.'

Jacques shrugged, unimpressed. 'And what of this John Markham? Does Wulf know who he is? Does he know he is being investigated? I think not.'

'I agree. Except, maybe he did know, but was trying to pretend he didn't. Maybe Francine threatened to reveal what he was up to and that's why Wulf killed her! Remember the note I found in her room?'

Mal leant forwards in her seat excited by her chain of thought until problems bubbled to the surface. Little doubts that fizzed and grew.

'Scratch that. How would Francine know that John Markham is a financial investigator?'

'Maybe Tinks told her.'

'Maybe, but that would be indiscreet and hamper a potentially ongoing investigation. Tinks strikes me as too good a barrister to do that.'

'You said she was angry with Francine last night. Maybe it came out in a row?'

They both fell silent. It wasn't convincing and if anything, it brought Tinks back into the frame for murder.

'Okay,' said Mal, sitting back in her seat. 'What could Wulf be being investigated for? I know he's your friend, but can you think of ways he might cut corners?'

'Alors.' Jacques scowled and Mal winced. Jacques only reverted to French at moments of strong emotion. 'The man is not my friend. I have just known him for a long time. It is not the same.'

'So why are you so reluctant to discuss what he is up to? Why do you keep advising me to leave him alone?'

'You are being stu—' Jacques flung his hands up and began to pace around the room. 'I am certain he is not doing anything illegal. But if he was, he is much bigger than you, and one woman has already died. You have a habit of poking tigers. I just think you should leave it to the police. Please.'

'If I promise not to go anywhere near him, will you humour me and answer my questions?'

'Mon Dieu. Yes. Ask.'

'What could he be doing on an island like this that is illegal? My first instinct is smuggling, people and goods. Do you think that is feasible?'

'Yes.'

'Ah, I thought as much. I've been considering all the financial tax write-offs which he could be up to his neck in. Then I wondered if the physical location could be a factor. Could he be hiding stuff down in the cellars?'

'It is possible.'

'I also wondered if Jordan could be involved.'

'Who is this?'

'Works down at the Wildlife Observation Centre. He's out watching the seas all day long and has a really close relationship with Wulf. It's possible he's spotting boats. I've seen his records, and he's already falsifying what he sees on a daily basis. Angela Davis looked really alarmed when she saw what he was doing.'

'And that's what you were doing when I saw you coming back across the island?'

'Guilty as charged.'

'Well, I don't know. Maybe Jordan is involved, but I can't see that falsifying the number of birds indicates criminal behaviour.'

Mal sighed.

'You're right. Maybe there is nothing to it after all. He just strikes me as an unpleasant sort.'

'Just because someone is unpleasant, they aren't automatically guilty.'

'Well, they're usually guilty of something, but you have a point. It was tuna, by the way.'

Jacques put the teacup down and stared at Mal.

'What did you say?'

'The records he was falsifying. It wasn't birds, it was tuna.'

Chapter Thirty-Three

Mal had never seen Jacques so perturbed. She failed to understand why it was tuna that alarmed him. But he was a fisherman, so maybe that was why.

'Tell me more about this Jordan,' he asked, his voice terse.

'According to Angela Davis, Jordan has worked at the observation centre for the past two years. He's a hard worker but doesn't play well with others. Never does more than the allotted task; never volunteers, but is the first one out in the morning and the last one back in, whatever the weather.'

'And how did you find out he was altering the figures?'

'Angela showed me his personal log. She had rescued it from the storm damage.'

'What was her reaction to him falsifying accounts?'

Mal thought back to this morning. Ange had gone from happy and chatty to closed-off and almost hostile.

'She was alarmed. Said it was clearly a mistake and told me not to mention it.'

In fact, Angela's and Jacques' reactions were quite similar.

'What am I missing? What's so significant about tuna?'

'They're a protected species.'

Mal wasn't impressed. 'So? Lots of species are protected. I appreciate that getting the numbers wrong is a big deal, but not the end of the world. Surely?'

'In Tokyo last year, a single tuna sold for one million pounds. Tuna is the most expensive commercial fish in the world and the fishing of them in these waters is highly illegal.'

Mal was astonished someone would pay so much for a fish.

'Was there anything special about that one? Was it super-sized, a particular breed?'

'They just go potty for tuna over there, but it's the same breed as has been turning up in our waters. Adult tuna are about 8ft long. A single fish can have around 200 pounds of meat on it.'

'So why aren't we fishing for them? How much are the ones in our waters worth?'

'We don't fish for them because they never used to come here. It's only in the past few years that they've been spotted.'

'And how much are they worth?'

'A single fish? I don't know, maybe £200,000.'

Mal blinked in astonishment.

'One fish. Here, swimming past us right now? My God, why aren't the seas swarming with fishermen?'

'Because they're protected. No market in the UK can legally sell them. Even landing the fish can earn you a prison term.'

'Prison?'

'Yes. There's a lot of monitoring of the fish happening right now. Several boats have a catch and tag scheme running at the moment, but even they can't land the fish. They have to reel it in and, when it's lying alongside the boat, then they have to measure and tag it in the water. And then they release it.'

'Good grief!'

'I know. And it's a really big deal, as you can imagine. The tuna numbers are swelling massively. They are voracious hunters and are beating the fishermen to the catch. They are worth a fortune, but should you catch one, you go to jail.'

'What if you catch it and sell it on the QT?'

'Then you are going to make an awful lot of money.'

Mal and Jacques stared at each other in silence. There was a fortune swimming just off the land.

'How is Jordan involved? How does him falsifying the records work? Surely, he wants to show that the waters are overpopulated with tuna and then the government will add them to the fishing quota.'

Jacques laughed. 'His Majesty's Government does nothing fast, and certainly not to help fishermen.'

'Help me, Jacques?' asked Mal. 'I don't understand what he could be doing.'

'I am guessing, but I imagine he sees a shoal go past, then calls a boat on a closed frequency and tells them where to fish. Those fishermen can land the tuna and sell them on the black market.'

'And no one's any the wiser because we don't have accurate figures for the numbers of tuna, we would usually expect off our shore.'

Mal sat back in admiration. It was so simple. Steal something valuable and no one would know if it was missing or not.

'But surely it's high risk?'

'Incredibly. The boys I was chatting to at the harbour said they had caught glimpses of unregistered boats. They suspect tuna poaching but have no evidence. As soon as these boats appear on the horizon, they disappear. And in bad weather, they're all but invisible.'

'Why don't they call the coastguard?'

'They have done, but it's a big sea. These boats are long gone by the time anyone comes out. Plus, there's no evidence. Just hunches. No doubt once the tuna is caught, the tag is dug out and thrown overboard.'

'Well, we have evidence now.'

'True. And I am glad this doesn't involve Wulf.'

'Oh no, Jacques, I'm sorry, but he's up to his eyeballs. When I was sitting at the table with Jordan, Angela, and Freddie, Freddie and Angela joked that Jordan and Wulf were as thick as thieves. When Jordan heard the police were coming to the island, he went pale as a sheet and dashed over to talk to Wulf. Later on, I saw them arguing. Now what would the owner of Castle Wolf have to do with a wildlife observer?'

Jacques frowned and paused, looking out the window. Mal took a moment to study his profile and smiled to herself. She liked his expression when he was thinking things through. A frown sat comfortably on his face and pulled his features into sharp relief. She knew it was a look that most people were familiar with, so when he smiled, it seemed all the more precious.

She mused out loud.

'If Francine found this out, she could ruin him. And we know she's not above blackmail.' She jumped up, remembering something. 'When we searched Francine's room, I found a note that said "Naughty Wulfie." He brushed it off, saying she had been flirting with him the night before. But what if it was the start of a blackmail note?'

Jacques strode across the room and grabbed Mal's hands, pulling them towards him. It was oddly intimate and Mal squirmed in her chair, keen to avoid the intensity of his stare.

'You do not talk to either man on your own. You are not to discuss them with anyone else. You are to do nothing with this information. Promise me.'

Mal tried to pull free, but Jacques held firm, his large hands enclosing hers.

'Promise me. When the police arrive, we will go together and tell them everything you have discovered, and then we'll let the police arrest them. Yes?'

Mal wanted to say "Yes" just to get her hands back, but for a second, she paused, simply enjoying the connection with Jacques.

'Malachite. Promise me.'

She gave him a small glare and then nodded.

'I promise. Besides, what more can I do? The girl is dead. We know why and we know who's involved.'

Jacques tilted his head, eyes narrowed as he released her.

'That's supposition. You have no evidence.'

'Look,' said Mal, with a playful grin. 'I promise. I will not mention them, talk to them, talk about them. I won't do anything. Cross my heart and hope to die.'

'Mon Dieu. I do not want you to die. Tonight I shall stay by your side for the entire evening.'

'Then I shall have a most enjoyable evening. Now, I believe dinner is at seven this evening. I need to change.'

Standing up, she brushed down her trousers and was slightly alarmed when Jacques walked to the door with her.

'I am not joking. I shall walk you to your rooms and then, when you have changed, I shall escort you to dinner.'

'What if I shimmy down the drainpipe?'

'Malachite. You are the most impossible woman. Now, I give you thirty minutes to look spectacular.'

'I could do it in ten!'

'You could do it in a heartbeat.'

Mal's snappy reply died on her lips. Instead, she smiled at Jacques and, reaching up onto her tiptoes, kissed him on the cheek.

Chapter Thirty-Four

Half an hour later, Mal left her room to find Jacques leaning against the wall opposite, looking splendid in a dinner jacket.

'You look nice, Monsieur Pellofey.'

'As do you, ma Reine.'

Mal paused to translate, then swatted him on the arm.

'Empress, at the very least, please.'

Arm in arm, they headed downstairs. Tonight, Mal was wearing a long grey gown. She wanted to wear her blue gown with silver sequin embellishments on the shoulder sweeping down to her opposite hip. She liked to refer to it as her mermaid dress and had packed it especially; but it no longer felt appropriate. Instead, she added a touch of colour to her dress with a green bolero jacket and a pair of green suede wedges.

As they reached the stairs, they were joined by Sebastian and Ariana, the young couple they had met on the second evening. The couple appeared to have been in the middle of an intense conversation.

'Good evening,' called out Jacques as they approached, allowing the couple the privacy to end their conversation before Mal and Jacques reached them. 'Are you dining?'

Sebastian was in evening wear, but Ariana was wearing the clothes Mal had spotted her in earlier. A pair of jeans and a white blouse.

'That is the very matter of our debate,' said Sebastian. 'I've told Ari that no one will mind what she wears but she—'

'She would rather have room service.'

Ariana thrust her hands in her pockets and looked awkward.

'Can I help you with anything?' asked Mal. They looked a similar size, although Mal had to concede that Ariana was much taller than her, and many decades younger. Her wardrobe would not hold much in the way of excitement for a beautiful young woman like Ariana. 'Although I think you look lovely as you are.'

'Thank you. I have plenty of evening gowns, but they're all rather OTT, if you know what I mean. This break was a chance for us to let our hair down and I packed accordingly. None of my outfits seem appropriate now.'

Mal nodded. 'I know exactly what you mean. I have a showstopper of a dress back in my room. An Oscar de la Renta. And when I wear it…' She laughed. 'Well, let's just say I know I look good.'

Everyone laughed at her confidence. And Seb shook his head at Jacques. 'My wife is the same. We have a room full of Dior and Balmain.'

'This season?' asked Mal curiously. She loved Balmain, but their last few collections hadn't been to her taste. 'Or vintage?'

'Oh, vintage. Everything I have is.'

'Well, I should have loved to see them and no doubt you may have even managed to just slightly eclipse me. Would you like to sit with us this evening?'

Mal wasn't certain why this young lady, with all her advantages, would worry about what people thought of her. In Mal's experience, the more privilege, the more likely people didn't care what others thought of them.

'We would love to,' said Sebastian. 'But Mr Clarkson has asked us to join him, and I already said yes before checking with Ari.'

'Ah,' said Jacques sorrowfully. 'You have done this to yourself. We men. When will we ever learn?'

As the joshing continued, the four of them walked downstairs and Ari seemed to relax.

'Did your sister's house suffer any damage in the storm?'

'None at all. The cover for the swimming pool was ripped off. I spoke to the boys this morning. They found a load of frogs in the pool. They all leapt in to rescue the frogs and Paddy, my sister, said they have been having the time of their lives.'

As they walked down the stairs, Sebastian looked back over his shoulder. 'Can't say the same for the poor frogs, mind.'

He gave his wife a small wink, and Mal envied the pair of them.

'It's a bit silly to be bothered about what people think of me. But I don't like to be the centre of attention. I like my clothes to repel people. If that makes sense?'

'It does. And don't worry about this evening. You will never see any of us again, and tomorrow, fingers crossed, you will be back with your children.'

They reached the bottom of the stairs.

'Now. Chin up. And remember,' said Mal, grinning, 'No one will be looking at you when I enter the room!'

Laughing, Ariana stepped forwards and gave Mal an unexpected hug, then joined her husband as the two of them headed towards Wulf. Jacques deliberately paused, causing Mal to stop.

'Remember,' he said, staring down at her. 'We are going nowhere near him tonight.' Jacques continued to fiddle with his cuffs until the small party entered the room, and then he steered Mal along the hall and into the lower entrance.

'You're being very bossy.'

'It seems the only way. Now, where shall we sit?'

Most of the tables were already full and Mal's heart sank when she saw the only obvious spaces was on a table with the Fitzgibbons and the Bondermans. Penny Fitzgibbon was in a plain long dress, its design dull as ditchwater, but in an attempt to offset it, she was glittering in jewels. To match her golden locket, she was wearing several other gold lockets all inscribed with "P" to the extent that Mal was instantly reminded of a Gypsy wedding. She even had a rather striking sapphire hairslide sticking up from a bun on the back of her head. It was easy to forget just how wealthy she was, especially when she was sitting next to Violet, who was currently making it her life's mission to ensure that no one doubted her wealth.

Not only was she wearing enough jewellery to stock Cartier's, but also a cobalt blue silk taffeta dress with ruffles up to her hips, and a neckline that plunged down to meet them.

As they approached the table, Teddy and Henry both stood up.

'Mal, honey,' said Violet, flashing her eyelashes. 'Did you forget your jewels? Jacques, what are you thinking? Mal is practically bare. Here, take a bracelet.'

She pulled at an emerald and diamond bracelet, and Mal shook her head in alarm.

'No, I-'

'Oh, go on,' laughed Penny. She tapped the hairpiece on her head. 'I am, look.'

Clearly Penny and Violet were bonding over jewels, swapping them like schoolkids sharing scented rubbers.

'No, I really—'

'Honey, are you trying to be respectful? That poor dead child is gone. May the everlasting Lord take care of her. But you're alive, sweet-cheeks. Live it!'

246

Mal had never been called "sweet-cheeks" before, and was thinking of ways to make Violet regret it, when Jacques stepped forward.

'I think Mal looks perfect just the way she is,' said Teddy, raising a glass.

'I quite agree,' said Jacques. 'Mal is, as always, perfection.'

He pulled out a chair for her and she was left with no option but to sit down or storm off for the second time in one day. The fact was, she was glad of Jacques' intervention. But how maddening. He had deemed her appearance satisfactory in his eyes and the other two women immediately acquiesced, as though his opinion was the one that mattered. Fuming, she looked around the room. The vast majority had also chosen to soldier on bravely in their diamonds and silks. The men in their dinner jackets proving the perfect foil for the colourful dresses.

There was no band or table magician as billed, because no one could get onto the island, but it didn't hamper the merry gathering. If a dead body hadn't quelled the enthusiasm for a good time, then the lack of live music was certainly not going to slow them. Piped music was playing across the room. Unsurprisingly, Mal recognised Wulf's dulcet tones as the piped music streamed through his greatest hits.

She watched as the man in question walked across the room, heading towards the hidden door, pausing and laughing with each table. At the last one, he stopped and had a word with Jordan, who was sitting with Johanna. Mal stared in surprise. Surely, she had better taste. Mal watched as Jordan left the table for a minute whilst Wulf spoke to him. Whatever he was saying, it was clear he was angry with the younger man. And Jordan seemed angry in return.

A hand tapped her own, and she turned to see Jacques staring at her, his eyebrow raised.

'The police will be on the island tomorrow.'

Mal smiled quickly at the others, nodding her general agreement that yes, wouldn't that be a blessed relief. By the time she looked over again, Wulf had gone and Jordan and Johanna were once again laughing together.

'Whatever has your eye, Mal?' said Teddy, and followed her gaze to where they were sitting. 'Ah, young love.'

Mal shuddered. 'I hope not.'

'You disapprove?' asked Penny.

Jacques stared at Mal intently and she sipped her wine.

'Not at all. But I was speaking with Johanna when we first arrived. She struck me as a girl with an amazing future ahead of her.'

'Well, we must all have some fun along the way. Surely?' said Teddy. Mal raised a glass in weary acknowledgement.

As the meal ended, Mal felt a deep lethargy wash over her. She was out of sorts with herself. She felt deflated that a girl should die over a stupid bunch of fish, and was unsettled by the whole affair. It all seemed so banal. That a life could be valued so cheaply.

'Excuse me,' said Mal, suddenly standing up. 'Today's events have finally caught up with me. I think I shall have an early night.'

Not giving Jacques time to accompany her, she left the table and hurried out into the hall. As soon as she was out of Jacques' sight, she doubled back, walked through the second set of doors, and snuck across the dining room floor to join Johanna and Jordan. By now their table had been cleared of plates and the two of them had sheets of paper, colouring pencils, and charcoals laid out between them.

Johanna's cheeks were flushed, her hair loose, and she was laughing loudly at a pair of sketches in front of her. Both sheets showed a rhino flying a plane.

'Mal!' said Johanna in delight. 'Which is better? Jordan and I are playing quick draw. We're taking it in turns to suggest the subject matter.'

Mal looked at the two images and couldn't decide whose was whose.

'They both look good to me.'

'No, you have to decide.'

'Very well, this one,' said Mal, pointing to the rhino that had a comically terrified expression on his face.

'Two-one to me,' laughed Jordan. 'Thank you.' He grinned up at Mal. She was momentarily surprised by how good looking he was, and how young. In Johanna's company, he had transformed from a surly, unpleasant troublemaker to a young man heartily enjoying himself.

'Mal, that's not fair. You were supposed to pick mine.'

'I told you speed was going to win out,' said Jordan, playing the table like a tom-tom drum. 'You take too long to get going with all your fancy studies and undercoats.'

'I hope you don't think speed is a virtue in all things,' said Johanna, and Jordan choked on the drink he had just taken.

'You seem in a remarkably good mood this evening, Johanna,' said Mal.

'Should I be mourning the death of a deeply unpleasant girl? I'm sorry for her parents. But that's it. Life is for the living.'

'That's the spirit,' said Jordan boisterously. 'My turn. I choose a bed!'

Johanna raised her eyebrows and then turned back to Mal.

'Excuse me. I intend to win this one.'

Mal had had enough. She had hoped Jordan might let something slip, but he was too enamoured with his companion. If she heard one more person tell her that life was for the living, she'd crown them. The whole bloody lot of them.

She trudged upstairs. Though she felt deflated, she was pleased she'd uncovered enough evidence for the police to interview Clarkson. But what did that mean for Jacques?

DAY FOUR Chapter Thirty-Five

Mac was tapping on the window trying to get in, but it was snowing and she wouldn't be able to get him any fish. The tapping continued, but now it was Mack's fishing rod banging on the patio door.

Mal tried to work out how he got a fishing rod up over the rooftops and then realised she had been dreaming.

A tapping on her door brought her fully to her senses. Grumbling to herself, she called out that she was coming, flung off the covers and went in search of the guest towelling dressing gown.

If asked, she would have sworn that she hadn't had a wink's sleep, except for the fact she had clearly just been dreaming. Pulling the belt in her gown tight, she opened the door and was surprised to see Jacques standing in the corridor, fully dressed. She was about to comment when he pushed past her and closed the door behind him, moving her out of the way.

'Jacques. What is the meaning of this?'

Instead of replying, he headed over to the sitting area and popped a capsule into the coffeemaker before turning around.

'Wulf Clarkson is dead.'

'What?'

'He was found half an hour ago near the wine cellar. He was bludgeoned to death.'

Mal stared in astonishment and suddenly felt something in her brain relax. She had gone to bed wound up and worried. Instead of being relieved they had solved Francine's murder, something had been bugging her. It had felt unresolved, although last night she hadn't known that was the source of her anxiety. With Wulf's murder, something became clear. There was more to Francine's death than they had assumed.

'Who else knows? What time is it? Why have I overslept?'

As she forced out a barrage of questions, she pulled some clothes out of her wardrobe, settling on a pair of jeans, a blouse, and a jacket.

'It's still early, only seven. But I'm afraid anyone coming downstairs will know. The staff are up in arms. The police have been called. Vivienne is in charge, but I said I'd offer her my support. I also took the liberty of explaining your familiarity with crime scenes, and she asked if you would help.'

Brushing her teeth, she glared at her reflection in horror. Her hair resembled the scene of a cockfight, her eyes like sunken pits of mud on a white lard surface. She pulled a comb through her hair, rubbed in some tinted moisturiser, dabbed on two streaks of eye shadow and slapped on her lipstick. Thank God for Collette suggesting tinted eyelashes instead of waterproof mascara.

Throwing open the bathroom door, she slipped her feet into a pair of deck shoes and nodded at Jacques.

'Let's go!'

Moving briskly, they made it down the first flight of steps, and then Mal stopped.

'First things first.' She headed along the lower corridor, only stopping when she got to John Markham's, and knocked on the door.

'Mal, what are you doing?'

'Getting answers.'

The door swung open and John Markham looked out curiously. He was already dressed and Mal could see some paperwork laid out on his bed behind him.

'I just thought you should know. There's been a second murder. Wulf Clarkson is dead,' said Mal abruptly, watching his expression carefully. His first response was shock, and he looked over his shoulder to the papers on his bed before he swung back to look at Mal.

'That's terrible news. How did he die?'

'He was murdered.'

'What? But that's terrible news. He was such a great man.' As he spoke, a change came over his face as though he realised the role he was playing wasn't quite working. 'Wait a minute. Why are you telling me?'

'Because Mr John Markham, or whatever your name is, you are here on this island investigating him and it's about time you came out of hiding and acted like the policeman you are.'

'I am not a policeman.'

'No? Well, you work for them. Don't deny it. Get them on the phone. Tell them we know you were investigating Clarkson.'

'Inside, now.' Markham swung the door open and ushered Mal and Jacques indoors. 'What the hell do you mean by a second murder? I thought you just said Clarkson was dead.'

'Francine Blake. Don't tell me your bosses didn't inform you?'

Markham looked distracted and tidied up the paperwork on the bed.

'No. I told them about the sudden death, and they said not to reveal myself. They'd get back in touch if they had more news.'

'And who are they, exactly?'

Markham hesitated.

Jacques exhaled loudly.

'Your cover is blown. What do you gain from further pretence?'

'Very well. I'm a forensic accountant employed by His Majesty's Tax and Customs. When we have enough evidence against Mr Clarkson, we shall place charges against him.' The wind seemed to billow out of his sails. 'But of course that's not going to happen now.' He put the paperwork down again. 'Why wasn't I told about Francine?'

'Probably the left hand not talking to the right hand. How often do major crime and the revenue talk to each other?'

'In my experience, they barely acknowledge the other exists.'

'Precisely.'

'But why didn't you tell me? You seem to know who I am, or at least you thought I was the law. If you knew she was murdered, why not speak to me then?'

'Because, you cretin, you were also investigating me and Jacques. I heard you discussing us on the phone.'

'Well, you have to admit, it was a coincidence finding Malachite Peck here at the home of a man suspected of money laundering and smuggling.'

'Half the people on this island probably have a curious relationship to money and the tax man.'

'But none of them went to prison over it.'

Mal shrugged.

'Anyway. That's why I didn't tell you. I didn't trust you.'

'And now?'

'Now we have two murders on the island and you're the only one with any legal standing. You need to keep law and order until the real police arrive.'

Mal headed back to the door.

'Come on. Time for you to stop creeping around in the shadows. Time to step up.'

Flinging the door open, she marched off down the corridor, Jacques was wisely keeping his opinions to himself but from the look of his face he didn't approve of her taking the bull by the horns with Markham.

She didn't care if Markham followed or not. No doubt he was already making phone calls, but she was glad the matter was now out in the open. She had hated being the subject of someone else's speculation, and now she had cauterised his investigation.

Chapter Thirty-Six

By the time she got to the ground floor, it was clear that anyone present knew what had occurred. Small groups were sitting around, their heads low as they muttered to one another. Mal ignored them all and walked briskly across the dining room to where Major Cartwright was standing in front of the door. As she strode forward, he stood to attention; the unstoppable force approaching the immovable object.

'Sorry, ma'am. No one is to go through. Orders.'

'My orders,' snapped Mal.

For a moment, the man looked baffled and then repeated himself.

'I'm afraid it's a crime scene. Evidence needs to be preserved.' He leant down towards her and spoke quietly, 'Plus, it's not a sight for ladies.'

Mal snorted, and he whipped himself back up to full height.

'Thank you for your concern, but Dougie has summoned me as I have experience in this field.'

'Crime scenes?'

'Murder.'

The major stared at her for a moment, then stepped back and turned towards the door. Knocking on it sharply, Mal and the major waited a few moments in silence before it swung open and Jacques waved her through. As Mal passed, she decided to get on the major's good side.

'Thank you for your diligence. The police will be here soon and you know what they can be like. If you spot anyone behaving amiss, could you let me know? Two murders have happened under our noses.'

'Two?'

'Exactly so, although I'm certain you already had your suspicions about Francine's death.'

His thoughts raced across his face, and Mal wished she'd had the opportunity to play him at cards. As they gradually coalesced into understanding, he tapped his finger on the side of his nose.

'Naturally, it was obvious to me, but discretion and all that.'

'Exactly. Now I know a man like yourself will have ideas. Let me know if you have any suspicions.'

With that, she moved past him and along the short corridor before heading down the staircase to the lower levels. The last time she had been here, she and Wulf had been laughing. Now as she arrived at his body, her memories blurred between his handsome open face and this bloodied pulp on the floor. He was lying face down. A shattered decanter lay in pieces ahead of his outstretched arm. Closer to his head was another decanter, this one was slick with blood and gore. Mal pulled out her phone and started taking pictures.

'What are you doing?' said Vivienne Chance in alarm.

'Who found him and when?'

'Anna found him just under an hour ago. The police have been informed, but they still can't get onto the island.'

'And that's why I'm taking photos. The detectives will need as much evidence as they can gather, even if only remotely. Move, please.'

'I don't think—'

'Clearly. Now move, please. You asked me here, remember? This isn't the first dead body I've seen.'

As Vivienne moved to one side, Mal took a few more shots and then dialled Sophie.

'What are you doing? You can't share those images. We have a strict privacy policy. Taking photos of Mr Clarkson's corpse definitely flouts that.'

Mal stared at the concierge in exasperation.

'I'm sending them to the police. Does that flout your policy?'

Mal looked at her phone in disgust.

'No signal down here.' She tapped her phone again, and the screen went black. 'Bugger. And now it's dead.'

Normally she was methodical about placing her phone on charge overnight, but with all the recent events, she didn't think she had charged her phone since she arrived on the island.

Mal could hear voices from the top of the stairs and recognised John Markham's confident tones as he made his way down them.

'Step aside, please. Mrs Peck, move aside please.'

'Look, I'm sorry,' said Vivienne, in a tone that expressed no sorrow but quite a significant level of annoyance. 'This is a crime scene, not a show-and-tell. All guests need to—'

'I am not a guest,' said John Markham, pulling a small wallet out of an inside breast pocket. 'I represent His Majesty's Revenue and Customs. Until the police arrive, I am now acting in an official capacity.'

Mal noted he didn't mention what that official capacity was. Was he taking matters into his own hands, or had he actually been seconded?

'Has anyone touched the body?'

'No. Well, yes,' stuttered Vivienne. 'Anna tried to see if he was alive. And Mrs Peck has been taking photos.'

Mal ignored the insult. Having heard that Markham was from the Customs, Vivienne's face had paled and she had lost most of her composure. Mal looked at her closely and wondered just how complicit she was. The fact she had started to sweat didn't bode well for her. To deflect attention, she continued to bad-mouth Mal.

'I told her not to. And I told her to give me her phone, but she refused. Also, she barged down here when I said no one was to come down.'

Mal pinched the bridge of her nose.

'You asked me for my help,' she reminded her again. Dismissing Vivienne, she turned to the tax inspector. 'I was simply gathering evidence. Mr Markham, I'll forward the photos when my phone is charged. Jacques here is acting as an independent witness.'

'Indeed?' Markham stared at the both of them, clearly still smarting from her dressing down minutes earlier. 'Can I ask how you knew about this secret passageway from the dining room?'

'It's hardly a secret, is it?' said Mal, looking across at Vivienne. 'Anyone with eyes could see the staff use it every day. Isn't that right?'

Markham looked to the concierge for confirmation. She nodded her head.

'It's the quickest way to the wine cellar, if you are in the dining room.'

'But you don't make a thing of telling the guests about it?' said Markham, pouncing on the detail and raising an eyebrow significantly when Vivienne agreed it wasn't a feature.

'And yet you noticed it, Mrs Peck?'

'And yet you didn't, Mr Markham.'

She stared at him as the silence filled the corridor. Eventually, he blinked first.

'Very well. You can all leave now. My partner, Kate Shaw, is currently assembling everyone in the dining room. Mrs Chance, we'll need to speak with you, so make sure you are available when we call.'

Turning his back on them, he crouched down to examine the body and then looked back over his shoulder at Mal.

'Are you still here?'

With his scowl seared into her memory, Mal headed back upstairs, as Jacques led the way. She had been impressed that Markham had taken control. However, from his expression as he examined Wulf's lifeless body, Mal felt certain it was the first time he had ever encountered a corpse. If he was in charge, Mal prayed the police got here as soon as possible. This killer was smart and would be able to run rings around the inexperienced accountant.

Mal knew she had been dismissed by Markham and warned off by Jacques, but she couldn't help herself. This was what she was good at. Knowing that Wulf wasn't the killer, she now had a suspect that made more sense.

Last night, Johanna and Jordan had been sitting closest to the doorway. Francine died first, and then Wulf. Johanna and Jordan were both closely connected to both murder victims. Was their proximity last night a coincidence? Johanna's alibi was apparently watertight for the night of Francine's murder, according to Tinks and Ferne. Did Jordan have an alibi? How could she find out? Once again, Sophie's voice was not so much whispering as shouting at her to leave it to the police.

Upstairs, the major was still standing guard, and Mal gave him a quick smile as he tilted his head towards the rest of the room.

'I see the experts are in charge.'

The room was slowly filling up with guests as Markham's partner gestured for them to sit down. Vivienne was back in control, walking between groups and talking softly. Some waiting staff were bringing out cups of coffee, others were already sitting down, a few were crying.

'Indeed.'

'Customs and Excise, eh?' chuckled the major. 'Wonder what they were doing here undercover?'

'Maybe they're investigating a crime syndicate of nefarious bridge players?'

'The only suspicious bridge playing I witnessed was their bidding. The man opened with a two of clubs and was only holding fourteen points!'

'Criminal,' agreed Mal.

'Mind you. I had my suspicions. I could tell he wasn't what he seemed to be.' He tapped the side of his nose again. 'He's not the only one hiding secrets, is he?'

Mal smiled blankly.

'Who amongst us doesn't have secrets?' She turned to Jacques, who had barely spoken a word since he had seen Wulf's body. His silence worried Mal, and she wondered for the hundredth time what favour he had done Wulf. What connected a French fisherman and an international rock star? Smiling up at him, she pulled a face. 'Will you excuse me? I need to charge my phone before the briefing starts.'

Chapter Thirty-Seven

Mal's head was full of questions as she plugged her phone in and came back downstairs. Jasmine had promised to text her back as soon as she knew anything, but Mal doubted she would remember.

When Jasmine had called her, she had just spoken to Julia, whom Mal knew had visited an obstetrician that morning. Add to the fact that Giles was with her when, by Mal's reckoning, he should have been at work, plus the pair of them were filling in paperwork, made Mal wonder if happy news was on the way.

As soon as she got home to Golden, she would write to Giles and tell him about her stay. He might reply and take her into his confidence. They had always had a close relationship and, whilst she still viewed him as a little boy jumping on trampolines and leaning out of his little boat to catch the smallest sliver of wind, she supposed that he really was a grown man now. And maybe there would be another generation of silly boys to come? Or silly girls. And who knows, maybe with Giles' and Jasmine's one brain cell combined, they may raise a clever-clogs? Although Mal was determined not to hold her breath. Whatever the child was, happy would be enough.

Smiling, she caught a peal of laughter and saw the bridal party make their way along the first-floor corridor. The girls seemed in higher spirits today, and she was glad of it. Youth should laugh. It raised everyone's spirits.

Theirs would be dashed again soon enough. Her own spirits slumped when she saw Jordan bringing up the rear, his arm slung possessively over Johanna's shoulder. Johanna's eyes twinkled, and it was clear from the way she leant into him that his proximity was welcomed.

'Mal,' called Tinks. 'We have all been summoned downstairs again. Do you know why? Can we leave? Jordan says the helipad isn't clear yet, but maybe he doesn't know everything?' Her voice was friendly but clipped. And Mal knew she was no fan of Jordan's.

'I've already told you, love. Unless you are really good at climbing a swinging rope ladder, you are not getting off the island today by helicopter.'

'That sounds like fun!' said Johanna. Jordan swung her around, giving her a quick squeeze and a rather passionate kiss before releasing her.

'You are just an adrenalin junkie.'

'You know me. I'm always after the next thrill.'

'Well, wait until you see what I have lined up for you later.'

He laughed, and Octavia made a gagging sound.

'I think we've had enough of your exploits for one night, Jordan,' she said, and the other girls burst into laughter, Johanna included.

'So,' said Jordan, looking at Mal, 'Do you know why we've been summoned?'

Mal stared at the smiling faces. She knew Markham wanted to tell everyone at the same time, but the chance to read their faces was too good to miss. Particularly Jordan's.

'I'm afraid Wulf Clarkson was murdered last night.'

The girls' faces fell. Imogen moaned in denial.

'Fuck!' Jordan stared at her. 'Is this a fucking joke?'

'No. I'm afraid—'

Mal didn't get a chance to finish her sentence as the young man barged past her and sprinted down the corridor towards the staircase.

Tinks got out her phone and Mal shook her head. 'It's not public yet.'

'How did he die? Is it definitely murder?' asked Tinks.

'Definitely.'

'But he could have drowned like poor Francine,' said Imogen tentatively.

'I'm afraid I have seen his body. He didn't drown.'

Tinks narrowed her eyes.

'That's two deaths in two days. Are you still going to pretend that Francine's death was an accident?'

The other girls gasped, but Ferne looked unsurprised and grabbed Tinks' arm. 'They're going to blame me.'

Imogen looked at her in confusion. 'Why would they do that?'

'Because I knew both of them.'

'I won't speculate. If we go down to the ballroom, we'll find out more. I understand a Mr Markham is taking charge of the investigation. He will, no doubt, be asking for everyone's movements last night.'

'Well, we all know Johanna's and Jordan's,' said Octavia, but the joke fell flat as the girls realised the enormity of what they were caught up in.

'Come on, girls,' said Mal kindly. 'Let's go downstairs.'

As they headed down, Mal walked ahead of them. Jordan's reaction had seemed genuine, but as Mal had already discovered, there was more to him than met the eye. He was a talented artist, a known liar, a poacher; why shouldn't he also be a gifted actor?

From what Jacques had said, the penalty for poaching tuna was a jail sentence. Jordan was clearly not acting alone. He and Wulf must have been working together. Jordan could have killed Wulf in order to cover his tracks, but did that mean that Francine had been blackmailing Jordan as well as Wulf?

Mal was certain she was missing an obvious connection.

As she saw Jacques across the ballroom, she stuttered to a halt. Were her feelings blinding her to an obvious line of investigation? If Jordan was tracking the fish and Wulf was facilitating the information, who was working with the fishermen? This wasn't an ad hoc arrangement. There was clearly an organised system in place. Wulf would have been coordinating with someone onshore, or on the boats, who knew the waters. Were the poachers British or French? If they were French, how much better if Wulf's contact was fluent in both languages?

'Are you alright my dear?' said Teddy from behind. His southern tones jolted her out of her dreadful thoughts. 'Can I get you anything?'

Shaking her head, unable to trust her voice, she made her way through the tables and sat down next to Jacques. She refused to believe he was involved, but for now, she had to pull herself together and start thinking clearly. She might have total faith in Jacques, but she doubted the police would be so quick to dismiss the connections.

'Are you okay?' he said. 'You look very pale.'

Teddy and Violet sat down at the table beside her.

'I said the very same thing. Let me get you some water.'

Teddy looked around the room, searching for a server, whilst Jacques stared at her intently.

'Mal?'

'I'm fine. Really, I'm fine. It's just the shock catching up with me.'

Teddy turned back to look at Mal and Jacques. 'The serving staff are all sitting with us. Is there more bad news to come?'

He narrowed his eyes, but Violet giggled.

'Oh, you gloomy Gus.' She patted his hand affectionately. 'He always thinks the sky is falling.'

'As you say, pumpkin,' said Teddy, smiling indulgently. But Mal noticed he had pulled out his phone and sent a quick text. As he hit send, he glanced across at Mal.

'Forewarned is forearmed. I don't suppose you know why we're all here?'

She was about to tell him when Vivienne Chance and John Markham walked up onto the stage and the room fell into silence. Mal looked around and located Jordan on the far side of the room. Even from here, she could see he looked out of sorts. He was wiping his palms on his trouser legs and muttering to himself, his eyes flicking across the room. In the distance, a door was banging in the wind. Vivienne frowned but cleared her throat.

'Ladies and gentlemen. I regret to inform you that our host Wulf Clarkson was murdered in the night.'

She broke off as those in the room, who didn't know, reacted in alarm. Mal watched as Teddy picked up his phone again and started another text. With a tap, he placed his phone back on the table and smiled at Mal, tapping his finger on the side of his nose.

'It's not insider trading if we all know.'

'Did you already know prior to the announcement?'

'Only when I entered the room. And I didn't know. I just knew something serious was about to be announced. I read the room and got ready to make a move.'

Mal nodded. Maybe he knew a few hours before everyone else, but then she dismissed the idea. He was small and old. Whoever had caved in Wulf's head was strong and of a similar height. Teddy was barely taller than she was.

Mal thought about it. You didn't get to stay a billionaire if you couldn't read a stock market properly. Mal was too long out of the game to know exactly how Wulf's death would affect the markets, but knew it would.

Jacques leant over towards Mal.

'You still look pretty pale. Can I get you some water or a coffee?'

She smiled weakly and shook her head. 'Honestly, I think it's all just catching up with me.' How could Jacques have anything to do with this? She had never met anyone more honourable. He was kind, clever and attentive. But she knew he was hiding something. He had been acting strangely around Wulf the entire weekend. She refused to believe he was involved in the poaching, but she was staying in one of the most expensive suites in the castle and, by his own admission, Wulf owed him a favour. What exactly was it? And was it connected to Wulf's murder?

Someone banged on the table and Vivienne thanked them as the room calmed down.

'Thank you. I know this news is alarming, but I'm going to ask Mr Markham here to carry on, as he has been appointed by Devon and Cornwall Police to hold the fort until they arrive, which will hopefully be this evening on the high tide.'

John Markham cleared his throat. Thanking Vivienne, he looked around the room. For a man in charge, Mal thought he looked nearly as uncomfortable as Jordan. As a financial investigator, he was never in the limelight. Now everyone was staring at him, hoping he could provide an end to their terror.

'Yes. Right. As Ms Chance said, the police will be here soon. In the meantime, they ask if you will all provide a brief account of your movements last night to myself and my partner. You are also asked to stay within the castle and to not go anywhere on your own. The staff will continue to provide lunch and dinner, but we ask you to remember they have just received a great shock and we thank them for continuing in their positions at a time of great stress. Now, I will take limited questions. After which you will each be interviewed in turn.'

The cacophony raised the roof and Markham stood there with his arms folded until Major Cartwright walked up onto the stage and roared in a voice fit to impress a drill sergeant. Silence fell again as the major glared out across the room.

'Questions will only be answered to raised hands.'

The door banged down in the corridor and he glared over at the open door.

'And for heaven's sake, close the bloody door.'

Penny Fitzgibbon was closest to the hall and stood up. Rather than leaving the room to find the errant door, she simply chose to close the door to the ballroom. Mal turned her attention back to the stage when Penny screamed out.

Mal sprang to her feet, her heart racing as she turned towards the source of the bone-chilling scream. Every person in the room had frozen, their gazes locked on the closed doors where Penny now stumbled backwards, her trembling hand raised, pointing in horror.

As Mal's eyes fell upon the door, she felt her breath catch in her throat. There, hanging upside down like a twisted work of art, was a large black bird. Its wings were spread wide, almost as if it were embracing the door itself. A single nail had been driven through one of its dark scaly feet, securing it to the wooden surface.

But it was the message that truly sent a wave of fear washing over Mal. Attached to the door, pierced by the same nail that held the bird in place, was a piece of white paper. And there, written in an eerie, dark red script that seemed to pulsate with malice, were two words that promised untold horrors yet to come: "You're Next".

Chapter Thirty-Eight

The next few minutes were awash with panic. Penny continued to scream and only calmed down when Henry handed her half a glass of whisky. She downed it in one and then vomited in the corner. As people rushed to help her, others went to remove the bird, but Markham shouted to leave it for evidence. By the time anyone heard him, the bird had been yanked off the door and the note had been handled by a dozen pairs of hands.

At the other end of the ballroom, a gong was banged and gradually everyone turned to see Sebastian banging it for all his might. His wife was standing by him, her hands over her ears until, when he had everyone's attention, she uncovered them.

'Everyone needs to calm down. Mr Markham will take your questions if you return to your seats. That bird and the attached note are evidence. Please stop touching them.'

There were a few cries of 'Well said', and the room calmed down. Penny was still crying, but her hysterical tears had at least faded.

Markham returned to the stage and looked out across the crowded room. He was clearly shaken, and Mal felt sorry for him. He had stepped up and taken charge, only to discover he had attached himself to a shitshow.

'I think we may now understand that the situation is unfavourable. I have placed the bird and the note in a bag and will give it to the police when they arrive. We will be speaking to everyone today. I will be asking if you touched either the bird or note so that we can rule out your fingerprints.'

There was a quick flurry of voices as people suddenly realised how their knee-jerk response could have implicated them in the event.

'We are going to take a roll call and start taking statements from everyone as soon as possible. Considering this recent development, can I ask that if you see or hear anything suspicious, please come and alert myself or my partner, Kate Shaw, immediately? Please do not take matters into your own hands.'

Mal could feel Jacques' gaze fall upon her, but she ignored his unspoken warning as Markham asked for questions, reminding people to raise their hands. The first question was not a surprise.

'Who are you? And what right do you have to interview us?'

Markham nodded his head. At least his first question was easily dealt with.

'As I said, my name is John Markham and I work for HMRC in connection with His Majesty's Constabulary.'

'Are you a police officer?'

'No. But I am working as their proxy until they arrive. You can choose not to answer my questions, but that will, of course, be noted.'

Silence fell amongst the more belligerent members of the crowd. As it was clear he had nothing more to say, hands shot up again, and he called on Henry Fitzgibbon. Mal wondered if this was the question that was going to put the cat amongst the pigeons.

'Were you here under cover?'

Mal smiled inwardly. Well, he wouldn't like that question.

'That relates to an ongoing investigation that may or may not be related to recent incidents.'

Whilst everyone tried to unpick that, Markham carried on.

'If there are no more questions, I would be grateful if, over the course of the day, you make your way over to the table at the far end of the ballroom. You may speak in confidence—'

'The other death,' said a woman's voice from a few tables over. 'That girl. Was that really an accident, or was that also a murder?'

Oh well, thought Mal. It was unlikely not to be asked. He had nearly got away with it.

'The death of Francine Blake is a matter for the police to determine. For now, we simply need to establish everyone's whereabouts last night.'

Another voice called out.

'That note said "You're Next." Is there a serial killer on the island?'

'Well, that's torn it,' muttered Jacques.

'Indeed,' said Mal. And what else was there to say? Two dead bodies and the threat of further violence to come.

Markham was shouting over the din of the crowd and finally grabbed a wooden chair, banging it on the podium until everyone turned his way. He was flushed red with the exertion and his perfect hair was now looking a tad scruffy.

'Speculation will not help us, but can I remind you that the situation is indeed serious? The police will be with us later on today and in the meantime, do not wander on your own. Thank you. Now, we will talk to people alphabetically and individually. Marigold Arthurs, please join us over in the far corner.'

Leaving the stage, he and his partner walked over to a long table set up on the far side of the room, a short woman that Mal had not spoken to before, following behind them. Whatever they had to say would not be overheard. Piped music played through the Tannoy system, and Mal unconsciously let out a sigh of relief.

'I take it you knew the young woman's death was suspicious?' said Teddy. 'It didn't come as a surprise to you.' Mal looked at him blankly, but he chuckled to himself. 'Very well. Keep your cards close to your chest, but your relief suggests you've been holding a dangerous secret.'

'Pumpkin, I'm scared. What if the killer tries to kill me next?'

'Well, he'll have to get past me first. And failing that, I'm sure Jacques here won't permit some varmint getting close to you either.'

Somewhat ungraciously, Violet looked at the two older men and then across at Jordan. Mal bit back a laugh and tapped the younger woman on the hand.

'Remember, one amongst us is a killer. Be careful where you place your trust.'

Violet yelped and Mal raised an eyebrow as Teddy chided her.

'Really, Mal. That's very dramatic.'

Mal was going to reply, but the conversation hushed as Kate Shaw made her way back across the floor, making a beeline for Mal.

'Mrs Peck, we have received a note from Devon and Cornwall Police that you might care to join us in collecting notes from the guests.'

Everyone within earshot turned and looked at Mal, who rose in silence and followed Shaw back across to the small table. Behind her, she could hear the speculation rise in her wake.

'Do you know why they asked for me?' said Mal, as Kate led them away from the other guests.

'Apparently you have form.'

'Form?' Was she referring to her criminal record?

'Yes. You've been involved in a few serious crimes. Why?' She smirked. 'What did you think I meant?'

Mal decided not to answer her, she was clearly goading her. Despite that, Mal found herself smiling, despite Sophie's very strict instructions to not get involved, the police were now actively asking for her help. She sat down next to Markham, forcing Kate Shaw to her left. Now Mal was sitting between the two investigators and trying to keep the grin off her face. Opposite them sat Marigold Arthurs, a lady well into her eighties, drumming her fingers.

'Do I have to go through this nonsense again?'

Mal smiled and shook her head. 'I doubt it. I'm just here to make sure the obvious questions are asked. Let me have a look.'

Pulling Kate Shaw's notepad towards her, Mal had a quick read of the notes and then sighed.

'Well, maybe just a bit longer,' she said to Marigold apologetically. She turned to Markham. 'Which of you is recording this?'

'There are no tape recorders. We were told this was informal. The written notes should be fine. Our record keeping is meticulous.'

'Not even an audio recording on your phone?' said Mal, turning back to look at Marigold and shaking her head.

'Okay, I'll keep this brief, Mrs Arthurs. I'm Malachite Peck. I do apologise. They've made a really great start, but we don't quite have all we need. Kate, can you take notes? And please also record my questions as well as their answers. John, can you record on your phone? Let's not waste any more of Mrs Arthurs' time.'

Without waiting for them to reply, Mal smiled at Marigold and began.

'Now we have details of your movements. Can I just ask you who you are here with? If you have been here before? If, prior to visiting the island, you had ever met Francine Blake or Wulf Clarkson? And finally, your height?'

Marigold answered the questions in rapid succession and then raised an eyebrow.

'I think I'm a little short to be bludgeoning people.'

As soon as she spoke, John Markham jumped on her words. 'How do you know he was bludgeoned? Only the killer knows that.'

Mrs Arthurs glared at him. 'Apart from the killer, everyone who found him also knows, I presume. Plus, by your words, you have also confirmed it. When Malachite asked for my height, it seemed an obvious deduction.' She glanced at Mal. 'Anything else?'

'No, that's it, unless you have something you'd like to add?'

She stood up abruptly and, with a quick shake of her head, returned to the other end of the room.

As she left, Kate slammed her pencil on the table.

'I am not your secretary and you are not the lead interrogator.'

'No? Well, I wonder why the police asked me to sit in, then? Clearly, they were concerned that you might not ask good follow-up questions. I don't think it even occurred to them you wouldn't ask the basic questions.' Mal looked around and then smiled at the girl who had served her on the first morning.

'Hello, Anna. Is there any chance of coffee, a jug of water and some glasses, please?' Anna nodded and then Mal called her back. 'And what about some biscuits? Let's make this as painless as possible.'

Turning back to her fellow investigators, she looked at John quizzically.

'Why haven't you got the next person on the list? Or would you like me to do that for you as well?'

As John left, Mal turned to Kate. 'And I can hardly take notes. You have the only pencil.'

Before she could reply, Anna returned with biscuits and John came back with the next interviewee, and the morning blurred into a pattern of question and repeat.

Chapter Thirty-Nine

Laurence Barta sat down and rattled out the required answers. But when it came to his alibi, he paused and looked over his shoulder.

'I had turned in early, leaving Morris to his dark thoughts. He had been most unimpressed with this weekend's activities and had a mind to inform our host. I couldn't sleep, worrying about his countenance. But finally the bedroom door opened at three, and I could hear him weeping as he came to bed.'

Mal and her fellow interviewers listened in astonishment. Kate started scribbling furiously.

'Oh, you mustn't read anything into his crying,' dismissed Laurence quickly. 'That was always his way as a child. He never could handle powerful emotions.'

John cleared his throat. 'Mr Barta, are you suggesting that your brother killed Wulf Clarkson?'

Laurence shook his head violently and jumped to his feet.

'I would never.' Then, without waiting to be dismissed, he marched back across the ballroom and tapped his brother on the shoulder. Mal watched as the brothers didn't look at each other, and then Morris Barta was walking towards them.

John leant across Mal and tapped Kate's notebook.

'Record everything carefully. We may well have our man.'

Morris sat down, picked up the glass of water, finished it and then looked enquiringly at the panel. His first answers followed the pattern of his brother's until he was asked his whereabouts for the previous night. 'I had turned in early. I had slept poorly the night before. The storm was relentless.' Kate stopped taking notes and tapped her pencil on her pad, and John frowned.

'You said you went to bed early?'

'I did. We had been playing cards with the Fitzgibbons, but I pleaded exhaustion and went to bed.'

'And after that?' asked John.

'I slept.'

Mal watched the man closely, but he was expressionless; sitting up ramrod straight, his hands in his lap.

'And did you sleep well?' she enquired.

'I did. Except, of course, when Laurence came to bed and woke me up. I know he was trying to be quiet, but he was washing his hands for at least ten minutes. It was most peculiar. What, I wondered, was he trying to scrub off so violently? I thought I heard him muttering about a spot he needed to wash off.'

John turned to Mal, shaking his head in disbelief and concealing his words with his hand, muttered, "Got them!" On Kate's pad, she had underlined the word "Guilty".

Mal shot to her feet, slammed her hands on the table and roared Laurence's name across the length of the room. The room fell silent as Laurence wandered across the room, smiling as he did so, and then sat down by his brother.

Mal sat and stared at the two smiling brothers in silence. Out of the corner of her eye, she could see John preparing to speak. She held up a hand and continued to stare at the men in silence until they began to twitch. Laurence tugged at his collar; Morris picked lint off his trousers. Mal continued to glare at them until Laurence spoke.

'If that's all?'

'Do you think this is funny?' asked Mal. 'We have two dead bodies and someone is taunting us with dead birds. Was that you?'

They recoiled and shook their heads vehemently.

'We would never.'

'Never what? Mess around with an investigation? Create false stories just to play about with the investigation? Do you have any idea how puerile your behaviour is?'

Laurence turned to his brother. 'I knew you'd overdo it. What did you say? I said you were washing your hands, saying "Out, damned spot". What did you say for me?'

'I said you came to bed at two, sobbing.'

The two brothers chuckled and then looked at Mal. 'Which one of us didn't you believe? It was the MacBeth reference, wasn't it? I'm no Lady MacBeth trying to wash away the blood of my sins.'

John and Kate finally caught up to the fact that the two brothers had been playing them for fools.

'I'm going to have you arrested!' said John angrily.

'What for?' asked Morris with a raised eyebrow.

'Wasting police time.'

'Ah, but you are not the police, are you?' said Laurence, a smile twitching on his face.

Mal looked at them in disgust. 'I take it you both have a rock-solid alibi?'

They looked at each other and shrugged.

'We were both online playing bridge all night. The site we play on has live video and audio feeds. It was a tournament event and thousands were watching worldwide.'

Nodding at each other, they stood up and left the table, leaving John spluttering in fury. He stormed after them, then addressed the rest of the room, shouting about wasting time, respect for the dead, and decent levels of behaviour.

Kate turned to Mal. 'I don't understand. Why did they do that?'

'A game. Nothing more, nothing less. They were bored, so decided to have some fun at our expense.'

'But this is a murder investigation,' said Kate, shocked.

'Which clearly doesn't bother them.'

After John had read the Riot Act, the room fell into an uneasy silence as the Bondermans came and sat down.

John was still furious and Kate was now scribbling frantically, time-stamping every utterance.

Violet had refused to be interviewed on her own and the two of them alibi'd each other, heard nothing of interest and saw nothing of interest. When John pushed the point, Teddy pointed out that he had volunteered this information freely. If he had further questions, he would be better off directing them to his lawyers. The plural was not missed by anyone as they left the table. John seethed.

'This lot are running rings around us.'

'Ignore them,' said Mal calmly. 'They are used to being in control. Just remember, one of them is a murderer. Our job is simply to take notes. The police will do the hard work. If we rattle someone, then all's well and good. But don't expect anyone to confess.'

'I did it,' sobbed Imogen Beasley. 'This is all my fault.'

'You killed Wulf Clarkson?' asked Mal kindly.

'No. of course not, but I may as well have done. First Francine and then Wulf. The paps are never going to stop hounding me. Everywhere I go, there's scandal.' She broke off, sobbing again. Mal called Anna and asked for a glass of whisky, remembering that the bride-to-be had been enjoying whisky sours the night before. A drink that made Mal's teeth shudder.

As Imogen calmed down, she gradually explained how the girls had had a quiet night. After Francine's death, they didn't feel like celebrating.

'I just want to get off this island. I think I'm cursed. I have brought death.'

'Drink up, dear,' said Mal, and was grateful when Imogen slugged it back, then coughed her way out of her melodrama.

'I'm sorry. I'm overreacting.'

'Not at all. You've had a horrible experience on what should have been a wonderful event with friends.'

Imogen nodded, took a deep sigh, and nodded as Mal continued.

'So, are you providing an alibi for the other girls?'

She nodded again. 'Yes, none of us were in the mood to stay up. We all turned in early. Well, except for Johanna,' she paused and chuckled bleakly. 'Her and Jordan were at it like rabbits all night.'

As she left, Mal considered the fact that she had also given Jordan his alibi.

The other girls also confirmed each other's alibis, and the rather enthusiastic Jordan. Mal wondered about them. They had all alibied each other the previous night as well, but it wasn't the most airtight. In the dead of the night, anyone of them could have sneaked out and returned again.

The Fitzgibbons were interviewed separately and, whilst both had had a late night, confirmed by other statements, Penny had noticed Vivienne and Wulf having a very heated exchange.

'But that was earlier in the evening. Besides, why kill your boss? You'd be out of a job.'

Kate and John were very interested in that revelation. As they watched Penny rejoin her husband, Mal drummed her fingers. The other two still hadn't said who they were investigating, but it was obvious by now that Wulf Clarkson himself had been their subject.

'Should we get Vivienne back?' asked Mal, curious to see their response.

Kate shook her head quickly, and John cleared his throat.

'No need. I think the next time Ms Chance is interviewed, it will be under caution.'

'You think she murdered her boss?'

'There are other crimes beyond murder, Mal. As I know you're aware.'

Mal considered snatching Kate's pencil and stabbing it into John's sneering face, but she took a deep breath and the interviews continued.

By the time Jacques sat down, she was grateful for a friendly face. From the beginning, Jacques was clearly uncomfortable. He smiled once at Mal and then addressed all his answers to John, refusing to meet Mal's eye. His refusal to look at her was bothering her, so she decided to take the lead in the questioning. It had been agreed because of her friendship with Jacques that John would take the lead, but now she broke protocol and asked him if he knew Wulf in any prior capacity.

Now he looked her dead on and said "No".

'Are you sure?'

'Well, I've met him here on previous bridge weekends.'

Mal stared at him in dismay. He was lying and she couldn't think of a single good reason why that should be. She knew they had some long-standing arrangement. She had spent the entire weekend trying to establish what it was, and now he was openly lying about it. She tried again.

'And you've never met him, beyond the bridge weekends, in a social or business capacity?'

'No.'

Mal stared at him as the silence became brittle.

'Well, yes, right, thank you. Unless anyone else has a question?'

The other two shook their heads and Jacques walked away.

'What was that about Malachite? Was Jacques lying?'

Mal stood up.

'Of course not. I'm so sorry, too much tea. Give me a minute.' And she headed off to the sanctuary of the loos.

Chapter Forty

Sitting in the cubicle, she found herself shaking. Why would Jacques lie? What was he hiding? And why was he being so blatant? He said Wulf owed him a favour. A massive favour, from the size of her suite. Why was he now denying what he had said to her previously?

She was washing her hands when the main door swung open and Imogen walked in. She looked over at the cubicles. When she was happy they were the only two people in the room, she blurted, 'I need to tell you something.'

'You've already given your statement.'

'I know, but I didn't want to cause trouble. And I will tell the police, but I just wanted to tell you and let you decide if it was important or not.'

Mal narrowed her eyes. This was completely weasel behaviour. Now the onus was on Mal to decide if what Imogen had to say was important.

'I don't trust those two from HMRC to not let something slip, and my friendship with Johanna means too much to me.'

'Is this about Jordan?'

'Yes. No.'

She looked confused and fiddled with her clutch bag.

'I don't know. Look, I have spoken to Johanna. It's not like I'm going behind her back. I mean, I am. But I told her I wasn't happy.'

'Why don't you just tell me?'

'It's about our alibis. Last night, I woke up in the middle of the night and went to the kitchen to get a glass of milk. I was barefoot, and as I walked across the hallway, I felt the carpet was wet and there was a leaf on the floor.'

'Is this hallway the main entrance to your collection of suites?'

'Yes. I didn't think much of it last night. I was half asleep. But now I think I heard someone coming back into our wing. I think someone had been outside.'

'And why do you think it was Jordan?'

'Because I know the girls. None of them go wandering outside at night. Plus, everyone said they were in the rooms all night long. Well, someone's lying. My money is on Jordan.'

'Do you think Johanna is covering for him?'

Imogen looked startled.

'Christ, no. That girl sleeps like the dead. Jordan could have been practising the tuba and Jo would have slept through it.'

'What did she say when you approached her?'

'She said I was tripping. And when I showed her the wet leaf, she just laughed.' She picked at her fingernails again. 'Plus, who wants to think the person they're sleeping with is a murderer?'

Imogen's words were still echoing in her head as she and the others continued the interviews. She was still worried sick about Jacques' reply. And now she was worrying about Johanna as well. Was the girl at risk? There was also another problem with Imogen's story. Johanna might have unwittingly given Jordan a false alibi, but, and loathe though Mal was even to think it, it also gave Johanna a false alibi. In fact, the wet boot prints and the wet leaf showed that someone in the presidential wing was lying. She wanted to talk it through with Jacques, but she had looked over at him twice and on both occasions he had spun away.

'What next?'

Markham's question shook her out of her reverie.

'We hand our results over to the police and we go have lunch.'

For the past hour, people had been having lunch, stepping away from the table for their interview. Now, as Octavia Winthrop finished her interview, the three of them were done. Pushing her chair back, she stood up and stretched. She didn't need a copy of the notes either written or audio. She had what she needed. Although looking across at the seated diners, she didn't want all that she had got. Jacques was still avoiding her eye.

Well, she'd get to the bottom of that after lunch. Choosing a table as far from Jacques as possible, she sat down beside Teddy and Violet. Their Texan optimism was what she needed right now, and she reminded herself not to tease Violet. Penny and Henry were on a neighbouring table and she was glad to see Penny had now recovered. The Barta twins, who had both refused to account for their movements, sat to the other side happily tucking into a plate of salmon Wellington and new potatoes. Mal's stomach rumbled, and she quickly ordered the same.

'There isn't much choice today,' pouted Violet.

'Hardly surprising, my dear,' replied Teddy, dabbing his moustache with his napkin. 'I think under the circumstances, we're lucky not to be in the kitchen ourselves rustling something up.'

'But Teddy, the price we pay, you expect a certain standard of professionalism. I mean, they are still getting paid.'

'Yes Pumpkin, but their boss is dead and there's a killer amongst us.'

'Oh, silly billy. What a drama you make of it.'

Raising her hand, Violet languidly waved for a waiter to refill her glass. Mal looked across at Teddy in surprise.

He mouthed back, 'Xanax.'

And Mal understood. That and the alcohol were clearly taking the edge off Violet's anxiety, if not eradicating it altogether. But this wasn't the right time to blunt one's preservation instincts.

'Don't let her out of your sight,' she whispered, as a server came and refilled the glasses. Mal gave Teddy an apologetic smile and, to his credit, he smiled back and mouthed that it was okay. She looked over to see if Penny was equally medicated and immediately caught her eye.

Mouthing to Mal, Penny asked if Violet was okay. Mal replied with her hands, indicating a drink or two.

'I mean, if it's not safe, they should get the army to come and rescue us,' said Violet.

Mal swung back and wondered if sitting with Jacques might have been the lesser ordeal after all.

'They'd send the navy, not the army,' said Mal gently. There was no point in being cross. She was out of it and wouldn't take on board a word that Mal said. 'But we're perfectly safe. The police will be here later today and—'

'They have guns, don't they?'

'I doubt it. This murder wasn't done with a gun.'

'It's two murders,' said Violet in an overly loud voice, causing a few heads to turn around.

'One murder. The other—'

'Oh, we know that's a murder.' She giggled and pointed at Mal, her finger waving unsteadily. 'You've got a coat hidden away in your room as evidence!'

Mal winced as Violet blurted out that piece of information. The last thing she wanted was to tip off the murderer. She would need to inform the police the minute they stepped onto the island so it could be properly secured. She was tempted to move it to the hotel's main safe, but that would risk further contamination. No, it was safe enough where it was.

'I'm afraid that's not true.'

'Yes, it is. The man who found the body told some of his staff and they mentioned it to one of the bridal party and Teddy overheard it and mentioned it to me.'

'And now the entire island knows,' said Mal with a sigh. 'I believe the police call that tampering with an investigation. Maybe you shouldn't comment anymore?'

Violet stared at her in shock and then her face seemed to melt into an elongated grimace as she began to cry.

'Pumpkin, I want to go home. I want to go home right now.'

Violet hiccoughed and hid her face in her hands. Then, sobbing prettily, she looked up at Teddy and fluttered her eyelashes.

'Please take me home.'

Teddy rolled his eyes and placed his napkin on the table.

'Will you excuse us? We're going for a lie-down.'

He stood up, helping his wife to her feet as Penny leant across.

'Remember to stick together at all times.'

With a small bow, Teddy left the table as his wife tottered out beside him, leaning down on his shoulder. A proud warthog escorting a newborn giraffe.

Mal returned to her food, her appetite all but wrecked. Now the killer knew she had evidence proving the first death was not an accident.

'Would you like to sit with us?' asked Penny, but Mal smiled, shaking her head.

The only person she wanted to share her meal with was studiously ignoring her. She wanted to storm over there and confront him with his lie, but it would be a cold day in hell before she laid on free entertainment in front of all these people. For now, she would slowly simmer and try to work out why Jacques had lied so blatantly, and figure out what it meant; not just for the investigation but also for their nascent relationship. She sighed deeply. That was what was really annoying her. She had to acknowledge that the time spent with Jacques over the past few months had been highly enjoyable. More than enjoyable; it brought meaning to her day and now she was having to accept that her future was unlikely to feature Jacques. How could she admire a man who was lying to her?

'Hello, Mrs Peck?'

One of the junior staff was standing expectantly by Mal's table. Mal remembered her blue nail varnish from the interview earlier. Anna Cartwright, nineteen years old, first season on the island being all of one month.

'Hello, Anna. How can I help?'

'I have a message for you from your niece. She said she couldn't get through to you on your phone.'

No doubt when Mal returned to her room, she'd find her recharged phone full of messages. Jasmine behaved as though the world were ending if you didn't immediately respond to her call or message. Worse yet, she seemed to invest her own self-worth into these messages. If Mal

296

didn't immediately respond, it was because Mal didn't like her or view her as important enough to drop everything immediately and reply. That she couldn't see how self-absorbed this made her made Mal chuckle. It didn't help that Jasmine was also, coincidentally, correct in her assumption of Mal's opinion of her.

Still, on this occasion, she did very much want to hear from Jasmine. But not here in public. Bad enough that everyone and his uncle knew she had crime scene evidence in her room. If Jasmine had something important to say, Mal needed to hear it, but certainly didn't want everyone else to hear it as well. She made to stand up, but Anna waved her hand.

'She says patience. That's it.'

Mal's jaw dropped. She had sent two text messages, and now she was being told to bide her time.

'Did she say anything else?'

'No, that was it. She said, "Please tell my aunt, *patience*."'

'Is your niece offering suggestions for new card games?' called out Major Cartwright, proving he had fewer manners than those sitting closer, who had clearly heard everything.

'Do you know what? I think Mal's niece has the right idea. As we are all confined to barracks, why not play a few hands of bridge? What say you, Mal? A bit of morale boosting. Yes?'

What Mal wanted to do was wring her niece's neck: try to work out what connected Francine and Wulf; figure out why Jacques was lying; and try to find evidence that placed Jordan at the scene of the second murder. Someone in the President's Suite had gone outside and lied about it. She needed answers, not cards.

Chapter Forty-One

The clock was ticking. A calm had gradually settled over the afternoon as groups played cards or talked in muted tones. Others were reading quietly to themselves or scrolling through their phones. In the hush, the grandfather clock could be heard softly ticking away the hours, counting down to when the police would arrive and release them from their fears.

For now, though, they did as people do when there is no other decent option: they kept calm and carried on. Mal's nerves were on a knife edge. People were drifting in and out of the ballroom, mostly in pairs. The major had declared quite loudly earlier on that he didn't require a chaperone to make use of the facilities and, since then, trips to the loos were solo escapades. Every time someone moved, Mal watched them, and then watched to see who was watching them. The tension was horrendous, and she was no closer to a solution. Wulf and Francine were connected, but as yet, nothing sprang to mind.

In annoyance, she realised she would need to use the facilities herself and headed off. As much as she didn't want to take her eyes off anyone, there was nothing to be done when nature didn't so much call but demand.

Her return to the ballroom was a scene of chaos. Even as she made her way back along the passageway, people were leaving the ballroom, chatting and laughing to each

299

other. Some people were heading up to their rooms; a few others were dashing to the front door, cigarettes already lit. Walking into the room, there was a clear sense of release. Some were picking up their cards, clearly interrupted; others were ordering drinks from the bar in an air of celebration.

Mal looked around for Jacques. Not seeing him, she made a beeline for Teddy.

'What's happened?'

'They've arrested one of the conservationists. Charged him with the murder of the young girl and Wulf.'

Mal stared at him in astonishment.

'The police have arrived?'

She'd only been gone a few minutes.

'No. It was those two from the Treasury. They called it a citizen's arrest. The major and some others accompanied them. Believe they are locking him in one of the rooms until the police arrive.'

'On what grounds?'

'On evidence you had uncovered, they said.'

Mal swore in annoyance, causing Teddy to laugh.

'Did they steal your thunder?'

'My thunder? Bloody hell, I don't care about that.'

She was going to explain herself, but broke off as Johanna dashed back into the room, looking around wildly. As soon as she saw Mal, she ran towards her.

'Tell them you got it wrong. Jordan didn't kill anyone.'

300

Imogen had come over and was now standing beside Mal and trying to comfort her friend.

'Johanna, we don't know what evidence they have.' She put her arm around her friend, but Johanna shook her off.

'None of this would have happened if you'd kept your mouth shut!'

'You heard him. He confessed!' wailed Imogen.

'That was a mistake. He was confused.'

Mal interrupted the two friends. People weren't generally confused as to whether they had killed someone or not.

'Johanna.' She spoke briskly and the girl broke away from arguing with her friend and glared at Mal. 'Tell me what happened.'

'The two from the interviews came over with the major and said, "We know what you did. We know you left the castle last night and lied about it. Confess, and it will be taken into account." And just like that, he said he was really sorry. It was a stupid thing to do. And that was that. The bloke and the major, along with some have-a-go heroes, grabbed him by the arm and marched him out of the room, and they've locked him in one of the pantries.' She took a deep breath. 'Do something!'

Mal looked across at Tinks and could see she was thinking the same thing. As accusations and confessions went, this was weak.

'If he was your client, how quickly could you get him released on bail?'

Tinks scoffed. 'Are you asking for minutes or seconds?'

Johanna groaned at her friend. 'You believe he's innocent?'

Tinks shook her head. 'That's irrelevant—'

'How can you say that?'

'Let her finish,' said Mal sharply.

'It's irrelevant because that's not what Mal asked. She asked if I could get him released on bail and, of course, I can. He's confessed to something, certainly. But what?'

'Well, to the two murders, obviously.'

Tinks shook her head again. 'Nope. Neither side mentioned anything of the kind. Sloppy accusation on behalf of the interrogator, and random response on behalf of the accused.'

'So get him released.'

'Not so fast,' said Mal. 'I assume everyone heard him confess?'

The two girls nodded.

'And he went willingly?'

'Sort of.'

'Well, then, in the eyes of most people here, he's guilty. If we get him released, people might take justice into their own hands.'

Looking around the room, there was certainly a mob air. Besides which, he may well be the murderer. Certainly, everyone in the room thought he was. The relief was palpable and as far as Mal could see, there was no harm in keeping Jordan where he was, whether he was guilty or innocent. Of course, if he was innocent, it meant that the killer could now relax and hope to get off the island scot-free.

'Where's he being held?'

'Over in the kitchens. But they said I had to leave as I was being difficult.'

'And since when, exactly, did that stop you from doing anything?' queried Tinks. 'Come on, you too, Mal. Let's see what this is all about.'

Mal followed the two girls out into the hall and headed back down to the kitchens. She hoped Markham was there and had a good mind to tear a strip off him. However, when she entered the kitchens, there was no sign of him. The chef looked up when they came in and, with an irate gesture, he pointed to the far end of the kitchens.

'If you all want to eat tonight, maybe you could get the hell out of my kitchen?'

Johanna turned to reply, but Mal twisted her around.

'Don't annoy the man that's feeding you. Besides, he has a point. Come on.'

At the far end of the kitchen, a passageway ran off towards a long narrow hallway. The floor was made of slate flagstones and, at the far end, the major was sitting on a chair.

303

'Well done, Mal!' he called as she approached. 'Never underestimate the memsahibs, that's what I always say.'

'Not convinced we have our man yet, Major. Markham may have jumped the gun. Mind if I have a word with Jordan?'

'Afraid I can't open the door.'

Mal considered whether it was worth the argument and decided it wasn't.

'Very well, I'll just shout through the door.'

He appeared to think about it, then, deciding he could see no harm in it, nodded.

Banging on the door, Mal shouted Jordan's name.

'Let me out,' he replied. 'These fuckers have gone mad!'

'They say you confessed.'

'Aye, I did that.'

'And that you went outside last night?'

'That too. But I didn't murder anyone.'

'So what were you confessing to?'

There was silence for a bit, and Mal looked at the two girls.

'Johanna, you try.'

'Jordan, it's me. I didn't tell them you went out last night.'

Mal heard a groan from inside, followed by a string of expletives.

'Aye, I know that, hen. You snore fit to raise the dead, so you do.'

'I do not snore!'

Johanna and Jordan laughed at the same time.

'Away with you. You're a proper snagger.'

Mal gestured at Johanna to get back on track. At this rate, the pair of them were going to descend into the dreadful, indulgent conversations of a new relationship. Any moment now she expected one of them to say, 'No, you hang up.'

The major's eyes were glinting and winked at Mal. He was clearly having the time of his life.

'We will discuss the meaning of snagger when you get out of there. For now, though, what the hell did you confess to, if not the murder of Wulf?'

'And your young friend,' interjected the major unhelpfully.

'I didn't kill anyone,' he yelled through the door, kicking it once for good measure.

'Then what did you do?'

Mal heard him groan again. There was a soft thud on the door, and Mal guessed he had just rested his head against it. Johanna must have thought the same, as she stepped up to the door and placed her hand on the wood.

'Jordan?'

'I did it for you.' His voice mumbled through the door.

'Did what?'

'You said nothing real ever happened in your life; everyone's emotions were always packaged up.'

Mal groaned as she worked out what he had done. Love truly made idiots of people. She didn't care for the boy, but she suspected he was right. He hadn't killed anyone.

'It was meant to be a joke. Make everyone scared. Give you something to witness. Remember what you said last night? That bit about wanting to experience life in tooth and claw?'

'I don't understand. Did you stage Wulf's death? Is it a joke?'

'Oh no, he's dead right enough,' said Mal, as she waited for Jordan to reveal his folly.

'So what then?' wailed Johanna.

'I nailed up the bird.'

Johanna stepped away from the door and just stared at it.

'You did what?'

'I thought it would be funny. You know. Make everyone think there was a killer stalking the island.'

'There is!' roared Johanna.

Jordan banged his head on the door again. 'I know that now.'

'Bloody hell JoJo, you sure do pick 'em,' said Tinks softly. The major was practically taking notes as he looked over at Mal.

'What say you? Truth or lie?'

Mal shrugged. She felt it had the ring of truth, but wasn't prepared to say as much.

'Jordan. Do you know why anyone would want to kill Wulf?'

'You asked me that already.'

'Yes, but I'm guessing you lied. So?'

'No, I meant it. I don't know why anyone would want to kill him. I imagine his debtors want him alive.'

'Are there many?'

'I'm guessing there are fewer grains of sand on the beach than people he owes money to.'

Wulf's financial issues hadn't come to light so far, but Jordan was right; if he owed people money, he was no good to them dead.

'What about the tuna?'

'What about them?' His voice suddenly changed from morose to wary.

'If someone knew he was poaching?'

'Who'd kill anyone over a fish? Not that I know what you're talking about,' he said quickly.

A lull fell as Mal tried to think things through. They were no closer to finding the killer. A sick practical joke had sent everyone into a tailspin and now everyone's guard was down. If there was a killer picking people off, they were now at liberty to hunt again.

'Are you going to let me out?'

'No,' said Mal decisively, and the major nodded his head in agreement. 'You can make your case to the police when they get here. Honestly, I think the safest place for you is in there. Have you got facilities?'

'I've a bucket and some bags of carrots, if that's what you mean.' His voice was flat, and Mal felt the stirrings of pity. 'Has she left?'

'Johanna?'

'Aye.'

'No. For reasons I fail to understand, she's still here. As is Tinks, her friend and barrister. And Major Cartwright. So mind your tongue.'

Leaving the three of them outside the door, Mal headed back through the kitchen, apologising to the chef as she went.

Chapter Forty-Two

Mal paused as she entered the ballroom. For the first time, the sky outside was blue, with white clouds drifting past. Looking across the white-topped waves, she could see over to the mainland and the occasional fishing trawler heading out to sea.

The buoyant scene outside was matched by the atmosphere within the ballroom. Music played across the laughter. As the drinks were poured, conversation flowed. It was a jolly scene and as Mal walked through the door, several people hailed her and she received a round of applause.

Struggling to contain her scowl, she smiled tightly and looked around for Jacques, but he, like others, was nowhere to be seen. This wasn't over; if he thought he could avoid her, he had sorely underestimated her.

Despite the various calls to join the crowd, she was looking for someone other than Jacques right now. At the other end of the room, Markham and Shaw were writing up their notes and Mal strode towards them.

'What the hell were you thinking?'

Markham looked startled, but Shaw just tilted her head and looked up at Mal through her eyelashes.

'Our job. It's what we do.'

'Don't talk rot,' spat Mal. 'You're forensic accountants. And now you've locked up the wrong person.'

They looked at each other and shook their heads before looking at Mal again. Shaw picked up her cup and took a sip, smiling as Markham cleared his throat.

'The facts speak for themselves.'

'Are you a total arse? The facts say nothing of the kind. All the facts say is that Jordan went outside and lied about it.'

'And his confession also doesn't speak for itself, I suppose?' said Shaw, putting down her cup. 'You know, you clearly think you are better than us. The great Malachite Peck, brought down by our esteemed financial agency. And I'm sorry to tell you that once again we have outsmarted you.'

'Give me strength. Are you stupid as well as lazy?' She stared at Shaw. 'Tell me you at least know how my crime came to light?'

Kate Shaw looked uncomfortable. Markham tapped his fingers on the desk.

'No? Very well, a conversation for another day if you don't want to draw attention to your partner's laziness.'

The fact that Mal had volunteered her confession before anyone was even aware of a crime had, in her mind at least, been the right thing to do.

'She isn't stupid,' said Markham, defending his partner.

'You both are.'

'Jordan Winters confessed.'

'To what?'

'To murder!'

'Did you note the conversation?'

'I did,' said Shaw, still flushed from being called lazy. She pulled out her pad and began to read. 'John Markham said: "We know you went outside; we know you lied. Why not save us all some time and confess?" And Jordan Winters replied: "It was a joke. I didn't mean for all this to happen."'

She closed her notebook and smiled up at Mal. Markham swore. Mal gave him a bitter smile.

'See the problem?'

'No one mentioned murder,' he said slowly.

Shaw studied her notebook again and joined in with the swearing.

'Even so, I still reckon he did it.'

'You reckon he killed both Francine and Wulf?' asked Mal incredulously. 'Why?'

'I think he followed Francine down to the water's edge, tried it on with her, she resisted. Maybe he pushed her, maybe she fell. Maybe she threatened him. Tried to blackmail him?'

'Blackmail? What sort of money do you think he has compared to her?'

Shaw's theories were preposterous. She was clearly floundering as she tried to make good her bungled arrest. 'And what about Wulf?'

'Maybe he saw Jordan follow Francine and confronted him. He was worried his boss was going to turn him over to the police, so he killed him.'

'The same boss who he's running a tuna poaching operation with?'

'Well, that's why he killed him. To shut him up.'

'If there's one person on this island who Jordan could trust completely to keep his secret, it would be his partner in crime. Why the hell would Wulf threaten him with the police when Jordan could simply shop Wulf and ruin his life?'

'He confessed.' Shaw glared at Mal in exasperation.

'He confessed to nailing up the bird!'

There was silence as the two inspectors digested Mal's statement and then exchanged a defeated glance.

'Now what?' asked Markham.

Having convinced them to keep Jordan locked up for his own safety and to keep the actual murderer unaware, Mal headed out of the ballroom. She was going to call Sophie, tell her what had happened; call Jasmine and see if she had anything useful to say other than telling her to bide her time; and then she was going to have it out with Jacques. By the time the police arrived, Mal had to decide whether she would tell them about his reluctance to share his relationship with Wulf.

As she was heading for the staircase, she checked her steps. Something Shaw had said rang true. Maybe Wulf saw the murderer. But it wasn't Jordan.

And maybe it wasn't Francine blackmailing anyone, but Wulf. He was clearly in financial difficulties, and then a goldmine landed in his lap.

Yesterday, he had told Mal the surveillance tapes were a waste of time. But what if he had lied? What if he had seen someone with Francine and, in his greed, turned to blackmail? Mal's mind was racing now. Which mean the murderer had to be hugely wealthy. Wealthy enough to rescue Wulf from the financial quagmire he was in. The problem was, with a guest list of multimillionaires, the field of suspects narrowed little. But it was better than nothing, and Mal felt the rightness of it relax the tension in her shoulders. She was on the right path. Now all she had to work out was why Francine had been killed in the first place and whom Wulf had seen on the videotape.

Chapter Forty-Three

Mal hurried along the corridor. What was the scandal that Francine had been part of? Deep in thought, Penny Fitzgibbon's sudden appearance startled Mal. The woman was a dishevelled mess, her hair loose around her face. Her pink skirt was muddy on the knees, and Mal was alarmed to see blood on her hands.

Grabbing her arm, Penny's fingers marked a cuff of blood on Mal's sleeve and she clawed at her feverishly, almost pulling her off-balance.

'It's Jacques. I think he's dead.'

Blood roared in Mal's ears. The hair on her arms stood up in shock and she wondered if she was going to faint. Jacques wasn't dead. He couldn't be. For a second, Mal was dragged along by Penny as the taller woman urged her towards a lower staircase.

'We should get help,' said Mal frantically, coming to her senses.

'I did. I got you. Oh, there's so much blood. I didn't want him to die alone. He said your name, and I had to run to get you.'

Mal didn't hesitate. Her stupidity in pushing Jacques away was about to prove to be her greatest regret. She had told herself she didn't need him and now she was facing the realisation that that couldn't be further from the truth. He had brought joy to her life when she hadn't realised it was missing; he made her laugh; he challenged her; he made her want to impress him, make him admire her. He was the first person she thought of when she woke up and her days spent in his company were the best she had had in decades. And now, because of her pride and her stupidity, he was dying alone in the bowels of the castle.

Pushing past Penny, she hurried down the staircase. As she reached the corridor, Penny shouted to take the next staircase down. Mal groaned. She should never have mentioned her idea to Jacques that Wulf was storing smuggled goods in the lower cellars. Had he come to investigate for himself and startled the killer?

She and Penny moved as quickly as possible down the second staircase. The worn granite steps felt as old as the castle foundations. What the hell had Penny been doing down here? As she reached the lower corridor, sodium lights illuminated every five metres, creating pools of orange light between the darkness.

'This way,' cried Penny, pushing past Mal as she came to a stop. Her question was now even louder in her head.

'What were you doing down here?'

Penny turned around, looking at Mal in confusion. She pushed her hair off her face, leaving a streak of blood smeared across her cheekbone.

'Mal, Jacques is dying!'

From further along the corridor, Mal heard a groan and peered into the gloom. Between two pools of light, she could just about make out a shape lying on the floor. She took two quick steps towards him and then looked back towards the staircase. A momentary spasm of fear clenched her belly as she looked back at Penny.

'Why were you down here?'

'I heard Jacques calling for help.'

He groaned again and Mal stood frozen to the spot.

'I'm going to get help.'

She turned and as she did so, Penny rushed her and shoved her as hard as she could. Mal stumbled forward, smacking the wall and slipping. In her struggle to regain her footing, Penny had grabbed her arm and shoved it up behind her back. Mal took a deep breath, ready to scream for help, when she felt the point of something cold and sharp against her throat.

'Make a sound and I'll stab you in the throat along with your precious Jacques.'

Dragging Mal to her feet, Penny walked her towards Jacques. He had fallen silent now and Mal felt hot tears of regret fill her eyes. In the darkness, she could make out one of his legs lying motionless.

'Jacques, I'm so sorry.'

'You can tell him how sorry you are in a minute. Hand me your room key.'

Jacques twitched and groaned. Mal thought he was trying to say no, but she didn't care. His voice was so laboured she barely recognised him. If giving Penny her room key could get rid of her, it gave Mal a chance to save Jacques. With her free hand, she pulled the key out of her pocket. As soon as Penny tried to take it, Mal would try to escape or disarm her.

'Throw it on the floor.'

Mal sagged in disappointment but did as she was told.

'And now your safe combination. I think you have something of mine.'

Mal swore.

'It was you wearing the coat.'

Mal felt the blade press against her skin.

'The combination. Now.'

'No.'

'Very well. I'll put an end to dear old Jacques.'

Mal thought quickly.

'If you do that, I'll escape and you'll be arrested.'

Penny laughed.

'True. But Jacques will be dead.'

He groaned again, but it was no good. She knew he wouldn't want her to give up the combination, but if she did, it would buy him a little more time. Penny had already killed Francine and Wulf. She wouldn't hesitate again.

'Sorry, Jacques. I'm not going to lose you.' She tried to take a deep breath, but the cold metal dug into her skin. 'One, three, five, nine.'

'There,' said Penny, smiling. 'That wasn't so difficult. Now Jacques,' she giggled, 'Could you pick up the room key?'

Mal tried to twist to see Penny's face. Her words made no sense, but she sagged in relief as Jacques' leg moved in the darkness as he rose to his feet. It made no sense. First Jacques was mortally wounded and then he was standing up at Penny's bidding.

'Jacques, don't do it. Together, we can overpower her.'

Penny laughed again as the man Mal had thought was Jacques stepped out of the shadows and she looked up into the unforgiving features of Henry Fitzgibbon.

Stepping past the two women, he bent down and picked up the card, then turned to Mal.

'If you lied about your safe combination, we'll know where to find you.'

He pulled his arm back, punched Mal in the face, and she collapsed into unconsciousness.

Chapter Forty-Four

Mal tried blinking, but the darkness was total. One of her eyes remained closed as she gingerly explored her face with her fingertips. A thick, sticky substance had coated one eye, and she followed the liquid up to the brow of her hair. Her head was throbbing as she discovered a gash on her temple. She didn't think she was still bleeding, and she stopped touching her head. Instead, she rubbed at her eyelashes until she felt that eye open, but the darkness remained.

She groaned as she tried to come to her senses. The Fitzgibbons must have dumped her down here. She was just grateful she hadn't broken her neck. Were they hoping that she would remain hidden until they got off the island? More importantly, why did they think she was on to them? She'd had no idea they were the murderers. If they had kept quiet, Mal would have had nothing to say to the police.

She decided to ignore that for a second and tried to understand where she was. Her trousers were wet, and she appeared to be sitting on a stone floor. Using her fingers, she began to explore her surroundings. Clambering to her feet, she yelped as her ankle collapsed under her. Gingerly, she bent down to feel her ankle and was relieved not to feel any obvious break, but her leg was tender to the touch.

Limping, she held her hands out in front of her, feeling the cold, rough walls under her palms. Now and then, they brushed over something slimy and organic hanging from the stone. Leaning forward, she sniffed the plant and realised it was seaweed. Sliding her hands across the wall, she felt the familiar undulating surface of mussel shells.

A wave of nausea washed across her, and she threw up. Throwing her hand forward to support herself, she felt a metal pole. Stepping forward, she made out the shape with her hands: a ladder fixed to the wall. Hoping she wasn't standing in vomit, she struggled up the rungs. Each time she put her left foot down, she pulled herself up, wincing as she put any weight on her ankle. A few rungs later, she hit her head. Holding on with one arm, she traced the surface above her. In the darkness, she traced a metal grille blocking her way. Leaning out, she could feel the curve of the wall wrapping around her. She was uncertain, but it felt like she was at the base of a shaft.

Desperately she traced her hand around the grille, but could find no way to release it. All she felt was the rough outline of barnacles. Were the Fitzgibbons planning to release her, let others know where she was? Or were they well aware of the tidal nature of her prison? Barnacles only lived in seawater. For them to be above her head meant this entire room would be underwater at high tide.

Weeping in frustration, she clambered down the ladder and explored the space below. She would not drown. If the sea could get in, then maybe she could find a way out.

Navigating around the shaft in the dark, she had found an exit and gingerly made her way along what she decided was a man-made tunnel. The smell of the sea was getting stronger as she reached a turn. Using her hands, she navigated in the dark, her fingers running over seaweed and barnacles. Reaching her hand above her, she couldn't touch the ceiling and assumed a smuggler could walk along here without hindrance. Wulf had said the island was riddled with tunnels and tall tales. She knew he was poaching tuna; was he also smuggling?

As she turned the corner, she began to see an outline ahead of her. The path was heading downhill, and she was certain she could also hear waves in the distance. Ten more steps and she knew she was heading towards an exit. She could clearly see shadows now and the sound of the waves was clear. She also thought she could hear voices on the wind.

In her excitement, she strode forward. The next moment her ankle gave way as she slipped on seaweed and hit the stone floor, jarring her wrists as they slammed into it. For a second, her head swam as she paused on her hands and knees, trying not to cry in pain. The floor was increasingly covered in seaweed. She could see a clear path through the middle and was certain this tunnel was in regular use.

Wincing, Mal stood up and limped forwards. She could barely place any weight on her foot now and worried she had seriously hurt her wrist as well. Touching her forehead, she looked at her fingers and saw her cut was bleeding again. She was also crying and hoped she would soon be standing in fresh air under an open sky.

She hadn't been mistaken. There were voices nearby. Taking a deep breath, she screamed as loud as she could and hobbled towards the light. As she turned the last corner, her heart failed. Ahead of her was a thin strip of beach with the waves swarming towards the exit of her tunnel. But between her and her freedom stood a metal gate stretching across the entire mouth of the tunnel.

Holding onto the bars, she shook the door, pulling at the padlock and screaming as loudly as possible. The voices paused, and she started shouting for help.

'Hello?'

Mal nearly collapsed in relief. She would know that voice anywhere.

'Jacques!' She sobbed in relief, then began shouting again.

'Where are you?' shouted an unknown voice.

'In a tunnel leading onto a beach. I can't get out.'

Several voices were now shouting her name as she continued to call out.

'Mal!'

Mal sobbed as she watched Jacques waded through the water, the surf swirling around his ankles. 'I'm here!'

He sprinted up onto the sand and ran towards her, shouting over his shoulder to the other searchers that he had found her.

'Mon Dieu. You are bleeding. What's happened?' As he spoke, he rattled at the gate, pulling at the padlock. He was accompanied by three other men. One was plain-clothed but the other two were in uniform. Finally, the police had arrived.

'Have you any bolt cutters on the boat?' asked Jacques. 'Can you call them back?'

'No,' said one of the men, a tall man in his forties and clearly in charge of the other two. 'Besides which, even if we sent them to collect a pair and return them to us, we'd be too late.'

Even as he spoke, another wave surged past them, covering their shoes before falling back. This time, as Mal watched the spume rush back along the sand, it didn't entirely uncover the shore. The tide was coming in and soon this cove would be submerged.

'Malachite Peck?' asked the man. As Mal nodded, he continued, 'I'm DCI Travers. I don't think we can get you out this way. How did you get in here?'

'The Fitzgibbons. They did this. Henry knocked me out and when I came to, I was in a dark room. I explored it and found this passageway.'

'What can you tell me about the room?'

'It had a ladder in it on the side of the wall. After a few rungs, it turns into a shaft or a well with a grid on top. I

323

think they dropped me down it, but I don't know where the entrance is.'

'Okay. We'll find it and have you out in a jiffy.'

Mal sagged against the bars in despair.

'That's all the time I have. The grate above my head was covered in barnacles.'

'Merde!'

Travers' eyes widened in alarm as he turned to the two younger officers. 'Call Dougie McDonald now. Tell him to find the location of this passageway. Someone on the staff must know.' Turning back to Mal, his expression was grim. 'Malachite. Head back to the ladder. I'll see you again shortly.' Then he was gone, wading through the surf as he followed his officers up to the castle.

'Mal.' Jacques' voice shook. 'I have to go.'

'I know.'

'I don't want to.'

'Shall we drown together, then?'

He gripped her fingers around the bar.

'Don't joke.'

'It's all I have right now.'

A large wave pushed in past them and Mal gripped the bars with her good hand as the surge threatened to wash her further into the tunnel.

'Jacques, get out of here.'

Her voice wavered between panic and despair. At least for now, she had a temporary retreat. But if Jacques stayed, he would soon be swimming. The waves were unrelenting and driving forwards; some small, some large. But inevitably they were rising, eating away at the cove.

'Get to the ladder,' he shouted over the waves crashing around them. 'And hold on. I will find you. Hold on.'

The surging water pulled back to the sea.

'Go!'

Squeezing her hand, he turned and strode through the retreating water. She watched until he was out of sight and then she turned towards the darkness. She had only managed a few steps before another huge wave rushed past her. Slipping, the water engulfed her and pushed her forwards. Blindly, she flailed her hands, desperate to grab purchase with anything to anchor her. She held her breath as the wave covered her. Icy water stabbed at her skin, and she panicked, feeling her lungs burn. A moment later, the water retreated, leaving her lying on the floor clutching a clump of seaweed. In the dim light, she could see the wave had carried her up the three steps.

Struggling to stand, she scrambled a few metres, but was finding it impossible with only one working hand. She screamed into the fading light, then pulled herself up, careful not to stand on any seaweed. If she fell again, she wasn't sure if she would make it. A small ripple of water washed around her feet. She knew waves came in sets. She had a few small waves in which she could make some progress before the next large set rolled in.

Hobbling as fast as she dared, her wet clothes dragged against her limbs, but she was grateful for the grip on her rubber-soled pumps. Never had an outfit been so well chosen, although in the freezing water, she wished she had chosen to wear waders that morning.

As her teeth began to chatter, she turned the corner into the pitch black. She could no longer see the water at her feet, but could feel it pulling at the hem of her trousers. Soon the surge of the incoming waves would be too strong for her to withstand and she would be knocked off her feet again. Only this time she would be battered against the long passageway, propelled forwards, then dragged back in the column of water, tumbling with nothing to hold on to. She had to get to the ladder and brace herself against the pull of the water.

As she waded, she noticed a change in the pressure of water around her legs. It was no longer just falling back; it was rebounding. She was nearing the wall. Holding her arm out, she sobbed in relief as she felt the familiar rungs of the ladder.

The water was now up to her knees. She wrapped her arm around one of the ladder's rungs and paused, panting. Her ankle and wrist throbbed, but she was grateful they were on opposite sides; at least she could climb. Feeling pressure on her calves, she felt the water drain away. The next big wave was coming. Grasping the ladder, she climbed as quickly as she could when she heard a distant roar of water surging up through the narrow tunnel. The force of the Atlantic Ocean was driving towards her.

Chapter Forty-Five

As soon as Jacques was free of the waves, he began running in earnest. He might not be a young man anymore, but he soon caught up with the police officers and quickly overtook them. The younger of the two officers was still holding his phone to his ear and shouted back to his boss that no one was answering their phones.

Jacques had to see Mal again. He had to explain why he was avoiding her. He had to tell her. Bursting through the main doors, he shouted for Dougie. If anyone knew where this particular cellar was, he would.

With the police officers at his back, they began shouting out for attention.

John Markham ran forwards, introducing himself.

'DCI Travers, I'm John Markham. It's a pleasure to see you. We have the murderer locked up. Let me take you to him. I think you'll find—'

'Where are the cellars? And answer your bloody phone in the future.'

His startled look would have been funny if Jacques had time to notice or care. Every second meant another wave pushing towards Mal, shoving her slight frame through the inky waters. He shook his head and spotted Vivienne.

'One of the cellars has a passageway out to the sea. Do you know where it is? Or where Dougie is?'

'I can get Dougie.' She looked confused by the group of four. Jacques was a guest accompanied by a younger man she didn't recognise and two uniformed police officers. All had wet legs and were dripping onto the parquet floor. 'Can I get you some towels?'

'Dougie, now!'

'Do you know where the passageway is?' asked Travers.

Jacques saw the alarm on Vivienne's face and knew in an instant that rumours of smuggling were true and that Vivienne knew all about it. She wasn't going to show the police and implicate herself.

'Vivienne. Mal is down there. She's going to drown. At the moment, you're only implicated in a smuggling operation. Do you want the police to add murder to their list?'

Vivienne blinked in alarm and then clenched her teeth.

'It's this way. But I don't know what you mean about smuggling.'

'Oh, mon Dieu, who cares? Take us there now.' Jacques knew he was being rude in his panic, but Mal was running out of time. When she had said the grille was covered in barnacles, he had felt his heart grip. For a moment, it had been hard to breathe as he understood her words. She had no exit. He pictured them looking down into the water and only seeing her beautiful silver hair swimming on the surface like seaweed, her lifeless body hanging underneath.

'Miles, Evans,' shouted Travers to the two uniformed officers. 'Find and arrest the Fitzgibbons.' Turning to Vivienne, he spoke quickly. 'We need to run. Is the room usually locked?'

Jacques could have kissed her as she sprinted along the hallway. 'It's not locked, but the entrance is down a short shaft that is blocked by a grate.'

'Is that locked?'

'No.'

'Can it be opened from underneath?' asked Travers, beating Jacques to it. In truth, he was having trouble catching his breath, keeping up with the younger men.

'No,' said Vivienne breathlessly as they ran down a staircase. 'It has a one-way latch for security. Wulf always used to joke that we should throw some of the more troublesome guests down there.'

Jacques groaned, and they ran along a second plainer corridor and down to another level. The lower levels of the castle were a warren. Would they ever get to Mal in time?

'One more staircase. Take care on the treads. This far into the bowels of the castle is pretty ancient. No one ever comes down here.'

She flicked on a light switch and they moved carefully down the steps. Jacques was certain he was wheezing and tried to steady his breath. He would be no good to Mal if he collapsed before he got to her.

The corridor down here was clearly unused. Cobwebs lined the brick ceiling, and white paint peeled off the dusty brick walls. Vivienne headed toward a wooden door and pushed it open. Leaning in, she flicked on a light and Jacques and Travers surged past her.

The room was brightly lit and smelled of the sea. Plastic crates and barrels were piled up against the wall. In the centre of the room was a wooden trapdoor. Grabbing the metal handle, Travers yanked the door open, letting it fall with a heavy bang onto the stone floor. Rushing forward, Jacques looked down into the darkness. A metre below was a metal grid. In a pool of light, Jacques peered past the rusty grid and saw Mal's blue eyes staring up at him, blinking into the light. The water swirled around her shoulders as she smiled and then laughed weakly.

'I hung on.'

Jacques fell to his knees and leant over the shaft.

'You actually did as you were told.'

'Never too old to try something new.' Her teeth chattered as she struggled to get her words out.

As she joked, a surge of water pushed up past her neck and her eyes opened wide in alarm as the water dropped away.

'Quick. Another big wave is coming.'

Vivienne showed Travers how the bolt released the locked hinge, then he and Jacques pulled on a chain, lifting away the barrier.

331

'Climb up,' cried Jacques in alarm as Mal struggled to move.

Mal stared up at him in shock. 'I'm trying, but I think my wrist is broken. And my other arm is cramped. I'm doing my best.'

Jacques stared down into the cold water; it was a serious threat.

'What are you doing?' shouted Travers.

Jacques rolled onto his waist, and sliding his legs over the side, dropped into the well. For a second, the freezing water rushing over his head shocked him, and then he burst back into the air. Grabbing the ladder, he hugged Mal.

'Are you insane?'

He laughed loudly. Wrapping himself around her, he carefully released her arm from the back of the ladder.

'Hold on. Time to get out of here.'

Laughing, his teeth already chattering, he climbed the ladder as Travers and Vivienne stretched down to pull Mal up into the light.

Chapter Forty-Six

When Mal emerged into the ballroom, the girls from the wedding party rushed around her and swept her away to their suite. A bath was run for her and the girls filled it with bubble bath, then helped her in and out, gently covering her in towels as she shivered the whole time.

Octavia had declared her ankle and wrist were probably unbroken, but heavily sprained. Without an actual doctor present, everyone was prepared to rely on the words of a yoga instructor. She had had the temerity to suggest a walking stick; Mal said that they would soon fall out if she carried on with that sort of defeatist nonsense.

'I'm sure Jacques will happily lend you his arm,' said Imogen coyly, and the girls all burst into laughter. Helping Mal dress in their castle loungewear, they rolled up the legs and sleeves, then wrapped her up in a thick dressing gown until her shivers gradually subsided.

Johanna offered her a hot chocolate, which she gratefully accepted, holding the mug carefully in one hand. There was a knock at the main door and the girls all turned towards it.

'It's DCI Travers. May we come in?'

'Mal, are you alright?' called Jacques.

Mal shook her head violently.

'Hang on,' called Imogen, then looked at Mal. 'What's wrong?'

'Lipstick,' said Mal quickly, handing her hot chocolate back to Octavia. 'Champagne. Did you get rid of the seaweed? How do I look?'

As the girls rushed to execute her orders, Johanna shook her head. 'Jacques doesn't care what you look like.'

'Sod Jacques. I care. The last time that detective saw me, I was a freezing battered old woman. I looked weak. Image is everything.' Johanna raised an eyebrow. 'Within reason, obviously.'

Taking a sip of champagne from her flute, she turned to the girls. 'How do I look?'

'In control.' Tinks smiled, and the others nodded in agreement.

'Very well. Come in.'

Mal swore as her voice failed to project. All her screaming in the tunnels had given her a sore throat, and she was grateful when Johanna rushed over and swung open the door.

'Malachite Peck will see you now.'

The girls giggled as the two men entered the room, and Mal grinned at their sport. Jacques walked towards her, and bending down, kissed her on both cheeks.

'Ravishing. You never fail to astonish me.'

Tilting her head in acknowledgement of the compliment, she patted the seat on the sofa next to her, and Jacques sat down.

'You scrub up nicely for someone that threw themselves into a well like a lunatic.'

334

'Well, why should you have all the fun?'

Jacques had changed into a pair of cords and a heavy-knit sweater. Mal wanted to squeeze his hand, but pulled back at the last second. The pain in her wrist was still throbbing, and she didn't want to remind Jacques of her injuries. She may have told the girls that she was trying to make a statement, and that was true. But she'd be lying if she didn't also acknowledge that she wanted to impress Jacques. She knew he had lied to her, and he needed to understand that. But when she thought he had been killed, all her feelings had crystallised.

DCI Travers took a chair opposite her. He looked capable, and Mal hoped this wouldn't take too long. She was desperate to sleep for about a week.

'Have you arrested the Fitzgibbons?' She was eager to get through this as fast as possible.

'We have, and they confessed to everything. Penny Fitzgibbon smiled through most of her confession. There was absolutely no regret. She even cut her own arms, pretending the blood was Mr Pellofey's'.

'Why did they kill Francine?'

'That was just Mrs Fitzgibbon.'

'But why?' asked Mal. It was the part of the puzzle that made no sense.

'They had a daughter called Patience.'

Mal groaned.

'What's wrong?' said Jacques quickly.

335

'I'm going to owe Jasmine the most enormous apology.' She patted his hand and winced as pain shot up her arm. 'I'll explain later.'

'Francine was at university with Patience,' said DCI Travers. 'Patience Fitzgibbon committed suicide after a prolonged campaign of bullying by Francine. It was well documented by the university, but all sides covered up Francine's involvement after the incident. Her father endowed the university with a new science building. In turn, the university wanted to keep things quiet as they were proven to be negligent in the care of their students.'

'That's dreadful,' said Imogen softly. 'I'm so sorry. I didn't know what Francine was capable of.'

'I can't believe it,' said Johanna.

'I can,' scoffed Ferne. 'God, that poor girl. How did she die?'

'She drowned herself.'

The detective's words fell solemnly.

'How did she get Francine down to the water?' asked Ferne.

'According to Mrs Fitzgibbon, Francine was extremely drunk, and it was easy to manipulate her. She'd had an argument with her friends earlier that evening and was feeling sorry for herself.'

Ferne and Tinks exchanged glances; Tinks shook her head.

'This isn't our fault, Ferne.' She looked at the detective. 'What happened next?'

'When they got to the water's edge, they struggled, but Francine's drunkenness worked against her. Mrs Fitzgibbon said the minute she saw her burst into the castle with the other girls during the storm, she felt this "Was a sign from God". Her words. Anyway, she said she saw Francine outside having a smoke, so she grabbed a raincoat and went outside to join her.'

'I have the coat in my room,' said Mal.

Travers nodded his head. 'Without you realising the importance of the coat, Francine's death may have remained as an unfortunate accident.'

'So what went wrong?' asked Jacques. 'Why did they kill Wulf?'

'Blackmail?' said Mal.

'Indeed. It appears Mr Clarkson had serious money worries. When he saw Mrs Fitzgibbon follow Francine out, he approached Mr Fitzgibbon with the evidence. At that point, his fate was sealed. Mr Fitzgibbon already knew about his wife's action and, according to him, he couldn't be prouder.'

Wow, thought Mal. Thinking back to her own ex, he would probably have rung the police himself. The idea of a man supporting her like that made her feel wistful. It was a waste of time thinking about how her life could have been, but it would have been nice to have a partner by her side that was completely in step with her over the major decisions. Maybe being bonded over murder was a step too far, but she admired their commitment to each other.

'So why did they attack Mal?' said Johanna. Mal noticed that Jacques hadn't asked any questions. No doubt he had already heard all of this from Travers on the way up here, but she was grateful for his steady presence beside her.

'When they heard she had the coat that Penny Fitzgibbon had worn, they were concerned about DNA evidence. But, apparently, it wasn't until they overheard Mal's phone message and their daughter's name that they realised Mal was about to work out who the killers were. They were hoping to immobilise her until they could get off the island.'

Mal picked up her glass and was dismayed to see her hand shaking. Taking a quick sip, she placed it quickly back on the stand.

'Well, this has all been very exciting,' said Jacques. 'But I, for one, need a bit of peace and quiet. Malachite, would you help this old lunatic back to his room?'

'We still need to take Mrs Peck's statement,' said DCI Travers.

Mal tried to stifle a yawn.

'Surely that can wait until the morning?' said Jacques. 'I'm sure she's not going anywhere.' He fixed the detective with a steely glare, and DCI Travers nodded his head in acceptance.

'Very well. We have your account from when we found you. A formal statement can wait until the morning. We'll take that time to interview Vivienne Chance, Jordan

Winters, and the rest of the staff. It seems from what Mr Pellofey has told us, that there have been some serious poaching and smuggling operations being conducted on the island. And I understand we have you to thank for that as well, Ms Peck.'

'Malachite,' said Tinks, 'Not Ms.'

Jacques leapt to his feet, belying his stated need for an escort, and lent Mal his hand, gently helping her to her feet. As she limped forward, DCI Travers frowned.

'Can I get you a crutch or a walking stick Ms...' he paused, 'Malachite?'

Before Mal could respond, Jacques shook his head.

'My girl does not need a walking stick. Mal, are you ready?'

Leaning on his arm, she smiled up at him and nodded. 'Let's go.'

Chapter Forty-Seven

As soon as the door to the girls' suite closed behind them, Mal slumped against Jacques and he looked down at her in concern.

'Are you okay? Should I have let the detective get you a stick?'

'Absolutely not!' She laughed weakly. 'But I do think this is going to be slow progress.'

'Would you like a piggyback?'

Mal looked up at him and laughed again. 'That is very tempting, but maybe when I can hold on better?'

By the time they made it to Mal's rooms, she was exhausted and sank gratefully into her sofa. The velvet cushions softly embraced her as she looked over at Jacques pacing around the sitting room.

'Sit down, you're making me tired.'

Jacques sat down on a dining room chair and looked uncomfortable. It was time.

'Why did you lie in your statement?' asked Mal. This man had come to mean so much to her and she was terrified that she had thrown her heart at a man who was entangled with a known smuggler, poacher, and blackmailer. She watched as Jacques took a deep sigh.

'I lied.' He paused before starting again and tipped his head, talking down to the carpet, rather than looking Mal in the eye. 'I lied to you originally. In my statement, I told the truth. I didn't know Wulf Clarkson beyond him as a host on this island once a year for the bridge weekends.'

Mal's wrist was throbbing and the painkillers, champagne, and exhaustion were beginning to take their toll. But she was determined to understand why Jacques had lied.

'Why did you lie?'

He groaned and placed his head in his hands.

'Because I'm a fool.' He paused and then rushed on. 'I wanted you to join me this weekend. I enjoy spending time in your company. So much.' He looked up at her and then continued. 'I knew you'd have a great time here, but I was worried it was beyond your budget. And I knew you wouldn't accept it if I offered to pay.'

'Absolutely,' said Mal, bristling.

'So I came up with the idea of pretending that the owner owed me a favour.' He shrugged and stared miserably at Mal. 'Like I said, stupid.'

'But one of the most expensive rooms in the castle? And how could you afford it?'

'The money's nothing. I know I don't make much of it, but my family is wealthy. Very wealthy.'

'But why didn't you have this room?'

'Because I wanted you to have it. After all you've been through, I wanted you to have the best. I thought you deserved it.'

He trailed off and shrugged. 'I'm sorry I lied.'

Mal laughed in relief. In a hundred scenarios, she hadn't thought of this one.

'Do you forgive me?'

'Forgive you?' laughed Mal. 'I could kill you. I was so bloody worried that you were tied up in some nefarious scheme with Wulf, and I was desperately trying to work out how to shield you from the police's attention.'

'You were? Why?'

'Why? Isn't it obvious, Jacques Pellofey? You mean the world to me.'

Jacques sprang to his feet, but instead of moving towards Mal, he began to pace, his heart pounding.

'That's what you mean to me, too. Since you moved to Golden, you have turned my world upside down. Ever since you first walked into Tommy's shop with your punctured float, I knew I was in the presence of someone very special.' Jacques moved over to the window and looked out into the night sky. 'I knew my life was about to change. I know we haven't known each other that long, but I'm old enough to know what I want. And I know when something is right for me. I just pray that you feel the same. Malachite Peck, will you do me the honour…?'

He turned around to finish his sentence and laughed softly.

Malachite Peck had fallen asleep.

Author's Note

Dear Reader,

Ever since reading And Then There Were None by Agatha Christie, I have wanted to set a murder mystery on an island. I love the idea that people can't get on or off, and the murderer is stuck in the same lack of boats as the rest of the suspects.

Living in Cornwall we have an abundance of offshore islands — only St George's at Looe, and St Michael's at Marazion are now occupied — but I thought we could probably fit another island in off the coastline of Falmouth. Sadly, Castle Wolf does not exist beyond our imaginations.

Tuna is indeed making a resurgence in British waters and is heavily protected and monitored. It is also incredibly valuable; an age-old motive for poaching. We are increasingly seeing them breach the water; their fast silver fins flashing in the sunlight before splashing back into water, throwing up a spray of white water. My brother has been out on the tag and release boats, and described the meticulous record keeping these fishermen undertake to monitor numbers. Who knows, maybe in years to come we will be eating Cornish tuna?

Once again, I should like to thank Anna Mullarkey for keeping me on track — her feedback remains invaluable —

and my editors, Julian Barr and Andy Hodge. Any errors sit firmly on my shoulders. I also have a team of early readers that warn me when I am staying off the path and to them I am eternally grateful.

As is ever the case, all mistakes that remain are mine and mine alone.

Yours faithfully,

Anna Penrose

p.s. Now, I always like to offer a little something extra at the end of each book and this time I thought I might share some information on how tides work. They rule our lives down here and I thought you might like to understand a bit about how they work.

https://bookhip.com/SJTCPHX

Yours sincerely,
Anna Penrose

BV - #0169 - 290424 - C0 - 198/129/25 - PB - 9781913628178 - Matt Lamination